Everblue

Also by Brenda Pandos

The Emerald Talisman
The Sapphire Talisman
The Onyx Talisman

Evergreen, Book #2, Mer Tales
(Coming summer 2012)

Everblue

Mer Tales ∽ *Book One*

By
Brenda Pandos

OBSIDIAN MOUNTAIN PUBLISHING

Cover design and layout by the author herself.
www.brendapandos.com
Cover Images Fotolia.com
© keller #26833195, © Yulia Podlesnova #13387223

Published by Obsidian Mountain Publishing
www.obsidianmtpublishing.com
P.O. Box 601901
Sacramento, CA 95860

Library of Congress Control Number
2011912922
ISBN: 978-0-9829033-9-1

10 9 8 7 6 5 4 3 2
Printed in the United States of America

To my husband,
for everything

1

≈

ASH

"So, tell me everything, Ash." Tatiana stretched out on her blanket in rapt attention. Her toes—complete with ruby-red polish—were out of her flip-flops and curled into the sand as if it was summer, though the chill of March lingered in the air and patches of snow dotted the coastline.

"Nothing exciting happened today." I shivered in my jacket, sitting on a nearby boulder with my arms looped around my folded legs to keep warm. "I swear."

"I'll be the judge of that."

Out of the corner of my eye, I watched her bask in a little bit of sunlight and wait in anticipation while the icy water lapped the beach just beyond us. Daily we did this—the drama report from South Tahoe High. Her home-schooled existence left little to no excitement, which meant I couldn't start talking about anything else until I'd dished out every dirty detail from my craptastic day.

"Fine." I rolled my eyes.

After I filled her in on the drama, I studied and secretly envied our differences. Tatchi, with her long, tan legs could have any guy at South Tahoe High School she wanted. Her iridescent blonde hair flowed like cascading water down her shoulders; a perfect match to her azure eyes. I, on the other hand, the Irish redhead that freckled in the sun, walked around school unnoticed by guys. Constantly smelling like sunscreen and chlorine didn't help either.

She lapped up my account like a lonely dog whose master had just come home. She never cared how similar the stories were. To Tatchi, my words were her lifeline to society, to a real life she craved—her live reality show with me as the narrator.

"Oh, wow. What did he do?" Tatchi rolled over onto her stomach and kneaded her hands together, hungry for more.

"Nothing. He acted like nothing happened. The whole thing kinda backfired."

Tatchi laughed and laid her chin on her folded hands. "Serves her right. Then what happened?"

The longing on her face tugged at my heart. I turned away to watch the endless span of sparkling water across the lake—only the snow-covered mountains gave away its end—and shook my head. "Nothing. I came home. Just another totally boring day."

"Not in the slightest," Tatchi giggled. "I can't wait 'til this is our life."

I smiled, knowing we'd be breaking out of this tourist trap soon enough and she'd be free. Then she'd finally see that living the drama was vastly different than hearing about it—especially when the heartache happened personally.

We sat in silence for a moment as the past drifted in like the tide in my mind. Tatchi would love nothing more than to finish her senior year in public school, but her parents were super strict—similar to mine. Only, their concern didn't lay with what kind of education she'd get at STHS or the influence from her peers. No, they hid a big secret. One I'd discovered a long time ago and was the reason I avoided her house.

"Do you have swim practice tonight?" Tatchi asked, interrupting my thoughts.

"No." I jumped back into reality. "There's some banquet for the teachers so it was cancelled."

"Nice to have a break, huh?"

"Meh. I like practice and it's not like you can do anything anyway. You've got a curfew—"

"Not for much longer. How many days again?" Tatchi sat up and copied my pose by curling her arms around her legs too.

"Like I have to tell you." I scrambled over and pulled the tattered brochure from my book bag. Every word on that thing had been read at least a hundred times.

Last summer, I'd gotten the hair-brained idea to get a post-office box so Tatchi could apply to colleges in secret. She wasn't thrilled about the idea, afraid how her family would react, but after we sent out applications and were accepted to Florida Atlantic University, we both became excited about the possibilities.

"Only five months and six days 'til we're free," she said with a coy smile, though nervously fidgeting with her charm bracelet, the vial of blue liquid sparkling in the sun just right.

I grabbed her hand. "Your family will be thrilled, I know they'll be. You're the first to go to college *and* on a scholarship. They'll be happy for your accomplishment."

Tatchi and her twin brother Fin helped run the family sailing business, Captain Jack's Charters. My Gran's curio shop, Tahoe Tessie's Treasures happened to be on the same pier. Without college, both of us would be slated to stay and eventually take over the family business, putting down roots like our parents.

"Well...," she said with a sigh, a glint of worry reflected in her eyes, "you just don't know them."

The childhood flashback of her dad's angry face shimmered across my vision. I gulped down my hesitation. She needed me to be strong for her when she finally told them.

With a deep breath and as much compassion as I could muster, I looked her in the eye. "How could they not be proud of you? Sure, they'll have to find someone to take your place in the office, but that's nothing. And you can't pass up a scholarship—"

"It's not that. It's other things."

My stomach clenched. Now seemed like an opportune time to

finally discuss what I saw so many years ago. Her dad had a serious problem. In fact, keeping the family secret to herself wasn't healthy, constantly living vicariously through my warped interpretations of other teens.

I'd just about broached the subject when Tatchi suddenly gasped.

"What's wrong?" I asked and glanced over to where she looked, afraid her father might be storming down the beach towards us. Instead, a red Jeep rolled over the ridge and down the rocky path that separated our neighborhoods.

She tsked. "What does he want?"

My mouth parched as I caught a glimpse of Tatchi's twin brother through his windshield. He wore his usual black baseball hat, and looked nothing short of adorable.

"He's coming here?" My voice cracked.

"Apparently." She pressed her brows together and looked toward her house. "Let me find out what he wants."

Fin parked and got out before she could intercept him.

"Hey, Ash," he called out with a wave.

My stomach flipped into a knot as I smiled and waved back.

They argued for a minute, but I didn't catch what about. I stood, trying not to gawk, as I shamelessly adored his broad shoulders and beautiful blonde hair. Under the bill would be his piercing blue eyes fringed with paintbrush lashes—the ones that always melted my knees.

My crush started years ago, right after we'd met when we were ten—right on this beach. With a deep breath, I tried to relax and not dream of a relationship that probably wouldn't be. As far as I knew, he didn't think much of me beyond meaningless flirting.

Tatchi threw her hands in the air and stormed back in my direction.

"Drama on the home front. I have to go," she mumbled as she snagged her blanket off the sand. "Sorry."

"Is everything okay?"

Fin watched us, which made me even more nervous.

"Yeah, it should be fine. I'll try to call later." She smiled and gave me a hug. But more of a "I'm leaving for a trip and saying goodbye" tighter kind of hug. I grimaced, unsure what to say.

She left with a sigh and headed toward their house, brushing past Fin without even a look. Once she was out of view, Fin turned and instead of going back to his Jeep, he walked towards me. My pulse quickened.

2

FIN

Ashlyn stood awkwardly as I approached. Her curvy hips and wavy red hair took my breath away. For a moment, I caught her scent and hummed—honeysuckle with just a hint of chlorine from her morning swim. Briefly, I imagined us playing in the water. She'd give me a run for my money in a race.

"What's going on?" I asked.

Her green eyes darted away. "Not much."

"Sorry I interrupted—" I pointed towards the imprint of my sister's towel in the sand.

"Oh," she said with a gulp and a smile, "it's okay."

She pressed her lips together and suddenly all I wanted to do was kiss her right then and there. I took a deep breath and glanced at my feet.

"Is school going good?" I asked, kicking a rock.

"Yeah." She shrugged and then shot me that look—one with a hint of yearning behind it. I couldn't help myself. I stepped forward and cupped her cheek. Her skin was soft as a rose petal, but within her startled eyes I caught my reflection—my very selfish expression.

Her whole life flashed before me. This kiss I desired to give her would change everything—her dreams, her life with her family, her future. Innocent and trusting, she closed her eyes and tilted her chin upward in anticipation anyway. My soul protested, but I did the only thing I could—the responsible thing.

"You've got something on your cheek," I said, wiping my thumb over her skin.

She opened her eyes and pulled away, her cheeks reddening. "I do?"

I stepped back and grimaced at myself. I was being one of *those* guys, the jerk who led girls on and toyed with their emotions.

"I'm going to go," she said, rubbing her hand where I'd touched, and faked a smile. "See ya later."

She quickly stumbled up the path towards her Grandmother's house before I could comment, but I heard what she said under her breath. *"I'm so stupid."*

I sulked back to the Jeep and slammed the door, hating myself for being such an ass. The only reason I'd come in the first place was to tell Tatch about the meeting we had to attend, not get distracted by Ashlyn's captivating beauty. And I'd made a complete mess of things.

I spun out of the spot, and drove the small distance back to our house.

When I went inside, I spotted Mom in the kitchen, eyes wild with frustration, her waterproof bag and random stuff spread out over the countertop.

"Where have you been?" she barked, hands on her hips.

"Sorry." I lowered my head.

Mom's right eye twitched, as if she couldn't decide whether to yell at me or just move on with things. I noticed she had changed into her most ornate, beaded bikini top and skirt—obviously for the meeting.

I casually took a seat on the bar stool.

"We've still got time," I gestured toward the bay windows. The sun still peaked above the horizon.

"Close enough. Your father has already left to meet with everyone. I guess you look okay. Just put on whatever you're going to wear to the hatch." She grabbed Great-Grandmother Sadie's sacred shell-encrusted bikini top. "Tatiana!"

Tatch came around the corner, taking a second to sneer at me.

"What?"

"I want you to wear this."

Tatch cringed. "What's wrong with this bikini top?"

"It's a special meeting. I want you to look your best."

"But that's for like ... a *promising* or something." Her face wrinkled up in horror.

Could this be a trick and not a standard meeting? Promisings in our world were the equivalent to weddings but prearranged between parents. Our parents, who fell in love before getting promised, didn't think the arranged unions were fair. They said, when the time came, we could make up our own minds. At least that's what I thought they'd said.

Tatiana blanched. "Oh, dear Poseidon. Please don't tell me you have arranged someone for me to—? Is it Azor?"

Mom chuckled. "Of course not. It's just an important meeting and I want us to look our best. Please, for me?"

Tatch groaned and grabbed the overly ornate thing from Mom's clutches and marched toward the bathroom, mumbling threats. I let go of the breath I didn't realize I'd held and darted into my room as well. Off came the jeans in a rumpled heap along with my shirt. I put on my tear-away board shorts and my waterproof sling pack over my shoulder—anything to stay on Mom's good side.

We reconvened in the living room at the same time and gave each other a fast once-over.

"Happy?" Tatch twirled in a circle, but I avoided looking at her chest.

"Beautiful." Mom's shoulders relaxed until she looked down at the lower half of her body. Tatch still wore her skinny jeans. "Are you planning to *wear* those?"

"No." Tatch rolled her eyes. "Sea serpents! Of course I'm going to change."

She stormed off and Mom resumed pulling cans of food from the pantry. Why would we need food when we were coming right back? Would we be staying the night?

"What's the meeting about, Mom?" Tatiana asked, walking back wearing her swim skirt.

Mom kept a straight face as she took dry goods out of the cupboards: flour, sugar, coffee, noodles, and beans. "We'll find out in a few minutes, but just in case, why don't you pack a few of your things."

"Are you serious?" Tatiana gasped. "Can I at least make a phone call before we go?"

Mom turned and tilted her head. "Who do you want to call?"

Tatch's eyes made their way to the linoleum. "Ash."

A jolt hit my stomach at the mention of her name.

Mom used her low lecture voice. "I'm not sure how long we'll be gone. What will you tell her this time? There's a family emergency? We've had a death?" She shook her head and tsked. Close human friendships were discouraged due to the risk of exposure and Tatch hid how much time they'd spent together, as well as her secret plans for college. "We have to leave in five minutes."

Tatch huffed and stamped her foot. But I already knew we were running out of time. Under my skin, scales began to form and ached for the refreshing cool water to relieve the growing itch.

But if we weren't returning for a while, then someone else would be assigned to guard the gate. Last time, the privilege became my Uncle Alaster's and his son Colin while we were in Fiji on vacation. Colin, who was our age, broke the lock on my closet and used all of my stuff. I couldn't let that happen again.

I ran to my room and put my belongings into the new secret hiding spot under the wooden floorboards: my laptop, iPod, all my shoes, and keys to the Jeep. I pushed my bed over so a leg secured the loose board in place. The rest of my clothes and underwear, I packed in a duffle bag and slid it into the attic. I shivered at the thought of him wearing my boxers again.

"Hey, Tatch. Will you lock this in your room?" I called across the hall, showing her my guitar.

"Yeah, whatever."

She was scrambling around, hiding stuff too. Luckily, my cousin never touched her room, but we could never be too careful.

"Fin," Tatch whispered. "Sweet talk Mom for me, will ya? Get her to let me stay."

"We have to go. Azor said."

"What?!" Tatch stood, wide-eyed and frantic. "He's going to be there, too? Why didn't you tell me?"

I shifted my weight from side to side, angry with myself for telling her accidentally. Azor, the King's son, made no secret of his desires for Tatch, but she couldn't stand him.

She shoved me aside and clutched her pink sparkly bag under her arm as she headed down the hall, her top jangling with each step. I half listened as she complained to Mom, begging to use the phone again.

I returned to my room, did one last sweep to make sure I'd hidden everything important, and grabbed a few extra board shorts for the road.

"Let's go, Fin!" Mom called from down the hall.

"Okay." I closed my door and paused, hoping this wasn't the last time I'd cross the threshold.

Mom saw me and sighed, frustrated with Tatchi's reaction—no doubt. I picked up the bag at her feet with little effort and offered my arm as we walked down the steps. She squeezed my hand to console me, but I remained positive things would work the way I'd envisioned.

Together, we walked across the bridge that stretched over the pool in our basement. On the other side was the metal hatch attached to the floor, leading out to the lake. Tatiana had already left, her pink bag resting on the cement ledge. With a shake of her head, Mom shoved it in with the rest of our things, sealed the bag, and dropped it down the hole. We watched it sink out of sight—the collection of our lives in one small bag.

"Don't be long," Mom said, and slipped into the water.

I frowned as I looked around at our huge recreational center, with the large TV suspended in the corner, swim-up bar with anything you wanted to drink hooked up to taps and swim mats to lounge on. Most likely, Colin and Uncle Alaster would soon be here, enjoying our stuff and having the time of their lives without having earned it. I wanted to punch something.

With two claps the lights shut off, leaving me in complete darkness. I ripped off my board shorts and plunged my body into the icy water. With an ache the muscles in my legs fused together and scales burst across my skin from my toes up to my waist. A wicked, black fin spread out where my feet used to be. I was sleek, fast, and dangerous—like a shark ready to hunt. I shot down the passageway and came out into the lake on the other side.

Riddled with guilt, I went back up to the lake's surface a hundred feet off shore. I looked towards Ash's house, already missing her. What was wrong with me? How could I let things go that far? I felt wretched for hurting her and vowed to never do it again. Feelings aside, I had to remind myself of the consequences and stay away from her. For her sake.

In the window, a silhouette of someone appeared. Was it Ash? I wanted to apologize in person and confess the truth about who we really were. *If only . . .*

"Sorry," I said right before diving down into the frigid lake.

I tucked my shorts in my sling pack and swam towards my family who waited a few feet underwater in the distance. When the sun returned, along with my legs, I'd need something to cover myself with so I wasn't walking around in the nude.

3

ASH

"Ashlyn Frances, is that you? Don't forget to take off your boots!" Mom barked from the kitchen. "And take your swim bag with you to your room—hang up your towel and suit too."

What am I, like five? With an eye roll, I kicked off my shoes as instructed and trudged towards my room. Yes, I'd forgotten to remove them, but the formal speaking of my name wasn't necessary. "Did you forget I didn't have practice today? And call me Ash," I said under my breath.

Mom poked her head around the corner and grabbed my arm, stopping me. I scowled while she put some of my stray hairs back into place behind my ear. "Your name is beautiful and you should be proud of it. It honors Grandpa, God rest his soul."

My middle name was after my late Grandpa Frances, or Frank for short. I used to like it until Mom said it every chance she got. I quickly turned towards the stairs to escape, knowing a probing conversation brewed on the tip of her tongue.

"You're home early. Is everything okay?" she asked behind me as I took the stairs by twos.

"Perfect," I grunted.

"Dinner will be ready in twenty minutes—"

I closed my bedroom door so I couldn't hear anything else and slumped down on my bed. Fin had flirted with me in the past, but that was—what was that? Was he about to kiss me and chickened out? Or did I read his signals wrong?

My cheeks burned remembering my willing response—hanging

my lips out there, ready to be kissed. And just when I thought I had a grasp on the situation, he'd do something like this to my emotions. Hot or cold—never easy for me to read.

"Oooh," I grunted, grabbing an innocent pillow and chucking it across the room.

I went to my window and looked toward their house. Trees blocked most of it from view, but his Jeep was visible enough. The sight of it rolled my stomach over. How one guy could be so adorable yet so frustrating irked me to no end.

If it weren't for the fact that I'd lose my best friend, moving away seemed ideal.

4

FIN

With a pop, gills opened behind my ears, allowing me to breathe as water rippled across my scale-covered skin. With a final exhale, I pushed out the last of the oxygen, lessening the resistance as we leisurely dove further into the inky depths towards the secret tunnel 1,600 feet down. Gel lenses slipped down over my eyes like goggles, enhancing my night vision and clarity. Our dive—easy for us to traverse—would be impossible for humans without some expensive equipment. Our mer bodies were unaffected by the glacial water and tremendous pressure.

Tatch swam alongside me; her worried thoughts met mine. *"Are we getting relocated?"*

I smirked, trying to keep our internal conversation from gaining mom's attention. Mer twins often had mind-talking abilities. *"Stop overreacting. If whatever Azor asks is going to move us away from here, Dad will decline like last time. Maybe he has to go somewhere and I'll get to guard Tahoe in his place."*

"You? Why would they pick you?" She clutched her charm bracelet that held her most prized possession—a tiny vial filled with a blue colored liquid—the *essence* of our life.

"I'd be the most logical choice," I said indignantly.

"Yeah, right. First of all you're not old enough and second, you're single."

"Nothing but technicalities."

Though the prospect of a bigger assignment when I got older was tempting, following in my father's footsteps and freedom apart from the colony appealed to me more. I just needed a chance to prove myself.

Tatch turned towards me, tilting her head. *"You could come with me and Ash to college you know."*

Tatch's response bitterly sliced through my excitement; I spouted out with internal laughter. *"Ridiculous."*

She looked downward towards our destination. *"No. What's ridiculous is how they make it seem like you control your destiny when you don't. This huge honor is just a disguise for a huge crap sandwich. Your life will always belong to the King and the rest of the Council. Luckily, Dad has groomed you specifically for this territory by setting up Captain Jack's, giving you some sort of freedom. But you'll still be owned by them and at any time, like now, they could take it from you. You know it and so do I."*

"Have you forgotten Dad is actually on the Council? He'd never let that happen."

We looked at each other for a moment—my twin, my little sister by five minutes. If she actually chose to leave us, to go to college and live "normally," the consequences meant erasing her memories and starting afresh as a human. People killed for our secrets and she was throwing it all away to be *normal*. No one in their right mind ever chose to leave.

I clenched my jaw. *"I doubt you'll be able to go through with it."*

"Don't make this harder than it needs to be."

I gulped down my emotion and shook my head. How could she act as if our family didn't mean anything to her? That our memories deserved to be heaved into a dumpster bin? The thought of losing her forever tore me apart the day she'd mentioned the prospect of college. Of course the decision would be easy for her to make—not having to feel the pain of losing the ones she loved. But I'd never do that to Mom and Dad, or to her.

I gritted my teeth. *"You get the good end of the bargain."*

"We've talked about this before. With the colony, there's no certainty. Dad's protection only goes so far. The King still has expectations. Leaving is my only choice," she said matter-of-factly.

"You could go to school close by. You don't have to leave leave."

"You just don't get it," Tatiana swam a little faster. "They'd still own me."

I gritted my teeth and silently followed behind. She was technically right. Everything *could* change after tonight. But I highly doubted we'd be leaving for good.

A statue of Tessie, Tahoe's Loch Ness monster, loomed in the dark as a joke, but ironically was a door to the meeting room. Mom felt under the statue's neck for the lever. As the statue's jaw lowered, the water undulated around us, disturbing the blind shrimp and other sea life. They scurried away as we swam through her mouth into the ante-chamber.

"This sucks, Fin."

"It'll be okay," I said, still hopeful I'd get my big chance to guard the gate.

Upon breaching the surface of the flooded cave, my heart barreled in anticipation of what could happen within the next few minutes. Bluish lighting—native to our world—danced across the abalone-encrusted ceiling, brightly illuminating the two-hundred square foot space. The cave, originally just a tunnel bridging Tahoe to Natatoria, was carved out by Dad to become a place for the Council to meet, far away from prying ears in the palace. A colorful mural of our city, inlayed with gems and shells, covered the main wall. I hadn't seen it yet and was blown away by the detail Dad had incorporated.

But to my disappointment, not only were Dad and Azor in attendance, Uncle Alaster and Colin were, too. Why would they be here?

Dad motioned for us to join them at the large granite slab that appeared to be floating in the center of the room. I swam up first and wedged my tail into one of the eight L shaped seats carved into the slab's ledge under the waterline, across from Uncle Alaster and Colin.

Azor, son of King Phaleon and second in command of the army, sat at the head of the table with his slicked back hair and cocky smile. His calculating dark eyes watched as we chose our seats. Mom took the spot between Dad and Colin, leaving a seat next to Azor and the one between Dad and I open.

"Tatiana, don't you look lovely. Please. Sit here," Azor said, ogling her blatantly, making my skin crawl.

She smiled, but chose the other seat.

"Ugh," Tatch groaned ever so slightly once she settled in. Out of the water, we couldn't mind-talk but I could imagine what she was thinking about Azor and what he could do with the seat next to him.

"Now that we are all here, we can start the meeting. Nice to see everyone," Azor spoke in our native tongue. The blue light gleamed off his white teeth as his glance darted across the attendees. "Let's get down to business."

Mom shifted in her seat. Of all the merpeople here, she was the only beta-mer: a human changed into a mer. That fact made her cower in the presence of the pure-born, the native tongue still difficult for her to speak without an accent.

Azor cleared his throat before starting. "First, I have to congratulate you, Jack, for your vigilance at the Tahoe Passage. Things have been peaceful and the rumors you've spread have been effective in containing curiosity."

"Well done, Brother," Alaster said, waggling his white eyebrows and giving a golf clap.

Dad nodded, keeping his posture stiff. He and his younger brother rarely saw eye to eye, especially with matters surrounding how to handle Tahoe.

Tatch sighed next to me as if to say "what a kiss-ass." I bit my lip to refrain from laughing.

"So," Azor said quickly, "that situation up North we discussed in the Council meeting has escalated. Jack, we need your expertise and advice after all. The King was hoping you wouldn't mind leaving your responsibilities in the hands of Alaster and helping us out."

I glanced at Uncle Al. His smirk under his white beard made my stomach flip. Why would they be allowing him to oversee again after the disaster last time? We still hadn't fully overcome the rumor mill over the fire and near sinking of the *Empress*. He was the last person I wanted in charge of our lake or our business. In quiet alarm, I waited for Dad to object, to insist I stay to protect Tahoe and run things in his absence.

"If that's what the King wishes, " Dad said to my dismay, "of course."

"Great. And then, as far as the family—"

I swallowed hard and clenched my jaw. Uncle Al taking over the lake? The last thing I wanted was to share living quarters with them.

"—Finley and Tatiana are having their eighteenth birthday soon, correct?"

Mom folded her hands on the table top. "Yes."

Azor smiled wide. "Perfect. The Coming of Age festival is less than a month away and there is much to prepare. We'll just have you stay in Natatoria for the time being. Have any prospects of promising been voiced?"

Tatiana hit her tail against mine. I kept a straight face.

"Not unless it's happened within the last hour," Dad said with a smile. "We're allowing Fin and Tatiana to choose, you know."

Azor's countenance fell. "Well . . . hopefully they'll find suitable mates before the festival."

From my peripheral vision, I noticed Tatch close her eyes, as if she'd sent up a silent prayer of thanks.

"Fine then," Azor continued. "Magdalene, you and Tatiana will be assigned to the palace to help prepare for the upcoming festival. Finley, I'd like you to join me in my command. One day, you might be given an actual gate of your own to guard so it's important you're trained."

Trained? Was he kidding? I'd been guarding the gate with Dad from the day I could swim. Maybe if he got off his pompous fin and actually spoke from experience instead of barking orders from his dad, I'd respect him. I bit back my retort once I caught Dad's cautious eye.

"As you wish, Azor," I said begrudgingly but shot a pleading look back. Dad still had time to suggest I stay in Tahoe in his place.

Dad kept a mask of strength and nodded his head. "I'm proud of you, Son."

"Excellent. Now that that's settled, I'd like to speak to Jack and Alaster alone. We have details to discuss." Azor raised his arm, directing us—the outcasts—toward the shimmering waterway in the opposite corner of the room. The tunnel leading to the city of Natatoria.

Dread crept across my scales. Our "convenient" assignments brought us right under the nose of the King. We'd have to fall in line and follow their rituals. No more jaunts on land for the time being. But the worst part was Dad's assignment.

What possibly could be happening up North that would shake him so badly? He'd never arbitrarily leave Alaster in charge of Tahoe and ditch us to deal with things like a pre-promising festival if there wasn't something big happening. Whatever the situation, though he tried to hide it, I'd never seen him so concerned before. When *would* we see him again? I suddenly didn't want him to go without me.

Tatiana responded to the gravity of the situation first and wrapped her arms around his neck. "Bye, Daddy."

He patted her on the back and his gruff exterior crumbled a bit.

"You take care of your mother. I'll be home soon."

Mom forced a smile and hugged my father next, but for much longer.

"When will you be home?" she asked quietly in English, caressing his face with her hands.

Azor interjected, answering to prove he understood her. "A few weeks, Magdalene. We'll take good care of Jack. It'll be difficult, but of anyone I know, you two can handle it."

Ignoring Azor, Dad hugged Mom and caressed her hair. "I love you," he said, distress lining his tanned face. "Always know that." They shared a tender kiss.

Anger burned in my belly. The fact that the King and his son had such control over us irked me. All the expectations sent a dagger into my chest. I wanted to jump up and demand Dad decline the mission. The whole thing reeked of danger. He shouldn't have to feel obligated to go if he didn't want to. What happened to the man who fought for his family? For honor? For what was right?

"Colin, stay close by. We'll start our stay in Tahoe tonight," Uncle Al said while my parents continued their goodbyes.

After several minutes, Mom reluctantly let go of Dad and joined everyone in front of the exit portal. Down the tunnel was a world I enjoyed visiting, but didn't want to live in. Colin dove into the glistening doorway first, making a big splash.

Tatch growled and wiped the water off her face. I didn't care. I had to know what was going on. I stalled, hoping to catch a snippet of conversation. But Azor stayed tight lipped, waiting for everyone to leave. Mom and Tatch finally disappeared underwater and I could no longer avoid the inevitable.

"Don't worry, Son," Mom said quietly as we swam towards our world. "Everything will work out."

I wanted to believe her.

Upon entry, our beautiful city wrapped me into its arms as the melodic songs of our people filled the void in my soul I often tried to ignore on land. I'd forgotten how enchanting our kind can be when you'd been away for so long. Located in between the ocean floor and the earth's mantle, the mers lived in harmony far away from the knowledge of man.

Light blue larimar lined the ceiling of our endless enclosure, giving the illusion of the sky. Above us hung one of many crystal balls that daily reflected beams of sunlight streamed in from pipes containing strategically placed mirrors. Tonight with only a half moon in Tahoe illuminating the sky, the ball was dim. Instead, light from trapped lava under gel-covered domes ricocheted out like a roaring campfire from the center of our colony. Structures of gold and silver, decorated with gems of every color, towered out of the reef in a circular pattern, reflecting the warm hue. In the distance, the palace loomed, teeming with excited merlife, enjoying their evening. If there was a heaven on earth, this was it—complete with streets of gold.

I inhaled the briny water and hummed. Tahoe's fresh water pulled all the minerals from our skin, leaving our scales void of color, but the salt content was far richer here than our melted-snow fed lake. Silver and emerald streaked down my tail, as if someone turned on a light switch under my scales. My fin was the last to fill with red and orange.

"I think waiting around might be a mistake," Mom mumbled, her accent in mer tongue prominent. "Tatiana, let's go."

Tatch frowned. Her tail, too, had changed color: blue, pink, and purple. Her hair floated in the water, framing her head in a golden halo. I had to agree with Mom, but for my own reasons. The quicker Tatch put distance between her and Azor, the better.

"Fin, this is exactly what I was worried about and I don't want to go to the castle without you, around all those uncultured sea serpents."

"Just play nice for now. I'll see you later. We'll get back to the

mainland soon."

"We'd better, or else."

She gave Colin, who seemed to be shamelessly checking out her tail, one last sneer.

"You look *nice*," he responded.

"Mermen are pigs," she spouted only to me. "Yeah, whatever. Let's go, Mom."

"Feisty." Colin chuckled and watched Tatiana leave.

I punched him in the chest. "Knock it off. You're her *cousin*."

"How does that matter?"

I rolled my eyes but everything in me wanted to beat the crap out of him. I gritted my teeth and counted to ten.

"You're going to lose the lake, you know. Your family has been getting a little too friendly with the humans and someone finally noticed. Maybe if you'd have stopped acting like you're better than everyone else and lived with the pure-born, you'd get to keep it."

"I'm not an idiot, Colin. Don't you have something you need to do?"

"Like move in? Yup. Just waiting on Dad."

I smirked, wishing I could be there to witness his disappointment when he broke into my room and couldn't find any of my stuff. But at the mention of our dads, I wondered what took mine so long. I wanted to at least talk to him before he left, see if I could come along.

I leaned up against the rock face and flipped my tail, disturbing the sand. Having fins in the water was useful to travel quickly, but the bulky appendage left much to be desired for exerting dominance. Something about being unable to sit, legs open, left me feeling feminine.

"You're going to be Azor's pet now," Colin said.

I looked away, ignoring his bait to argue.

"He'll do anything to get in good with the twin. He's set his sights on Tatiana and he gets what he wants."

"My sister gets to choose who she wants to marry."

"Marry?" Colin belly laughed. "She's gonna pick a human, huh? That's gonna go over *real* well—"

Crap. "Promise. Marry. Whatever. Weren't you just in there? She gets to choose. Or has the King turned on its people and changed the law?"

"Don't get your barnacles in a bunch. I'm just saying."

He ran his hand under a rock and pulled out a crawfish. With his razor-sharp teeth, he ripped out a huge chunk of flesh from its tail. "Man, is this going to take all day?"

I scrubbed my hand over my face. It was hard enough to find out my uncouth cousin would be messing up my room, but what kind of mission required so many details?

Dad's reputation obviously landed him the job. He was respected on the Council and among his peers, even though he lived outside of the walls, and was married and promised to a beta-mer.

Where is he?

"Thanks, Jack," Azor said, exiting the tunnel first, while clapping my dad on the back. "I knew I could count on you. Go ahead and assemble your team." He turned towards Colin with a slightly annoyed look. "Alaster is waiting for you."

"Awesome," Colin said, tossing his half eaten crustacean into the current. "Bye, Cuz." He shot me a mischievous look right before disappearing through the darkened Tahoe gate.

"So?" I asked, expecting to hear he was putting me on his team.

My father looked over my shoulder and raised his eyebrows at Azor. "Is that all?"

"Yes—"

"Then, I'd like a private word with my son. I'll have him join you momentarily."

"Sure thing, Jack." Azor formed his lips in a straight line. "Finley, meet me on the south side of the palace when you are finished."

"Yeah," I said and watched Azor leave, thankful I didn't have to follow his orders. Little did he know, I'd be leaving with my dad. "So what's going on and when do we leave?"

"Son—" Dad put his hand on my shoulder. "We've had an incident and unfortunately, I can't risk taking you."

"What? Why not?"

"I want to bring you—" Lines of concern pressed grooves into the skin around his eyes. "Just trust me this time. I need you here with the girls. Besides, how bad can it be working with Azor? He'll help you improve your skills."

"Why can't I come with you? I don't understand."

"I—I'll tell you why when I get back."

He pressed his hand on my shoulder, but his words didn't convince me.

"This doesn't make sense."

"I know. Please, Fin. Trust me." He ran his hand through his hair and grimaced.

"Do we have to stay here? Can we go to the lake house instead?"

Dad looked away. "Your mom isn't allowed to be there without me. You know the rules."

The rules. Mermaids weren't trusted outside of a merman's protection. Their powers of seduction might get the better of them, causing loads of trouble and risk of exposure.

"But Alaster is there and I'm almost eighteen."

"Maybe if you were, you could, but not this time."

I swallowed my pride and pretended the rejection didn't hurt. He could take me if he really wanted.

"Son, I need to go assemble my team. Thank you for understanding."

He grabbed me and hugged me hard. Then with a flick of his powerful red tail, Dad disappeared into the folds of the city. He had *men* to recruit and apparently my stupid birth date prevented me from making the cut—still a boy in his eyes. My chest ached with fury. I wanted to be anywhere but here, trapped in the center of the earth with idiots like Azor. Why wasn't I born a couple of months sooner?

Tatiana was right. My situation *was* a huge crap sandwich.

5

⌒

ASH

No cup of coffee cleared out the morning cobwebs like a douse of 70 degree water at early morning swim practice. Though warmer water would have made the first lap a little more bearable, the pool slowly began to feel like bathwater once I got going.

Bubbles of air escaped from my nose as I glided underwater. This quiet haven was where I could think in private, away from noise and distraction. I broke the surface and stretched my arm forward, propelling my body through the current one stroke at a time. Thirty five laps to go to finish my warm-up.

After my last lap, I looked at the board—same old thing. Three miles worth of laps split into individual medleys and sprints. Piece of cake.

"Psst," Georgia, my closest girl friend at school whispered from the lane next to me. "You finished with your warm-up yet?"

"Yeah," I answered, and rinsed out my goggles.

Her shoulders dropped. "Really? Already?"

"Enough chit-chat! Let's go ladies!" Coach Madsen barked.

Georgia stuck out her tongue when Coach wasn't watching and pushed off the wall with a splash.

"You finished, Lanski?" Coach directed at me while twirling her whistle.

"Yeah." I sank into the corner of the wall to rest before the next set.

"Nice job," she said with a slight smile, then proceeded to yell at a pair of slackers a few lanes down from me.

After practice, the locker room buzz was all about Senior Ball when it should have been about the big swim meet in two weeks. With a quick check of the clipboard, Meredith Hamusek, my nemesis from Squaw Valley Academy, and I were slated to race one another in the 100 yard butterfly—which left my stomach in a knot.

The dance did, however, loom in the recesses of my mind, but my fantasies involved Fin as my date and no one else. Tatchi had pestered me about taking up Ryan's invitation. He was cute, but I'd already told him "no." She couldn't know the real reason. But after what happened yesterday, maybe a date with someone else would be what Fin needed to finally make a move.

Attached to my gym locker door was a picture of the three of us, hanging out at Fannette Island when we were thirteen—my only picture of Fin. They'd bet I couldn't swim the entire distance, all of 500 feet. The freezing water cramped up my calf, but I did it without a whimper.

With a quick brush of my finger over my lips, I touched his exquisite face. Why couldn't he understand we needed to be together?

While Holly, my locker neighbor, sauntered about in her pink bra and skimpy panties, bragging about the cost of her dress, I pulled my hair up into a ponytail, slathered on my favorite honeysuckle lotion, and applied a little mascara. I just wanted to be on time to English.

A quick exit into the hall accosted me with bigger drama than fancy dresses. A cluster of girls whispered in the corner, eyeing a red-eyed Brooke who had her own soirée surrounding her. What could the head cheerleader and girlfriend of Lake Tahoe High's sexiest guy at school, Callahan, possibly be crying about? Then I heard—they'd broken up.

Tatchi is going to love this one.

I pressed my lips together to suppress a smile and ducked into the classroom. Mrs. Keifer had already written our assignment on the board—more chapters due from *The Scarlet Letter*. I pulled out my book and marked the pages. I could identify with Hester Prynne, but my chest felt branded with the scarlet S for shy.

"So, Brooke huh?"

I looked up to find Holly standing over me like a vulture, finally clothed.

"I guess." As if I cared about the dirty details. Tatchi on the other hand would be all over this.

"Rumor has it Callahan's got someone else on the radar to take to Senior Ball." As she slid into the neighboring seat, her apple blossom scented lotion assaulted me.

I smirked. The whole charade had to be a stunt. Why would the potential King and Queen break up two weeks before Senior Ball? "Your point?"

"Oh come off it. Like you don't know."

"Know what?"

She sniggered. "I heard he's got his eye on you. He knows you don't have a date."

My gaze swung around to meet Holly's devious look. "Brooke and Callahan will get back together before the dance. You'll see."

"I don't think so. It's all you, girl. Stop playing like you don't know. Did he ask you already?"

Holly's boldness overwhelmed me. Luckily she quieted down as more students filtered into the classroom. Georgia took the seat in front of me, out of breath.

"What did I miss?" she swiveled around in her seat, her hair completely coiffed, grabbing my book to note the page. My guess was she forgot to wear her glasses again.

"Nothing." *Yet.*

Then Callahan walked in, light brown hair flopped over his forehead like a surfer. His big, chocolaty eyes pierced mine and my heart roller-coastered against my ribs. I looked away and pulled my book back from Georgia's grasp, hiding behind it.

Callahan? Me? This couldn't be true?

"What's with you?" Georgia said, and turned to look.

I knew she saw him. What girl didn't lose all ability to speak coherently in the beguiling all-star pitcher's presence? Callahan defined handsome in every girls' internal dictionary and took a close second to Fin for me any day. But no one of his caliber ever paid attention to me—the geeky girls' swim team captain. Out of the corner of my eye, I watched him sit down a few rows over. So did Georgia. The thought he might possibly want to take me to Senior Ball made my stomach tremble. Holly always exaggerated. There was no way he'd ask me.

Taking a deep breath, I refocused my attention on Mrs. Keifer after hearing the buzz of the second bell.

"All right, let's get started. I thought we'd read in class today—"

The door opened, interrupting her talk, and Brooke sauntered in with swollen eyes. A pang of guilt wracked my chest, though I'd done nothing wrong. Her glare met mine anyway and my cheeks burned. I slouched down in my seat. Why couldn't I have been home-schooled instead of Tatchi? Great. Today's cover story featured me.

"Nice of you to join us, Brooke. Holly, could you start reading chapter eight outloud?"

The sound of shuffling pages filled the room like a delicate rainstorm falling on dried leaves. When Brooke found her seat somewhere behind me, a burst of hushed whispers followed. Cold stares prickled down the back of my neck while I tried to listen as Holly stumbled over her words. Could Callahan really like me? Did Brooke and her flock of friends already know, prepared to swoop down and ambush me later? I bit my lip and pushed away the notion as ridiculous.

The next few periods zipped by and I'd managed to stay far away from the drama. But as I walked into the cafeteria with Georgia, I spotted Callahan's brown head of hair right away. He sat off to the side with his friends, looking utterly gorgeous. My pulse jolted thinking about what Holly had said.

"Nervous about Saturday?" Georgia asked after we found seats, a celery stick hanging from her mouth.

A ball of dough from my peanut butter sandwich lodged in my throat as my gaze swept over to Callahan. I quickly sucked down a sip of Sprite. "No. Why?"

"Did you not look at the board? You're racing against Meredith Hamusek and she's wicked fast. "

"Right." *The meet.* I stuffed a corn chip in my mouth, embarrassed. Holly mentions Callahan once and my brain becomes total mush. "I guess we'll have to see."

"You have to win. We need it for the championships but I hope we get out of there at noon. I have a hair appointment at two. Plus I need to get different shoes. Do you want to come shopping with me? I'm looking for something strappy but not too gaudy, you know? I'm so glad I got a little bit of color from working out in the pool, but I need to put bronzer on the tan lines, unless you want to help me? It's lame you aren't coming."

Her explosion of words blew me back into my chair. "Did you have a lot of caffeine today?"

"Why? Am I talking too fast? My mom always says I do. I had a few cups of coffee and a diet Coke earlier. Why?"

"Nothing. Go on."

"So, no one even asked you to go?"

I contemplated lying, but told her the truth. "Ryan did."

Her jaw dropped. "And what happened?"

"I said no."

"What? Why?" Georgia slammed her apparent second Diet Coke down, clanking it against the table with a splash.

For once I'd knocked Georgia speechless. I marveled in the quiet for a moment as her eyes—lashes heavy with mascara—watched me in wonder. Coyly, I smiled back.

"The guy I want to go with didn't ask me, so . . . I'm not going," I shrugged and crunched on another chip.

"Who?"

"No one you know."

"Does he go here? 'Cause I know everyone at this school."

"No, but it's fine." I looked away, avoiding the confrontation.

"Whatever," she said with a huff and prattled on, completely oblivious to the fact that people were strangely gawking at me.

Sixth period came and went with more odd stares from my peers. At the bell, I went straight to the pool without stopping to drop my books off at my locker. Drama with my name was apparently underfoot and I had no wish to indulge it. Only a good workout would calm my nerves.

I was the first at the pool for practice. A dash of talcum powder helped me slide on my swim cap. Swim blocks lined the wall, newly installed for the meet. I stepped onto the lane three block. Rough sandpaper secured my feet on the otherwise slippery metal as I laced my toes over the edge.

In a week and two days, a crowd would fill the empty bleachers and Meredith would be standing to my right. I imagined the gun popping and leapt into the air. The bubbles rushed past my ears as I glided like a torpedo. One stroke . . . two . . . three . . . deep breath . . . flip-turn. My body flew up and over the water. I had to be untouchable—faster. I finished the set and pulled my head up to check the time. I did it. My best time ever.

"Cannon ball," Georgia screamed and careened into the water next to me, interrupting my imaginary win.

As she surfaced, I pushed her head under.

"Did you see?" She popped her head up further away, half of her smiling mouth under the water.

"See what?"

She laughed and splashed me. "You have to go to Senior Ball."

"What do you mean? No, I don't."

She took a water-logged piece of paper out of her suit top. "Oh yes you do. Look."

I grabbed the dissolving pink filaments and stared. On it was a list of candidates to vote for Senior Ball royalty. My name, the third one listed, jumped out at me under the heading Senior Ball Queen.

"Where'd you get this? Georgia? Georgia!"

She just laughed and swam away from me. With tepid cheeks, I looked around at the other swimmers who'd started their warm-up, curious grins on their faces. Apparently, this wasn't a joke and explained all the staring.

6

∽

FIN

Unsure where to go the next morning, I hung out by the palace—the place I was supposed to meet Azor the night before—and waited. Standing him up wasn't the most brilliant plan, but I wasn't thinking straight last night. A steady stream of females went inside while the mermen headed towards a sandy field behind the palace. I drifted in their direction, looking for a familiar face.

The crystal ball shot sunlight into the city, making my tail ache to change back. Rarely did we spend the night in Natatoria, let alone the next day. Normally, we hung out in our retrofitted basement swimming pool with easy access to the lake through the hatch.

Unused to being solidly underwater, I attributed Natatoria's atmosphere to the claustrophobia that slowly started to choke me. But what I missed most was coffee, something impossible to brew, let alone drink down here. Plus the few pieces of fish I'd eaten for breakfast had already burned through me and I craved some substance like French toast or pancakes.

If it wasn't for Dad's mission, I'd be on the deck of the *Empress* right now, sipping a good Sumatra and showing tourists the bay in full sunlight. Instead I was listening to some guy named Chauncey explain the rules for today's hand-to-fin combat tournament. The only reason I paid attention was because the winner got a golden trophy cup filled with rubies—not a bad reward.

When Chauncey finished his rhetoric, I floated among the group, trying to look like I fit in. Where was Azor?

"Aye, son," a redheaded merman with a thick Irish accent said.

"You'd be Jack's son, right?"

"Yeah," I said, unsure if that was a good thing.

Without hesitation, he swam over and gave me a bear hug. "I'm Badger. Good to meet ya. You'll be my partner today. How's that?"

"Okay." *I guess.*

I followed him over to the edge of the field. Memories of Dad talking to me about him vaguely came to mind.

"What's with you, lad?" Badger asked.

I pressed my thumb against my temple, willing away my caffeine headache. "Don't you ever crave something other than fish?"

Badge threw his mane of hair back into the current and laughed. "Aye, lad. Every day. I'd love me a thick Guinness right about now and me mum's fried shredded potato."

His full-bodied holler echoed over the field, which lightened my spirits. "That does sound good."

"Ya missin' the food from the Pacific already, aye?" He raised one hairy eyebrow.

"Dad's on a mission, so I'm stuck here training on temporary assignment until he returns."

"That's what I've heard. Well, we aren't half as bad as ya think, but then, most of these boys would start blubberin' like wee girls at the first sign of combat." Badger flared his fin to reveal the deadly barbs just under the surface. "You're with the best."

I smirked, suddenly remembering the time Dad came home from Natatoria with a limp. Badger was the one he was sparring with that day. "So I've heard."

Badger beat his hand on his tattooed chest, inked with obvious important issues of his past. "The Irish Republican Army is where I got me battle scars. But me thinks ye be needin' some real home cookin' to deal with yer homesickness. Sandy's makin' me somethin' special tonight." He looked left then right and whispered. "Somethin' from me country."

"How'd you get—?"

"Oh, I've got me ways. And with that air gizmo, it'll be something to savor. Me mermaid's an excellent cook." He nodded and under his knobby beard, his lips pulled into a smile, revealing a gold incisor. My taste buds watered at the possibilities of what she'd make on a real stove in an oxygen-filled kitchen. "Now let's get to sparrin' so I can bring home that cup 'o rubies fer me doll."

"Oh, like that's gonna happen." I swam back and poised my tail, barbs out. "On guard."

Badge shot past me like a cannon, knocking me right into the coral. I shook my head and leveled myself.

He floated above me and held his belly, howling. "Son, ya need to keep focused." He grabbed my hand and yanked me off the seabed. "Get yer head out of yer arse and hold your fin up like this."

He positioned himself to show me how to hit my opponent by just bending at the waist and angling my tail for a faster hit. I copied his example.

"Aye, there ya go," he said with more confidence. "Try again. But whatever ye do, don't let me pass."

Badger rushed me, faster this time, and with ease promptly knocked me on my backside into the sea kelp. I spit out the sand and cursed under my breath.

"Now don't start blubberin' on me. You'll get better. Keep yer eyes open. That was yer last freebee."

Freebee?

I growled. Part of me wanted to close-line him with my arm the next time he passed. But I was to learn the proper way to tail-duel, as stupid as it was. Shooting each other evil glares, we floated in the current for a moment, ten feet apart with challenging stances. I pawed my hand forward, inviting him to try it again. He gave me a nod. I smiled. This round would happen my way.

Over his shoulder, though, I caught a glimpse of a girl with long auburn hair, holding a tray with something on top of it. A hint of honeysuckle infused the water around me.

Ashlyn?

I'd lost my preparation. Badger had already set off to retaliate and fire rushed up my fin, seizing my muscles. Then the world went hazy.

:::

"Sorry about earlier, laddy," Badger said while relaxing on his moss-covered lounge chair, smoking his pipe and wriggling his hairy toes. The golden trophy stood on the tabletop in between us filled with a small fortune in rubies sparkling from within.

I yanked my hand from my injuries, realizing I'd been massaging the spots where he'd stung me earlier. After our short practice, he really let loose and took me out on the first round. "Oh, it's fine."

In the privacy of Badger's air-filled home, he sat in his kilt and I in my board shorts, stretching our legs. We indulged in pints of freshly squeezed orange juice—though I suspected his had a little something extra added.

Sunlight hit various mirrors staggered on the walls, allowing self-willed conversion from fin to feet. From the kitchen, like I'd hoped, onions and garlic simmered in some type of butter sauce and the delicious smell wafted into the cramped living space, making my mouth water.

"This is the secret, lad. Ya need to be watchin' at all times. All it takes is one stupid moment ganderin' some pretty lass's tail and ZAP, yer a goner." He laughed and scratched at his hairy belly before perching his hand into his beltline.

The sting from his barb felt exactly like the electric shock I'd experienced when I was ten. After Dad and I had installed electrical lines in the basement for our entertainment center, he turned on the juice but I wasn't finished taping the bare wire. My body still throbbed in memory of the pain.

"Who was that girl anyway?"

"That be Sandy's niece, Lily. She's a cutie and available, if yer askin'."

"No-o," I stuttered. "I—just—she looks like someone I know, that's all."

"Oh, I see." He winked then relaxed his head back and made O rings with the smoke. "Ah, this is just what I needed. Well, a peek at TV might have been nice."

I laughed and looked around the room—very untypical of a mer. An oil painting of a ship at sea hung over a simulated fireplace, one that could never be lit. On the mantle were more sparring trophies, a spyglass, and some empty bottles. On the other wall was a wooden plaque that said *Sea Queen* that hung on a chain from rusty nails. Next to it was a ship helm and a Celtic cross inlayed with green stones.

"From me ship. I was a fisherman before my Sandy came along."

"Was that *your* ship?" I pointed to the painting.

"Aye," Badge nodded his head. "The *Sea Queen* was a beauty before she sank."

"Is that how you got here? Did Sandy save you from drowning?"

"Well, now. That wasn't entirely my doing," A sweet voice filtered into the room as Sandy emerged from underwater through the porthole doorway in the floor. She pulled herself onto the ledge and slipped behind the dressing curtain dangling next to the doorway. After phasing into legs, she walked in the room and arranged a bunch of algae sprigs and sea anemones on the table.

"Ah, I was a miserable bloke before the mer, fightin' and drinkin' away me regrets. Me first wife died of the influenza while I was off tryin' to conquer the sea. I couldn't forgive meself and wanted the sea to end me pain. But Sandy here, she looked past me mean exterior and saw me hurtin' heart. She says she only found me that day, but I know different. I saw her flirting a few other times before, but that day she became my angel. The promise does a world of good on a poor man's bleedin' heart, let me tell ya."

"That it does." She winked at me before she walked over, her glass beaded skirt tinkling as she moved. Their eyes sparkled at one another before she planted a kiss on his lips.

"You're one fine merwoman." He spanked her on her backside. "And look what I won ya, doll."

"Oi, man." Sandy slapped his hand away, flitting an embarrassed glance my way. Her cheeks were as red as the rubies. "Lovely, Badger, thank you," she said and hurried off to the kitchen.

I looked away. This was nothing new to me. My parents did the same thing all the time.

Badger's grin parted his beard. He cupped his hand to his mouth and leaned in. "Now listen to me. You be sure to get yerself a lass with some gold in her tail, ya hear me?"

"Bairtliméad!" Sandy barked from the other room. "Don't you be filling this boy with nonsense. I won't have it in my house."

"Oh quiet, woman! Let me talk—you stick to cookin'.'"

"You better not speak to me like that! I'm not your mermaid!"

I cringed, expecting a fight to erupt when a ruckus of laughter poured from both rooms. I wrinkled my forehead, unsure what was so funny.

Badger winked. "Get it? She's not me 'mer' maid? What a sense of humor she's got."

"Oh," I said, then forced out a laugh. "Yeah, hilarious."

I heard something slam shut and the aroma of freshly baked bread filled the small space. She came out with the hearty loaf and a tray of cheese and butter. "Mind your manners, or only the boy is getting this treat."

"Oh you, vixen. Where'd you manage this gift?"

"You know I have my ways." She cast off a wicked smile. "Now sit at the table and eat."

I didn't dare comment.

7

ASH

As soon as practice was over, I went directly to the dance chairman and asked to be removed from the ballot. With a puzzled expression, he informed me voting had already begun. My time to decline needed to have happened when nominations took place in homeroom earlier in the week.

I'd been late to class Monday. Georgia insisted we talk to Coach Madsen after practice because someone stole her swimsuit out of her locker over the weekend—which she later found at home. The vote must have taken place then.

Colorful signs requesting support for Brooke and other candidates littered the halls and mocked me as I left his office. Whoever nominated me had played the worst joke ever and when I found out who, they'd get a piece of my mind. Even still, I wasn't attending.

Shivering from my wet hair, I jumped into Mom's car in the student parking lot and cranked on the heater. Work duties prevented her from picking me up as usual.

I zipped through town, anxious to talk to Tatchi. With a screech, I parked on the pier and briskly walked across the wooden railroad ties of the dock toward the life-sized cutout of Captain Jack, Tatchi's dad, propped next to the door. He and Fin would more than likely be on an excursion, showing tourists the bay. Oblivious of the closed sign, I yanked on the locked door with the wrath of a woman scorned, and hurt my arm.

"What?" I mumbled as I looked through the plate-glass window into a darkened interior. "Where are they?"

Confused, I knocked hard against the glass, but there was no answer.

"Mom?" I asked, while walking into Gran's shop and dropping her keys on the counter. "Did they run any charters today at Captain Jack's?"

She looked up at me over her bifocals and took the pencil out of her mouth. "What?"

I pointed towards Captain Jack's. "Are they closed today?"

"Ummm. Are they?" She glanced behind me. "I don't know. Could you help me organize these?"

In a box at her feet were oodles of new T-shirts that said "Don't messy with Tessie." I pursed my lips. Last thing I wanted to do was fold shirts. I had to find Tatchi—quick. I'd go to her house if I had to; my life was at stake.

"I need to get home. I've got a lot of homework—"

"Ashlyn Frances. You can help me for fifteen minutes."

"Fine." I dumped my gym bag and marched over. "What do you want me to do?"

"That's my girl. I'll inventory the shirts and put them in piles. Tag a price on these, then hang them on that rack by size. The leftovers go in bins over here, folded."

Fifteen minutes, yeah, right.

"Mom, I'm only helping for a few minutes, and then I seriously have to go."

The pencil was back in her mouth and she was counting again. With a roll of my eyes, I started on the first stack.

After thirty minutes passed, I was still hanging shirts on hangers. It took all my self-control not to rip down the papier-mâché plesiosaur that hung over the top of the display.

This is all your fault, you know.

She stared back at me with empty black eyes. Tessie, the biggest hoax in history, was an invented monster to trap tourists into buying the kind of crap Gran sold. The dinosaur's picture covered everything: cups, hats, bottle openers, stuffed animals, postcards, calendars, key chains—you name it. And every week, Gran and Mom were thinking up new slogans and promotions to spin the fad. They even worked out a special "Tessie watching" charter with a free shirt if you saw the beast, which everyone did because there was a mini-golf dinosaur statue planted underwater.

Though I could have as many free T-shirts as I wanted, I wouldn't be caught dead in one with Tessie on it. As a kid, all my clothes came from the store anyhow. But now, the only Tahoe related apparel I wore said "Keep Tahoe Blue" or something more eco friendly.

When Mom finally left the room, I piled the shirts on the rack and shoved the rest in the bin. "Done, Mom. Bye."

The door chimed behind me, signaling my escape.

From there, I wasn't sure what to do. Half of me wanted to walk past Tatchi's house and the other dared not to. Either way, I was desperate to find her. Would she tell Fin later? Would he even care? Could I be so bold as to drop a hint that I wanted Fin to be my date?

My feet trekked down the rock trail and when I had to decide if I'd turn towards Tatchi's house, I chickened out and skittered towards the beach. It was safer to check there first.

At the beach, seagulls claimed the spot where we were yesterday. I sat on a pile driver and decided to wait. The sun melted from the sky over the mountains, painting a light show of blues and golds. I didn't know why I waited. She'd have been home by now anyway. Sunset was her curfew.

Frustrated and freezing, I grabbed my bag and headed home.

"Ash? Is that you?"

Dad popped his head out of the kitchen. Garlicky aroma from firehouse spaghetti blew past me, rekindling my hunger.

I blinked back at Dad in surprise. "You're home tonight?"

The caterpillar of fur on his upper lip formed a smile. "I decided to let some of the young bucks get an overtime shift tonight. I missed my girls." I walked over into his awaiting bear hug. He kissed me on the top of the head. "Is your mom with you?"

"She's buried under a new shipment."

"Sounds dangerous." He let go and went back to stirring his sauce. "Can you call her and see if she's clawed her way out? I'd like to eat together."

I slumped down at the kitchen table. Last thing I wanted to do was give Mom an opportunity to chew me out for bailing. "I just left the store and I'm sure she is right behind me," I fibbed.

"Perfect. So, how was your day?"

I chuckled. *Absolutely ridiculous.* "Fine."

"That doesn't sound like plain ol' fine to me." Dad winked before he tossed two half loaves of bread, slathered in garlic butter, into the oven.

"I don't know. Same old crap." I looked down at my fingernails, noticing they were in dire need of a manicure. "Just preparing for the big meet on Saturday."

"That's right. I'm going to be able to make that meet after all." Dad dusted his hands off on his jeans and parked next to me at the table.

"Really?" With his erratic fire-station schedule, he rarely made any of my swim meets.

"I'm home," Mom called from the back door. Her keys hit the countertop in the hall much louder than normal. My body tensed involuntarily. "Is Ashlyn home? I need to speak with her!"

"Ruh-roh," Dad whispered, giving me a raised eyebrow. "What did you do now?"

"Nothing." I batted my eyelashes innocently, then faltered under his questioning stare. "Just left early. She tried to rope me into doing the entire display."

"Go on then," he shooed me up the stairs. "I'll talk to her."

Behind me I heard her complain I'd abandoned her and made a mess of all the shirts in the bins at the store, doubling her work. Dad soothed her frustration by pouring her a glass of wine. After a few minutes of griping, she settled down and their conversation became low mumbles. I tiptoed into my room.

Lying on my bed, I looked up at the glow-in-the-dark stars peeling off the ceiling. Tatchi's house had one solitary light illuminating the interior. The Jeep remained parked where it was the night before. My cell phone on my nightstand taunted me to call her and hang up if someone else answered.

Then like magic, it rang.

I lunged for it.

"Tatchi? Where the heck have you been? You weren't at work today and I've been waiting to talk to you all day. Why was Jack's closed? I have to tell you what happened. I've been nominated for Senior Ball royalty. Can you believe it? Holy crawfish!"

"I know," said a low voice I didn't expect—one belonging to a guy.

My pulse quickened. "Who is this?"

"Callahan."

My breathing stopped, leaving both of us in silence.

8

FIN

Dinner at Badge and Sandy's was what I needed to help with my mainland homesickness. And afterward, Sandy brought out fresh chocolate chip cookies which made my night complete. When I'd questioned how she got all the ingredients, Badger broke down and swore me to secrecy. Apparently, Sandy's cousin, Dorian, guarded the Loch Ness gate under Scotland and let her come and go as she pleased—completely breaking Natatorian law because she didn't have the King's permission.

With a flip of my fin, I dolefully swam with an uncomfortably full belly towards my water-filled mer home, which was vacant most of the year. Though we did well financially on land, we didn't have much Natatorian tender of jewels and gold to buy an air interior like Badger's, nor had we needed to. I would have stayed longer to stretch my legs, but their incessant flirting made me uncomfortable so I made an excuse to leave.

"*Fin.*"

I stopped and spun around to scan the nearby kelp bed at the sound of my sister's panicked voice.

"*Tatch?*"

She slowly rose up from the weeds in her new technicolor glory. Whatever they did to her at the palace today, my sister now resembled a Christmas ornament. I tried not to overreact, holding my face as straight as possible.

"It's okay. You can laugh." She slumped down on a nearby rock and put her face in her hands.

"You look—"

"Ugly, just say it." She held up her multicolored tresses encrusted with beads and shells in disgust.

"I was going to say colorful."

"Colorful? They dyed my hair! And put these stupid things in it. I'm never going to be able to get them out. And look at these weird tattoo things." She scrubbed at her arm, but nothing came off. "It's horrible! How can I go back to the mainland looking like this?"

"It's not that bad." Purple and aqua painted vines wrapped around her shoulders and down her arms. They were so realistic they seemed to move with the water, and pulled at me with some hypnotic ability.

"Fin, get real. Fin?"

I snapped out of the trance and looked at her eyes framed in green lashes. Out of nowhere, she broke down into raspy sobs.

"It's only been one day and look what they've done to me. Imagine what I'll come home looking like tomorrow. Or the festival. For the love of the kraken!"

Unsure what to do, I awkwardly patted her on the back.

"We only have to endure a few days until Dad gets back, and when he does, we'll return to the mainland and wash this crap off with something stronger than soap."

Tatiana pulled her face up, mid snivel. "Fin, Dad isn't coming back anytime soon."

My eyes met her crestfallen expression. "What do you mean?"

"He whispered to Mom when they said goodbye that he might be gone for several months. Months!"

"What?" *Why didn't he tell me? Why didn't he take me?*

I moved away and pounded my fist on a nearby barnacle-laden rock. Why was I the last to know?

"Sorry. Mom didn't want me to tell you. She hoped the mission would end early."

Suddenly, I felt as if lead weights were attached to my flukes like the mobsters at the bottom of Tahoe. Dad's absence meant we'd be stuck here. For once, I finally understood what Tatiana was complaining about. I'd joined the ranks of merwomen trapped in Natatoria's big fish tank under the earth's crust.

"Come our eighteenth birthday, I'll get us out of here."

"You can't be a chaperone unless you're promised."

"It could work. I'd be the male figure, and Mom the chaperone."

"That's not until May." Tatch rolled her eyes. "No, what we need to do is disappear and go to Fiji. We could stay on that desolate island we vacationed on last summer."

I shook my head. If we ran away, I'd forfeit all chances of acquiring Tahoe in the future. We'd have to stick it out and hope the King would let us go back as a family in May.

"Holy crawfish!"

She dashed for the kelp bed as I turned to spot Azor, swimming in our direction.

"Please, get rid of him," she whispered in my head.

"Finley," Azor called as he approached.

I tried to act casual. "What's happening?"

Azor looked beyond me and scanned the surrounding landscape. "I'm looking for your sister. Have you seen her?"

"For the love of plankton, get him to swim away from here!"

I cleared my throat to cover my laugh. "Did you check the house?"

"I was just there. Magdalene said she hadn't come home from the palace yet."

"Oh, well, maybe she's still there . . . you know how she *loves* to get all dolled up." I shot Tatch a sly wink.

"Finley! Stop it! I'm going to kill you!" Tatch screamed in my mind.

"Hmmm," he placed his index finger on his lips, "that she does.

Maybe she didn't receive my message to meet afterwards at her house. If you see her, tell her I was looking for her, would you?"

"Will do."

He swam past me, headed towards the palace.

I watched him disappear over the sand dune. "Azor wants you."

"Shut-up!" She punched me in the arm, but the water prevented her fist from actually doing harm. "Oh my starfish, you are so dead. Let's get out of here."

"Oh, let's," I said with a laugh, until her tail flipped back and hit my bloated gut, this time causing me pain.

9

ASH

I stood shaking with the cell phone in my hand.

"Are you still there?" Callahan asked.

"Yes." My voice squeaked as a flame of heat rushed to my cheeks.

"I'm sorry—are you expecting a call? Should I call back?"

"No. It's fine. I can talk." I swallowed as my hands grew clammy. "How did you get my number anyway?"

"I tried to catch you after practice, but you'd left. So, I asked Georgia for your number."

Georgia? Georgia! Oh, no. Images of her ambushing me with a million questions before morning practice already started to haunt me.

"I had to leave early."

"Oh." He took a deep breath and cleared his throat.

Blood hammered in my ears while I waited for him to speak. Was this really happening? Callahan O'Reily, the hottest guy in school, could not be calling me. This had to be another horrible prank.

"I—" He hesitated. Then another painful silence. I wanted to say something, anything to rescue the conversation.

Speak, Ash. "If this is a bad time for you—" *Stupid, of course it's a good time for him or he wouldn't have called. Please just tell me why you called already.*

"Uh, no, it's good. So, Senior Ball."

He said it. He called to talk about the dance. Was Holly right?

"Senior Ball," I echoed like a dummy as my nerves rattled like loose change.

"Are you going with anyone?"

My heart hammered harder. "Um—hadn't planned on going."

"Really? But you're nominated for the court."

I chuckled nervously. "Funny you'd mention that. I don't know how that happened."

"You . . . don't want to be in the court?" His voice sounded confused, like he had no clue why I'd be upset about that. I'm sure in his mind, all girls wanted to be nominated.

"I—I'm honored," I lied. How could I explain to him that I was mortified someone pulled this prank on me?

"You should be. It's not just a popularity contest."

Yeah, right. I couldn't help it. A snort slipped out.

His sigh sobered me up. "Well, then blame me."

"Why would I blame you?"

"I nominated you."

"You . . . what? Why?"

"The ballot said to nominate someone who they believed represented the ideal student. Someone who's kind to everyone, of high character, and scholarly. I immediately thought of you."

My mouth opened but only air whooshed out. No snippy comeback, nothing.

"See? And even in the admission, you're humble. I rest my case."

I clenched my jaw. "Not fair."

"How's that not fair?"

"I was late to class that morning. I couldn't remove myself from the ballot," I stammered.

"Exactly." I heard the grin in his voice and my knees weakened.

"Ashlyn, time for dinner." My mother's voice floated upstairs—a little more urgent than normal, like this was the second request.

"Dinner," I mumbled.

"Do you need to go?"

No. "Yes." If it weren't for the fact that at any second my pesky sister would be barging through my door, I'd ignore my mom and keep this magical conversation going forever.

"Can I ask you one last thing before you go?"

"Yeah, I guess." I bored holes into the back of the bedroom door with my eyes, wishing my lock actually worked. Dinner didn't need to center around the first phone call I'd ever received from a boy. Callahan, unfortunately, needed to get on with it.

"I know it's late, but would you go to the dance with me?"

The world slowed down as his words fluttered into my ears and the door flew open at the same time. Lucy huffed and perched her hands dramatically on her hips.

"She's on the phone!" she barked down the hall.

I blinked at my sister and clenched the phone, my hand shaking. *The little brat.* I made a "knock-it-off" motion by slicing my finger across my throat and fervently pointed for her to leave.

"Ash?" I heard Callahan ask, slightly pained.

"Ashlynnnn," Lucy whined at the same time. "Come on. I'm starving."

Unable to get Lucy out of my room so I could talk some sense into Callahan, who obviously suffered over his break-up with Brooke, I caved. "Yes. Yes, I'd love to. I have to go, though. Sorry, bye."

Lucy rolled her eyes. "About time!" She stormed out of my room.

I stayed an extra minute, blinking at the contraption that just bridged me into the world I'd only talked about with Tatchi. Was this happening? Did Callahan actually invite me to the dance? As his date? In the mortal words of my best friend, "Holy crawfish!"

I saved his number in my phone and floated down the stairs to dinner. Elbow to elbow, everyone else swarmed the kitchen counter like ants and loaded up their plates with noodles slathered in tomato sauce, giant meatballs, and salad. I waited in a daze until they finished. Once we settled in our seats at the table, Dad took a moment to say grace before he pronounced we "dig in."

"You seem to be in a good mood," Mom said to me, after passing the basket of garlic bread to Dad.

"Um-hm," I mumbled with a mouth full of noodles. Though my stomach still played the cha-cha from Callahan's phone call, I did have an appetite. I pinched my fingers together like a crab to signal I wanted a piece of bread too.

"I'm glad to see all my beautiful ladies around the table with me," Dad said, passing the basket towards me.

From a choice between a slice and a heel, I snagged the slice before handing it to Lucy. She stuck out her tongue.

"There's more in the oven," Mom remarked to Lucy after giving me a disappointed look.

"Did you say beautiful?" Gran lifted her glass of red wine into the air, and everyone followed. "I'll drink to that."

"Salud!" we all said in unison.

"So, Ashlyn," Mom said while cutting her noodles with a knife. "You came into the store and asked about Jack's today? Did you find out why they weren't opened?"

"No." I set down my glass of milk and swallowed my bite. "No sign or anything. They were just closed."

"Hmmm. That's weird. They usually let me know if something's up. I hope they're open tomorrow. We've got customers interested in the Tessie tour."

I scoffed. "I'm not surprised. This was bound to happen. Jack is kinda unpredictable."

Mom stopped mid-bite and stared at me. "What do you mean by that?"

I squinted back while visions of the past floated by—his booming voice, the crash of broken glass, Tatchi's anguished cry. "You know. He's an—" I glanced at my sister's huge inquiring eyes and tried to think of a way to disguise what I wanted to say. "A-L-C-O-H-O-L-I-

C."

Dad looked upward and mouthed the letters.

"All colic?" Lucy wrinkled up her nose. "Ewww."

"You don't mean—?" Mom stopped when I opened my eyes really huge to say "shut-up." She squinted. "Ashlyn, that's quite an accusation—"

I dropped my fork. "Don't you remember what happened? When he got upset—when I asked if Tatchi could spend the night? You *told* me he was one."

"I did?" She looked to Dad, who finally caught onto the conversation. She shrugged. "When? Just recently?"

"No. It was a couple of summers ago. Her dad broke the glass hutch with his fist! You seriously don't remember? I told you and you said *that* was probably what was wrong."

Mom looked at the table and pressed her lips in a line. "I must have been mistaken. Jack appears a little gruff, but we've been friends for years now. He's an upstanding businessman and a gentleman. I highly doubt he's got *that* kind of a problem."

"Does colic mean he's got a lot of gas or something?" Lucy asked.

"Garlic cleans you out. That's what it does," Gran said with a bang of her knife against the table, obviously not wearing her hearing aid again.

Everyone chuckled but Mom.

"No one is colic and I couldn't agree with you more about garlic, Mom. But I think we need to change the subject. We'll talk about this later, Ashlyn." She gave me a stern warning look to drop it. "Anything exciting happen at school today?"

Lucy answered, assuming it was her turn, starting on her regular banter. I pursed my lips and pushed the meatball around my plate—slightly nauseated.

The summer I'd met Tatchi, back when we were only ten, I'd invited her to spend the night. In excitement, we ran to her house to ask her parents' permission. To be polite, per my mother's instructions, I waited on the porch for the answer. But instead of the "yes" we'd expected, her father burst into a rage and punched his hand into a nearby cabinet, shattering the glass door and a shelf full of china. My feet hit the pavement as I burst into tears. When I told Mom what happened (after she calmed me down, of course), she simply responded, "Poor thing. Her father must have a drinking problem." At the time, the statement made absolutely no sense.

But after I got older I figured it all out. The fact that Mom claimed she didn't remember the incident angered me. She could say now he was upstanding, but she wasn't there. She didn't see how mad he got.

"Can I be excused?" I blurted.

Mom scanned my plate and then locked eyes with me. "You've barely eaten and your sister is sharing. Once we're finished, you can be excused."

"But she's always talking. She never stops talking!" I stood up and suddenly wanted to throw something. I needed air. "I don't feel very good."

With fast strides, I headed for the door.

"Ash—"

I slammed it behind me before she could finish. She had a lot of nerve.

Marching away from the house, I tugged at my flimsy cardigan sweater and squished across the slushy ground, wishing I had something more on my feet than my slip-on Keds. Outside of the swath of light from the porch, I stood and stared at the lake. The smell of snow lingered in the air as dark clouds salt-and-peppered the evening sky. The creek serenaded me in the distance, but all I wanted to do was scream. Behind me, the door opened and shut, and someone traipsed down the lawn. I braced myself for my mother's voice.

"What's wrong, Pumpkin?"

Dad.

The lump in my throat dissolved. "I'm having a crazy day and I'm sick of Lucy," I muttered.

"Crazy day, huh?" He stood close to me, left arm stretched out. "Does this have anything to do with what happened with your mom at the store earlier?"

Dad still wore his work attire—black jeans, steel toe boots, and navy T-shirt with Lake Tahoe Fire silk-screened on the back. When tucking myself under his arm, I noticed the firehouse smell lingering on his clothes—a mixture of old leather and cigar smoke.

"I'm not mad at Mom. I just don't like when she expects me to do stuff without asking me first." I drew circles in the mud with a toe of my shoe.

"Have you told her this?"

"I shouldn't have to."

He hummed. "I still think you should tell her."

I shrugged and picked at my fingernail. "She'll just yell at me."

"You won't know unless you try."

I grunted.

"Is there something else bothering you?"

"Besides my best friend being MIA, the star pitcher on our baseball team asking me to be his date to Senior Ball, or the race on Saturday against the fastest girl in the league—yeah, I'm having a day."

"A date for Senior Ball. Now *that* sounds serious." Dad smoothed his black mustache and nodded his head. "Would I like this boy?"

I bit my lip to keep from smiling. "Yeah. I think so. He's nice."

"So, I imagine you'll need a dress."

"Yeah, probably."

"And I'll need a gun."

"Dad!" I tried to move away from him.

He chuckled, holding me tight. "Just kidding. I don't see the problem. My daughter's bloomed into a beautiful young lady and this *respectable* gentleman, as you've confirmed, has noticed."

I hid my blushing cheeks next to his chest. "Dad."

"Of course, there's going to be an interview, polygraph, and I'll need his social security number."

"Oh geez. I shouldn't have told you."

"Okay, an introduction will do—"

I let out a large sigh.

"—But as far as Tatiana goes, no one's been reported missing, so I bet her family probably left on an emergency and will be back soon. And you'll do fine on Saturday. Keep your head down and pretend a shark's behind you. I'm looking forward to watching the race."

I peered up into his face. The porch light shone around his head, creating a halo effect. "Just don't be the loudest on the bleachers this time, okay?"

"I've got my air horn all ready."

I tried to twist out of his grasp again but he gave me a playful noogie on my head.

"Dad."

He laughed and let me go. "No, seriously. I'll do the dishes tonight. Take all the time you need." He smiled and then went back inside.

The chilly breeze moved my hair and tickled my cheek. After working through my frustrations from Mom, my queasy stomach fluttered with butterflies. Never in my wildest dreams did I imagine the outcome of today's events. But here I was, going to Senior Ball with Callahan. Only then did I jump up and down in elation.

10

FIN

"Wow." I surfaced to find a newly installed air bubble inside our mer house. "When did this happen?"

"Today." Tatiana ran her hand through the light from a sun-mirror and phased out of her fin, then leapt up onto the stone floor. "Mom? Mom! I can't stay here anymore. Look at what they did to me!"

She disappeared around the corner which gave me the perfect opportunity to phase and throw on my shorts. Apparently Mom hadn't had time to put up a privacy curtain.

"Mother of pearl!" Mom yelled from the back room.

I cringed. Not the reaction I hoped for. Sobs from Tatch followed. I ducked into my room and stopped in my tracks.

In the corner, a lava lamp illuminated a new hammock, complete with a downy comforter and feather pillow encased in a green striped sheet. A poster of my favorite band, *The Classic Crime* hung on the wall and a few of my favorite books lined the shelves. My childhood *Star Wars* action figures sat on a stack of T-shirts.

I thumbed through the pile, pulled on my favorite "#TessieLives" shirt, and laughed. No mer in Natatoria would have any idea what it meant, let alone understood the concept of Twitter.

With a smile, I curled back on mesh netting. Since we slept on the bottom of the pool at night, my bed at home only served as a household prop. But with the continual sunlight available through mirrored tunnels, I could have my legs all night. I wiggled my toes, enjoying the refreshing change. Mom thought ahead this time.

"Good," she said while peeking around the rock doorframe.

"How did you know? When did you do this?"

She smiled. "Dad took this stuff down right before the meeting. He guessed we might be spending an extended stay in Natatoria, so I thought this would help with the transition."

I sat up. "Tatch said Dad's not coming back."

Mom walked over barefoot, wearing a sequined skirt that shushed when she walked. She sat next to me on the hammock. "He's coming back. I'm just not sure when."

"Where is he?"

"Today, in the palace, someone accidentally mentioned it's top secret, so not even I'm allowed to know." Mom folded her hands in her lap, keeping a sullen expression.

I swallowed hard. Top secret sounded dangerous and Mom appeared to be stuffing her worry. "So now what?"

"We wait, we do as we're expected and when your father returns, we go home." She patted my knee.

I groaned. I didn't want to stay any longer than we had to. Fresh oxygen and the sun hanging in the sky still rated higher than some fancy mirror labyrinth and a bubble. "But what about the business?"

"Hopefully Alaster doesn't burn up our fleet," she said with a forced laugh. "We'll just fix his mistakes when we get back. Next time you'll be old enough and this won't happen again, though Al's made no secret he wants Tahoe. I'm hoping you'll have the gate and the business one day. But your chances will increase if you have a wife. You should use this time to meet other mermaids your age."

Ashlyn's smile fluttered into my mind. She'd been the first and only girl that captured my attention. "Mom, it's not that easy to meet girls."

"Then go to the courting room."

I rolled my eyes. Only desperate mermen went there. "Geez, Mom."

"So you're not planning to attend the festival?" Mom's eyes studied mine, piercing me through to my unpromised soul. "Are you planning to leave the mer life instead?"

I clenched my jaw. "Of course not."

She closed her eyes and sighed. "I'm concerned you're going to choose to leave because we never tried to help you fit into Natatoria's way of life."

"It's not that, Mom. I like the fresh air and sunshine."

She looked at me with tears in her eyes. "Being a mer is a wonderful thing. There's no sickness, endless youth, and long life. The promise gave me my soul mate, your father. That's all I've ever wished for you and your sister."

"You don't have to sell it to me." I patted her on the shoulder. "I like being a mer. I just want to find a girl on my terms."

Tatiana peeked around the doorway, her hair bound up in a towel.

"Come here." Mom opened her arms wide. Tatch joined in and the three of us sat swinging, encased in mom's hug. "Listen. I know this change has been rough. Tatiana, I'm sorry you've become the Barbie doll of the Queen. And Fin, for being stuck with us. It's only temporary. Dad will groom you to take over Tahoe, like you want when he gets back. And Tatiana, I'll help you get into a college in Tahoe or even" —she took a deep breath— "let you date since you don't seem keen on any mermen here. Let's just get through this, all right?"

"Okay," Tatch moaned in agreement, followed with a sniffle.

"Sure, Mom." I didn't know what else to say.

11

ASH

I walked into my room from being outside, shivering and anxious. My cell phone on the nightstand signaled I had a missed call. I picked it up and looked at the display before playing the message, hoping for a call from Tatchi.

"You've got ten new messages. First message—"

My mouth gaped open. *Ten messages? What?*

Georgia's voice roared through the earpiece and I rushed to turn down the volume.

"Where are you? I've been dying to talk to you. You'll never guess what happened. I have to tell you in person. Call me back right away. Okay? Just call me back—"

My chest constricted.

"Next message—"

Georgia again. "Where the heck are you? I have to talk to you—"

Irritated, I clicked the delete button.

"Ashlyn, gosh, where—"

Delete.

"Are you like out or something? I have—"

Delete.

"It's Georg—"

Delete.

"I—"

Delete.

I jumped when the phone vibrated with another call, just when I was about to hit delete if I heard her voice again. Caller ID said it was none other than Georgia.

Great.

If I let it ring, she'd just keep calling and eventually fill up my voice mailbox. And, just in case Tatchi called, I didn't want to shut my phone off.

"You rang?" I said in a monotone voice.

"Ashlyn! Where have you been? I've like called a million times—" I held the receiver away from my ear at a more comfortable decibel. "—are you there?"

"Yes. What's up?"

"Oh my gosh. I have news. Big news. Are you ready?" She took a huge breath, then giggled. "After you left practice, Callahan came over and asked me for—"

"—my phone number, I know."

I smiled at her sudden silence.

"You know already? Did he call? What did he want?"

I felt bad for stealing her thunder, but after knowing she'd left ten messages, I wasn't in the mood for her usual chirpy chatter.

"He called to ask me to Senior Ball," I said, my stomach rolling around like a cement mixer.

"He did?" Georgia squealed. I pinched my eyelids shut as a dull headache formed in my temple. "And what did you say?"

Telling Georgia the news before I told Tatchi felt like a cardinal sin against our friendship but her sudden absence left me no choice. "I told him I'd go."

She squealed again, but her excitement was more grating than thrilling. All I wanted to hear was Tatchi's more mature enthusiasm on the other line. Drained and suddenly worried about Tatchi, I just wanted to get off the phone.

"Georgia, I hate to do this, but I'm really tired. Can we talk about this in the morning?"

"Are you kidding me? The cutest guy in school asks you out and you're tired?"

"I know—it's just been a super long day. Tomorrow, I promise."

She pushed out a gust of air, her voice filled with disappointment. "Okay. I guess. Talk to you tomorrow."

I hung up and slid onto my floor in a heap, tempted to turn off my phone entirely. My gut quivered in excitement and my heart hurt with worry. The biggest news of my life and the one person I wanted to tell wasn't home. Where did Tatchi's family go in such a hurry anyway?

::::

In the morning, I managed to sneak downstairs, snag a piece of toast, and escape before anyone converged in the kitchen. With my swim bag in hand, I pulled on my thick coat and trudged down the street through a dusting of new snow. I'd already decided to take a little detour and walk past Tatchi's house on the way to the bus stop.

I stopped and stared at the wood siding for a second, my heart pounding. But no matter what I told myself, it was as far as my feet would could go. Disgusted I couldn't even knock on the door, I turned to leave when someone tall and blonde walked around the corner, cursing something under his breath.

I gasped. His electric blue eyes met mine.

"Why *hello*," Handsome Boy said, flashing a crooked smile and sauntering towards me. "Can I help you?"

"Tatiana," was all I could mutter, my tongue glued to the roof of my mouth.

His eyes, deep and cool, sucked me into a watery vortex I wanted to sink into and look at forever. My mind and muscles went numb, like the time I'd secretly drunk Uncle Roger's beer in the cellar on a bet at the annual family reunion six years ago.

"Well, aren't you fun?" He walked closer and I couldn't stop staring. "Actually, my loathsome cousin isn't here and honestly, I hope she never returns."

I wanted to be concerned and ask how he could talk about her like that, but his lips, so soft and luscious, called to me to kiss them. I took a step forward. He reached out, about to touch my face when a gruff voice echoed from within Tatchi's house.

"Colin! Did you find those darn keys yet?"

Handsome Boy turned his face away from me and frowned—breaking the spell. "No. I'll be there in a second!"

I tore my eyes away and looked at the ground. The fuzziness began to melt away, drawing me back to clarity. I rubbed my forehead.

"Um," I garbled, "tell her to call Ashlyn when she gets back or whatever—"

As my senses returned, danger warnings screamed for me to get out of there—now! I stumbled backwards and high tailed it up the hill towards the road without looking back.

"Don't be a stranger, Ashlyn," Handsome Boy (I could only assume to be named Colin) called after me with a voice rich like chocolate.

My throat hitched as something inside wanted to turn around and look into his eyes again, but my feet kept moving forward, taking me to safety.

My heart thudded at an elevated rate the entire ride to school; partially from the weird interaction with Colin, but also in anticipation of seeing Callahan. Did this all happen, or was the whole thing some weird dream?

Georgia's expression after I walked through the gym doors confirmed it was real. Beyond us, a few zombies shuffled in and changed into their swimsuits. I focused back on her, knowing what she'd do next. Nothing like a squeal from Georgia to wake everyone up prematurely.

The shrill made me pinch my eyes shut. Then we were bouncing up and down, in joyous giggles.

"So, I guess I need shoes too," I said midair, letting her excitement creep into my life, finally.

That launched her into a monologue, words and questions speeding out of her mouth so fast, not even a court reporter could keep up.

"Whoa." I held up my hands as we walked across the deck towards the pool. "Let's take one thing at a time. I need to get a dress first."

"Oh totally. Let's go shopping after practice."

"Okay." I bit my lip, hoping Mom would be cool with that idea too. "And as far as transportation, we probably *could* all ride together in the same limo, but I don't know what Callahan's got planned so far."

Georgia grinned. "Okay."

I dove in the pool to escape her, thankful for the silence when an ecstatic scream could be heard echoing underwater.

This is going to be a long day.

12

FIN

The smell of breakfast roused me from my sleep. Groggy and unaware, I popped open one eye and peered out the window. Where redwoods and sunlight should have been, fish swam by in the dimly lit water.

"Ugh," I put my head in my hands.

My throbbing legs, covered in scales, were unsure if they should remain appendages or fuse into a fin. Mom's blithe song stopped me from my rant. I rolled out of the hammock and headed towards the lovely sounds and smells drawing me to the kitchen.

On the wall, the world clock said the time was noon in Tahoe. Underneath, an illuminated section highlighted where the sun shone over a replica of the earth with little black dots to show all the gates into Natatoria across the world. Homesick, my eyes zeroed in on the one I cared about and wondered what Colin was up to. Probably still trying to figure out where I'd hidden my clothes, no doubt.

Mom turned to me with a grin before adjusting the overhead mirror to shine sunlight onto her workspace.

"These burners are sure different," she said as she flipped pancakes in one pan, and stirred scrambled eggs in another over a sparkling new lava-heated stovetop. "I'm having a hard time judging how hot they are."

I bent down to inspect the lava bubbling under the gel covers of each hot plate. Mom lifted her hand and brushed a few damp tendrils of her hair aside. On the skin of her ring finger, the ornate tattoo I rarely saw caught the light—the mark of her promising to Dad.

Normally, her diamond wedding ring covered the ink that she said magically appeared shortly after they kissed for the first time. But the absence of her most prized possession left me wondering.

"How did you pay for the air bubble and the new stove?" I asked hesitantly.

"The what, honey?" she asked, pouring more pancake batter into the pan and licking the excess off her finger.

"The bubble." I gestured my arms around the room.

She quickly turned her back to me and pulled plates from the shelves carved out of rock. "I was able to barter for one."

At the mention of bartering, my stomach dropped. "What did you barter?" I asked, fearing I already knew the answer.

She turned back around and gave me a guarded look. "It's nothing to worry about."

I watched her finish dishing up our breakfast and motion we sit at the table. Her silence added to the dread already gnawing in my stomach.

"I'm loving the oxygen, aren't you?" She buttered and layered strawberry jam on top of her pancakes, then motioned for me to do the same as I stared at her.

I couldn't. I had to know the truth. "Mom, where's your ring?"

She stopped in the middle of salting her eggs and hesitated. "I traded it in," she finally said.

"You did? But, why—"

Mom traced her thumb over her bare finger. "It's fine."

Speechless, I stared at the steam wafting up in circles from my food, my appetite ruined.

"Since we are going to be awhile, there were a few things we needed to be comfortable. It's not like they can take my debit card, so I had to make a decision. The stones can be replaced. Your father will understand."

My eyes stayed firmly glued to my plate, though I clenched my fists under the table. She should have at least talked to us first before selling her most precious possession. We could have come up with another way to pay for the air bubble or done without for a little while.

"Really, it's fine. I'm not upset. This is our home under the sea. It needed some love."

I shook my head, amazed at how lighthearted she was about the whole thing. We both knew the real reason we couldn't be in Tahoe right now. She wasn't allowed on land without Dad. But unlike what everyone would have you think, it had nothing to do with the wiles of a mermaid's reputation. The King's insecurity over the loyalty of beta-mers, promised or not, insisted they be chaperoned.

"This sucks, Mom. We could be in Tahoe. It's all because of fear and technicalities that we aren't."

Mom held up her hand to stop me. "I'm fully aware why the laws are the way they are. You and your sister aren't aware of the horrible things man can do. Their greed would put us in laboratories in a heartbeat, and for many millennia the law has kept the mer safe and pure of heart. Your father is one of the few who has enough street smarts to live close to humans and remain undetected—God protect his soul. But I've had some time to think and I've realized something—this predicament we're in is actually a blessing in disguise."

My jaw dropped. "What do you mean?" I asked, cocking my head to the side.

"I mean, look at where we are. It's wonderful here. No crime, love is all around us, people are happy and it's the most gorgeous scenery ever. And, other than missing your father, it's like a vacation."

I scoffed. "But you complained just last night you were having a hard time adjusting here, without the sun and stuff."

"I know what I said, but after a good night's sleep, I've had a change of heart. It's growing on me and, with the bubble, it feels like home. But really, we need to start thinking of the big picture. I was talking yesterday with some of the other mermatrons, and I wasn't aware of all the opportunity there is for you kids. You both need to seriously embrace the culture, and me too. We all could use some friends of our own kind."

Who took the woman who'd consoled me last night and replaced her with this robot? We'd avoided this place like poison and now she wanted me to embrace it?

"And I was thinking, goodness, you both are around the most eligible mers of the land, you could introduce each other to someone. And maybe if Tatiana is dating, Azor will back off."

I blinked at the tsunami of information Mom spewed at me. In her sleep, she must have sprung a screw loose. This was insanity.

"You've got so much potential. What if there's something better than Tahoe? Maybe a larger gate or—" Mom gasped, "what about sun tunnel excavation?"

"Mom, I don't think—"

"And once you get promised, don't wait too long to have merlings."

At that, I choked, almost spitting eggs out of my mouth as she looked at something invisible in the horizon with a smile—the first real smile since we'd arrived.

"What's this about merlings?" Tatchi asked as she shuffled into the room.

Perfect timing.

"I'm glad you've decided to join us. Get some breakfast and have a seat," Mom said, her voice overly cheerful.

I wiped my mouth off on a napkin and took a moment to breathe before taking another bite. Tatiana turned up her lip and marched over to the kitchen counter to inspect the buffet. Never again would I be the first to breakfast in case of another bi-polar ambush.

"Let me guess. This is about the festival," she quipped while drowning her pancakes with syrup.

"Well—" Mom took a sip of her coffee. "No, not entirely."

"There's coffee?" I asked in surprise. With the distraction of Mom's absent ring, I'd completely missed she'd made some.

"Yes. It's on the stove."

I hopped up, planning to snag a cup and run for the door before another mention of merlings came up. Tatiana shot me a look that said, "oh, great. Can't wait to hear what this is all about," which she couldn't say telepathically because we weren't immersed underwater. I smirked back. She needed this lecture way more than I did.

Mom continued to eat and speak nonchalantly. "I was just expressing some new ideas I had about how we can turn our frowns upside down."

"Is she okay?" Tatiana mumbled.

"Oh, just wait." Mer had hearing like a hawk and Tatch had to have heard the prior conversation. Obviously, her hunger overcame common sense to wait longer and avoid Mom's "hurray for Natatoria" pep talk.

Tatiana blew out a gust of air. "Look. I get it's safe and all wonderful down here, but don't you see what the cost is? Azor's going to be outside this house as soon as I leave for the palace in an hour and stalk me until I agree to his hand. He is the prince after all. How is that the 'land of opportunity'?"

"Tatiana, don't be so dramatic. I was just going to suggest your brother escort you from now on and I'm also going to have a talk with Azor. Just because he's the prince doesn't mean he can bend the rules. No mermaid is to be alone with a single merman, period, and he knows that. He's not swimming all over me because your father isn't here. Besides, I was suggesting to your brother you hook each other up with dates anyway."

Tatiana coughed. "Find Fin a date?" She howled in laughter.

"What's wrong with that?" Mom asked and raised her eyebrow.

"Yeah," I chimed in.

She smirked and went back to shoveling food into her mouth while standing at the counter, like she planned a quick exit, too.

Mom huffed. "Can't we all eat at the table please? Come sit down, both of you."

Tatch and I exchanged glances. A layer of fear lay behind her eyes, hidden beneath a tough exterior. For Mom to think Tatch would suddenly embrace Natatorian culture just because she asked was crazy. That in itself would require an act of God, especially since the night before, Mom had promised her something completely different.

Mom took our hands once we joined her. "I love you both and want what's best for you. It's hard enough for me to be without your father, but I can't deal with four to five months of constant pouting and bickering. We're a family and merfolk. So let's accept this, find the good, and stick together."

"Fine," I lifted up my hands and went back to my breakfast.

"Yeah, sure, but I don't need Fin's help to find a date," Tatiana said with a smirk, letting go of Mom's other hand.

"Me neither," I muttered with a mouthful of food as Tatch stuck out her tongue.

"Good," Mom said.

Tatch started in on her breakfast again. "So you're all of a sudden okay with this because you want to be a grandmother?"

"Well, something Portia said yesterday about her daughter's new little merling on the way got me thinking."

"Good sea snails!" Tatchi exclaimed. "But what about last night? You promised me I could go to college and date a human guy."

"Well . . ." Mom took another swig of her coffee. "That's not entirely out of the question. But for now, I want you to try to make things work here. You never know, you might just like it."

Tatiana sighed dramatically. "Yeah, well—I'll play nice for now, but I refuse to be trapped here forever. And so far, there hasn't been one solitary merman like Dad who's cute *and* enjoys the land more than the sea. So, I'm going to be taking you up on your offer, Mom."

Mom shifted in her seat. "That's fine as long as you two look out for each other."

Tatiana and I glanced at one another, and she stuck out her tongue. I jabbed her arm with my elbow. Though we were cordial again, the pressure still lingered right under the surface. Without Dad things would continue to remain tense, as Tatch's desire to leave grew stronger. My only hope was she'd meet someone. If not, her ultimate decision to leave was going to break my parents' heart. And mine, too.

13

ASH

I sat in English, heart pounding as I slyly watched each person walk through the doorway, anticipating Callahan's entrance. Georgia entered with a grin, looking like the top of her head was going to zip right off, and plopped in the chair in front of me.

"Where is he?" she whispered, gawking at his empty seat.

"How would I know and stop being so obvious." I ran my hand through my bangs, trying to keep cool as I inconspicuously hid my searching eyes behind my wrist.

Then he walked in. A moment passed before his spine-tingling gaze landed on mine and held it. My breath froze. The warmth behind his mouth-watering chocolaty eyes made my stomach do cartwheels.

He mouthed a "Hi". I evaporated into nothingness for a quick minute before I whispered one back. He kept a flirtatious eye on me as he sauntered over to his chair, a beautiful smile upon his tantalizing lips. I rested my chin inside the palm of my hand to hide my enjoyment of our silent interaction.

"Oh. My. Gosh," Georgia mumbled.

I hit her with my book and turned to watch Mrs. Keifer get up from her desk to begin the discussion on *The Scarlet Letter*. Callahan's golden smile continued to skip rope across my heart, breaking all my concentration and taking over my thoughts.

I did listen somewhat about Hester Prynne's unwillingness to divulge the identity of her baby's father, as I watched Callahan joke with Evan through the curtain of my hair. Inside, my excitement and anxiety grew, wondering if I'd still be able to find a dress in time. Could this really be happening?

Behind me, harsh whispers interrupted my dream world. I nonchalantly glanced back to see the source, meeting Brooke's glare head on, then gulped and turned away. *She knows.*

"Who'd you tell?" I wrote on a paper and passed it to Georgia.

"No one, yet. Why?"

"Brooke is staring at me."

She smirked. *"Let her."*

Georgia was thrilled I'd been elevated above the pecking order, unaware of the cold front blasting me from behind. My heart beat hard thinking about what Brooke might do to me later—a sundry of options playing through my head. Luckily girls didn't throw girls into dumpsters like boys did.

When the bell rang, I was the first one out of the classroom, unprepared to talk to anyone face-to-face yet. With a mad dash, I plunged through the double doors and sloshed through the soupy slush to the History modular across campus. Neither Callahan nor Brooke were in this class, which would give me enough time to figure out what to say once I did get the chance.

"Wait up," Georgia called behind me, out of breath. "What's with you?"

She grabbed my arm to slow me down.

"I'm not sure I want to go with Callahan after all."

"What?! Are you insane?" Georgia's shrieking voice made me want to put my hand over her mouth.

"Shhh, geez. I'm just confused why he wants to take me. Brooke's friends are going to kick my ass for ruining Brooke's life, you know?"

"Forget them. She's all bark, no bite. Besides, they fight all the freaking time over everything. It's a good thing for both of them," Georgia said with raised eyebrows.

"But still—" I took a deep breath. Icy air stung my nostrils.

"They'll find a way to punish me. I know it."

Georgia put her hand on my shoulder. "He likes you. Just accept it. And have fun. You deserve this."

I want to.

We stepped inside the warm classroom and I appreciated the time to think. But lunch came quicker than I wanted and the new blanket of snow made the outside picnic benches a no-go. I surfed into the cafeteria amongst the sea of bodies looking for shelter. I didn't intend to avoid Callahan for as long as I had, but at this point—shy or not— I needed to get over my insecurities and talk to him in person. Worried his presence would make me a bumbling mess, I quickly ate my turkey sandwich.

"Nervous?" Georgia asked, while chewing on her celery stick, eyeing the cafeteria like a prairie dog.

"No," I lied and cocked my head to the side. "I don't know how you have energy to swim only eating rabbit food."

"I gotta stay slim for the slinky dress, don't ya know."

"What about the peanut butter cup I saw you eating earlier?"

"Nice. I was starving and—" Georgia's mouth remained open, but the sound stopped pouring out.

I licked my lips as my neck prickled. "He's behind me, isn't he?"

She nodded ever so slightly, as soft footfalls stopped behind my chair.

Here we go.

"Hey, Georgia. Is this seat taken?" I heard a beautiful masculine voice ask.

I turned, accosted by his brown eyes and enticing scent at the same time. My voice betrayed me, paralyzed in my throat as he sat down.

"Nope, have a seat," Georgia cooed.

For once I was thankful for her gift of gab. He set down his lunch tray and they started chatting about the snow pack at Heavenly Ski

Resort where Callahan worked. He continued to watch me with a boyish grin but my good-for-nothing cardboard tongue didn't want to move, so I snacked on my corn chips, and smiled instead. I didn't have much to contribute since my world revolved around the swim team. But there he was, Mr. All Star Pitcher, eating his burrito and looking incredibly gorgeous, sitting next to me.

"So, everything's cool with Senior Ball?" he asked me quietly once Georgia got distracted and started to chat with Shannon and Gracey, who happened to pass by but couldn't keep their eyes off of us. Callahan didn't notice.

I nodded and rolled my eyes. "Yeah. Sorry about hanging up so quickly. I have an annoying little sister who seems to know when I'm on the phone and likes to barge into my room."

"I have one of those, too." He smiled and his eyes sparkled under his brown hair that practically begged me to run my hands through it. I giggled and melted into a puddle for the second time that day.

The school day ended better than expected, minus the run-in in the hall with Myranda, one of Brooke's clones who bumped me, purposefully knocking my book on the floor. Other than their evil looks, that was it. I'd expected so much more.

But Callahan liked me and asked *me* to Senior Ball. Neither my uncouth conversational skills nor reeking chorine-infused skin seemed to bother him. Instead he walked me to my last two periods and asked if he could call tonight. I'd already decided to prop the chair under the door knob to keep Lucy out when he did.

Snow continued to fall as I jumped from Georgia's passenger seat with damp hair from practice. We'd made plans to go shopping. I just needed to ask permission and get some money.

The bell to the store chimed as I entered. I scuffed off the ice from my boots and waited as Mom stood behind the counter, her cacophonous voice filling the small enclosure. With flailing arms, she continued on with her story as she rung up the merchandise, oblivious her customers were antsy to leave. I stayed back by the window so Georgia could still see me, secretly scrutinizing the closed sign at Captain Jack's with hopes Tatchi would walk out the doors.

"I know you'll be happy with the quality of those sweatshirts," Mom called out to the blissful couple. "Have a nice day."

I smiled as they exited; mom's gaze fell on me.

"Thank God for the snow. Lucky for us, they packed for warmer weather. So how are you doing today?"

"Great, Mom," I said with a smile, actually showing some teeth and her face stayed lit up.

"Well, that's wonderful to hear. Something exciting must have happened today."

"Kind of." I removed my gloves and smoothed the front of my jeans with my hands. "I don't know if Dad mentioned anything, but—"

Mom snapped her fingers and pointed. "That's right. Senior Ball. So I guess we need to go get you a dress, don't we? Just give me a minute to close up here."

The reason for her joyousness made sense now. She hoped we'd go together, a mother-daughter bonding moment. I swayed as the last shopping trip came to mind. She'd held up every ugly or too-much-skin revealing outfit and mocked the designer while I tried to blend into a rack of clothes next to me.

"Actually, Georgia's in the parking lot right now, and we're going together this afternoon, if you don't mind."

Her curled lips fell into a straight line. "Oh. I see."

Guilt hit me hard, pulling my shoulders forward. "Sorry, Mom. She offered and I thought you'd be busy."

"It's okay. You're right." She began to refold the shirts fanned out on the display table in front of her. "I do have to finish sorting that shipment."

"I knew you'd understand."

She continued to straighten the shelf and brush off the invisible dust while I stalled, waiting for her to offer up cash.

"I—I need some money."

"Right. How much are formal dresses nowadays?"

Honestly, I didn't have a clue. "Like a hundred or so—?"

"And shoes, I imagine." Her eyes glazed over as she mouthed something inaudible. I braced for a discussion when she walked over and opened the cash register. "Here's two hundred. Spend it wisely. Oh, and don't forget to order your date a boutonniere."

I blinked at her as she put the bills into my hand and went back to arranging the display. Whatever Dad said to her yesterday had worked. This was much less painful than I expected.

"Thanks, Mom." I left before she could change her mind.

14

❧

FIN

I paced the length of our small living room, checking the sun clock yet again. If Tatch didn't hurry, I'd be late to the practice field. "Come on, Tatch. It's all going to wash off when you get in the water anyway."

"Shut-up, Fin. I'm almost finished," Tatch yelled from her bedroom.

I blew out a gust of air and sat on the couch. For me to get ready took all of two minutes. There was no need to get dressed or take a shower and the bathroom was technically outside, which grossed me out at times.

After ten more minutes passed, she finally walked into the room, looking no different than she had at breakfast. "Finally." I shook my head.

She glowered and stuck out her tongue. "Stop being such a stickleback."

I ignored her and marched over to the new privacy curtain mom just hung up that partially obscured the porthole entry. As I took off my shorts, pulled back the rock door, and dunked my legs into the water, little bells tinkled from a string that fed through a pipe in the floor I'd never seen before.

"What's that?" I asked.

"The door bell," Mom called from the kitchen.

"Sea stars, it's Azor!" Tatch gasped. Her feet slapped the smooth rock floor as she retreated back to her room. "Tell him I'm not home."

I sat on the rim of the porthole and pulled back the curtain, unsure if I should phase back into my legs or not.

Mom walked around the corner, looking as angelic as ever with a beaded skirt and tasseled fringe top. "Invite him in," she said, her voice filled with posture—the tone that said she meant business.

I quizzically studied her confident demeanor, confused at the change from her normal insecure manner in the presence of the pure-born, then shrugged and dove underwater to find Azor waiting outside.

"Azor," I said with a nod.

"Finley, I was hoping to escort your sister today. Is she at home?"

Conflict erupted inside me, unsure what to tell him. I could lie like Tatch wanted and protect my mom from the confrontation, or follow her orders and invite him in. I glanced up at the one-way window, knowing Mom probably watched us from the other side.

"Yeah, come on in. I hope you've brought something to cover yourself. We've had the air interior installed."

"Oh, really?" He looked upward and noted the bubbles escaping from our rooftop. "I do," he said smugly, placing his hand on a small rectangular box attached to his utility belt. My leather waterproof one was much cooler.

"You're welcome inside then." I held out my hand to lead the way.

Azor swam up through the porthole and disappeared into the house. When I surfaced behind him, he'd already phased into legs and wore a black man-skirt and matching sock-like boots. I tried not to snicker. He didn't pull off the kilt look like Badger did.

"Why hello, Magdelene," Azor said, his voice laced with charm.

Mom smiled sweetly but gave him a stern look. "Azor, I'd like to be called Mrs. Helton, if you don't mind. And while you are here, please—" she motioned towards our moss covered couch, "have a seat."

Azor grimaced slightly before following her instructions. I guessed it wasn't often that someone corrected him.

Again, I chuckled on the inside, but sat on the porthole rim, still finned up, uncertain what Mom wanted me to do. She gave me the "stay put" look as she took a seat in a chair on Azor's left hand side.

"Tatiana, please come here," Mom called over her shoulder.

A smile spread on Azor's lips. I squinted, unsure what Mom was up to, but I knew it wouldn't be in Azor's favor.

"Yes, Mom?" Tatiana said timidly as she came around the corner, but didn't make eye contact with Azor—pretending he wasn't there.

"Your brother has offered to escort you today and Azor has conveniently stopped by. I need to discuss a few things with him before I join you at the palace. Is that all right?"

"Oh . . . okay, I guess." She gave Mom a kiss on the cheek, then turned towards Azor with a fake look of disappointment. "I didn't see you there. Hello," she said curtly, then pivoted towards me with a huge grin on her face and plunged into the porthole feet first.

As soon as I was underwater, all I could hear were peals of laughter in my head.

"Did you see his face? Sweet urchins! Mom is going to let him have it."

I laughed back. *"I know. He thought Mom was calling you out to see him, not to get a lecture. And she is on a roll today."*

"This day has totally turned around," she said, sounding jovial for the first time since arriving. *"I'm going to be laughing about this for days."*

"Me, too."

With a hard flick of our tails, we sped off towards the palace, laughing like we use to in Tahoe.

15

ASH

I spun around in front of the mirror, wearing my new emerald-green gown. A solitary sequined strap crossed over my collar bone and looped around my neck, hugging my shoulder like a big hook. Never did I imagine a sleeveless dress would complement my overly muscular shoulders, but it did. The soft silk against my skin and the elegant way it hung to the floor made me feel like royalty. For a moment, I wished Senior Ball could have been tonight—not in two weeks.

The girls waited noisily downstairs for the fashion show as I slipped on my shoes. With small steps, my ankles wobbled as I traversed down the stairs. When I came into view, Mom brought her hand to her mouth and Lucy gasped.

"Aye, aye, aye," Gran said with a golden gleam. "Aren't you a picture?"

I smiled—just the reaction I'd hoped for.

"So who's your beau?" Gran asked after I came into the room and twirled a few times.

I twisted my lips and looked at Mom. "Bow?"

"Beau is another word for your date, or guy *friend*," Mom said, as she walked over and tugged on the seam under my armpit. "Is that comfortable?"

I nodded and she inserted a straight pin from her pincushion.

"His name is Callahan. He's the pitcher on our baseball team and a really good snowboarder." Joy burst from my heart as my feelings flowed freely from my mouth. For once the conversation revolved around me and not Lucy, who was still mute at the moment. "He's got brown hair and big brown eyes—" I daydreamed for a second, imagining us dancing together in the center of a dimly lit room.

"Well, in my day," Gran said with a sparkle in her eye, "things were very different. My parents were strict. In high school, they wouldn't let me go to a dance alone with a boy, but I could tag along with my older brothers."

I looked at Lucy and smiled evilly. She'd die if Mom and Dad did that to her when it was her turn.

Gran put her hand on Lucy's knee and squeezed. "So, I'd go with my brothers and meet up with your grandpa at the dance. We didn't do the wild moves you kids do now, more like dancing cheek-to-cheek or jitterbug. I was pretty good, but your Grandpa . . . he wasn't coordinated. Maybe it was his big feet, but we'd have a good time anyway."

"I've never heard this story," Mom said, pausing from pinning up my hem.

"Oh, I'm sure I've told it before," Gran laughed.

And this is how her stories surfaced. Out of nowhere Gran would pop out a story none of us had heard before, as if she kept them for special moments such as these. I'd resorted to studying the pictures scattered around the house to fill in some gaps of what their life was like together. The sparkle in their eyes told me they loved each other very much back in the day.

"Did you ever wear any pretty gowns like in the movies, Gran?" I asked while eyeing a particular picture where Gran pushed Mom in a baby stroller while Grandpa walked next to her, arm draped over her shoulder.

"Oh, no," she said with a chuckle. "We wore our everyday dresses and saddle shoes, not those—" she waved her hand at my strappy ones. "But I would have loved to. Boy, are you stunning."

I felt my cheeks grow hot. "Thanks, Gran."

"Oh, that reminds me. I have something for you." She rose from the couch and headed toward her room.

I looked at Mom who smiled knowingly. She returned with a brown garment bag. From inside she pulled out a white fox stole. "It was my mother's. I'd like you to wear it on Saturday."

My mouth dropped open as she draped the soft silky side over my shoulders and fastened the jeweled clasp front. I rubbed my cheek against the luscious fur, instantly enveloped in warmth. "Really?"

"Of course. The weather is supposed to be dreadfully cold, so it's perfect."

"Can I wear it?" Lucy asked, standing up and dragging her hand across the front of the stole.

"When you have a special occasion, darling, I'll let you borrow it as well." Gran took her arm and guided her back to the couch. They sat and she pulled Lucy into her shoulder. "Isn't your sister lovely?"

Lucy's sallow skin matched her sour expression as her eyes raked over the fur. She reluctantly nodded. I held my shoulders up and smiled, enjoying every second of the attention.

"I'm done," Mom said. "Go ahead and carefully take off your dress so I can sew it before the weekend."

I gingerly pulled the edge of my dress off the floor and did a Miss America wave. "Thank you everyone for voting for me."

Mom chuckled and looked to me with pride. "I can't wait for your father to see you."

"Me, too." *And Callahan.* I bit my lip and grabbed the garment bag before floating upstairs on a cloud of glee. Would I really be doing that the night of the dance? Did I have a chance to win?

In front of the mirror, I held up my hair to simulate an up-do. Georgia had offered to practice hairstyles on me Friday night since my little stash of cash was all gone. "Tiara hair" she called it.

What would Fin think of me now? No longer the plain girl next door. I smirked, wishing he'd be home when the limo pulled up and I walked out, drop-dead gorgeous on another guy's arm. I peered out the window towards his house, plotting my evil deed and spotted Colin pacing back and forth in front of Fin's Jeep, tapping something on the palm of his other hand. I gasped as he shoved the tool down into the window slot and pulled upward, a Slim Jim. With a flip of the handle, he opened the door.

"Don't you dare mess with Fin's Jeep," I said and positioned my index finger and thumb so I could pretend to squish his head.

He turned, looking down the street toward my two-story window as if he heard me. The hair prickled on my neck as I moved out of view. Through my chiffon curtains I watched him stare with a peculiar smile. He proceeded to crawl inside and dig around for something on the floor boards before he slammed the door and walked back into the house.

My breath came out choppy for a moment, feeling caught. How could he have heard me? I stayed rooted to my spot, wondering why he was breaking into Fin's Jeep. What was he looking for? If Fin knew he'd touched his Jeep, let alone broken into it, Colin would be dead.

I bit my lip, remembering how beautiful his eyes were—clear and blue like Fin's. And that an overwhelming desire to kiss him had flooded me. How could that have slipped my mind so easily? But did he actually say he hoped Tatchi didn't come back?

Suddenly, my blood boiled and I wanted to smack his sassy smirk right off his face. He knew where the family was and if I didn't hear anything from Tatchi tonight, I'd be paying him a visit tomorrow.

16

FIN

I dropped off Tatch and headed straight over to the practice field. Chauncey mentioned yesterday we'd get to drill with actual weapons today and I needed to hurry before everyone picked over the armory selection. My chances of defeating Badger could improve with something like a sword in my hand.

I tried to clear my mind and think only of the upcoming duel like Badger had instructed, but Tatch mentioned wanting to tell Ashlyn about what happened with Azor, which ended our jovial morning. At the mention of her name, my craving rekindled for the outdoors and the sun along with the desire to go home.

"Aye, yer late. Get over here before I give you a wallopin'," Badger said and threw me into a headlock, rubbing his knuckles into my skull.

"Hey." I wriggled free and took a fighting stance, barbs out. "Who made you my keeper? I had something I had to do." *Like babysit my sister.*

"Yer da' would want me to be keepin' watch over ye, and I don't want ye to be gettin' no demerits."

"Demerits? Ha! I wouldn't worry about that today." Out of the corner of my eye, I spotted a black tail zip by—Azor returning from our house with a wounded ego, no doubt. "So where are the weapons?"

Badger winked at me and took out a trident from behind a nearby rock. My smirk disappeared off my face. He continued to grin as he pulled out a golden javelin too. *He snagged two?* My hands ached at the sight of such fine pieces of workmanship, surprised the armory held weapons of such caliber.

"Aren't you a greedy charlatan," I said quickly, while clenching my jaw, figuring I'd probably end up with a wooden sword or worse—nothing, if everyone took more than one.

"You underestimate me, lad," he said, holding both pieces out toward me. "Pick yer poison."

I cocked my head to the side. "What?"

"I got two so ye could choose yer favorite."

"Really?" My smile returned. "Yer a good man, Badge."

"I know."

Grommet, the youngest of our group, sang a high pitched series of notes to signal the army to move into ranks. Azor hovered close by, stoic and visibly pissed off as the excitement heightened from the group. My enjoyment of his earlier tongue-lashing from Mom was hard to contain; I couldn't wait to tell Badger what happened. Azor impatiently flipped his tail a few times, stirring up the current to get our attention. The group silenced.

"Mermen," he said after clearing his throat, moving to float a few feet higher so we had to look up at him, "it is time we learn how to fight and defend our city!"

Everyone erupted into a sudden cheer, startling me. Was this the first time they'd ever had access to the armory?

"They say you can tell a lot about a merman by the weapon he takes into battle." Azor's scowl fell on me. "And we are at battle, gentle-mermen, don't be deceived. Man may look like you, he may sound friendly, and he may even give you the promise of his word, but never forget that his ultimate desire is to kill, destroy, and steal what is rightfully ours. Humans are never to be trusted. We must always remember that they are our enemy!"

Badger joined the hoots and hollers, beating his fist against the metal breast-plate over his chest. I stayed still, content to observe with my javelin in my hands behind my back. His agreement surprised me. He of all people, who once was a man, didn't strike me as one so apt to condone blanket condemnation of his previous kind. Before I could mention something, Azor continued.

"We must defend our city to the death. For here in our utopia, we have the delicate balance of peace, love, and happiness that the humans cannot understand. They do not have the capacity to progress to this level and never will. So, take your weapons and master them. Make them become an extension of you! Of us! Of Natatoria! For we are the master race!"

More hoopla rang out from the group as mermen clashed their weapons against one another's in a chorus of thundering metal. Badger raised his trident toward me.

"Look the part, lad. Someone's watchin' ye, thinkin' yer gettin' soft on the human folk."

Out of the corner of my eye, I caught Azor's glare. Instantly, I raised my javelin and clanked it against Badger's, growling on the exterior, but disagreeing in my heart. There were plenty of virtuous men on land, like Ash's dad who was a fireman. Not all of them were lost to greed. Unfortunately, Azor never had an opportunity to find out himself, being a snob in his underwater kingdom, content to preach fear.

"Come, lad. Let's get to fightin'," Badger said quickly, gaining my attention.

"But you don't—"

He grabbed my arm and shook his head. "Not here. Come."

I followed him to our dueling spot, feeling slapped for doing nothing wrong. Once we were out of earshot he turned abruptly with fire in his eyes. "Son. A word of advice. Don't be gettin' bold and assertin' your displeasure of what Azor be sayin'. For the most part, he be talkin' just to hear hisself talk, but you don't want him on your bad side. Ya hearin' me?"

I backed away. "What's the big deal?"

Badger got back in my face. "The deal is, he's royalty and if they suspect you're gettin' soft on the humans, they'll yank yer chain so fast yer head'll spin. I don't think you'll be takin' too kindly to stayin' here the rest of yer life!"

"What?" I rolled my eyes. If that were true, we'd have been grounded a long time ago. Dad was a total rogue.

He sighed and pawed his hand through his wild hair. "Aye. I wouldn't be tellin' ya if I didn't know so."

"But you don't agree with what he's saying, do you?"

"Of course not." Badger took his hand and splayed it against his forehead. "I knew men that would cut their parts off to save me life. All he knows is he needs to keep peace and doesn't want another uprising like they had in '93."

"Uprising?"

He looked up toward heaven. "Oh, dear Lord of mercy, don't ya be knowin' your own history? I'm goin' to have a talkin' to your da' once he gets home fer not teachin' ya the important stuff of our ways. You don't know about Montauk and the massive town mind-wipe?"

I shook my head. As a family, we never discussed stuff like that. And now that he mentioned it, Dad didn't talk about the past at all.

"I don't be havin' time now to be schoolin' ya. You just come by me house tonight, and I'll fill ye in on what happened."

I pressed my eyebrows together. This sounded a heck of a lot more important than banging our swords together, especially if we never intended to fight for real. "But Badger."

"Don't be badgerin' me! Sparrin' is what we're supposed to be doin' now. We'll talk later, in private."

I glowered but moved into position. I knew if I didn't, Badger would knock me on the seafloor without warning. As we fought, I continued to stew. Why was I even here? Dad had no idea the ignorant fool he left me with, spewing asinine propaganda and running crappy drills with weapons we'd never use. If it weren't for Badger's company, I didn't know how I'd survive.

Once we arrived at Badger's house, I felt less heated and glad we decided to talk in private. Over the day, more questions came to mind, including if he heard any news about Dad.

Badge curled his toes and blew smoke circles while draining his Guinness—something Sandy must have scored last time she visited the mainland.

"Aye, man. I don't even know where to start. Weren't ye even partly curious about yer own folk?"

I shifted in my seat and looked at the ground; my orange juice suddenly tasted tart in my mouth. "Not really."

"Let me see," Badge leaned back and closed his eyes, "it was back in the spring of 1693. Frederick and Marta Fairchild were charged with the Montauk gate. Why, I don't know. They weren't the sharpest tools in the shed. It started out innocent, as they got real friendly with the neighbor folk. But after a bout of the fever, Frederick took to healin' the people with his secret elixir, our blood hidden in tomato juice.

"Word got out about the cure and more people flocked into town needin' help. Everythin' went smooth until people began demandin' the recipe, showin' up at all times of the day and night. Of course the mer weren't around durin' the night, which started the folk questionin' but finally someone caught them drainin' their blood which made a hash of everythin'.

"Only thing they could do was mind-wipe the town and disappear. The gate was sealed, and Frederick and Marta were never heard from again. Rumor has it, they were stripped of their mer and forced to live as humans."

I looked down at the ground. We weren't healing anyone, but we were pretty active in the community with our charter business. If this was such a huge fear, why were we allowed to do so? "Are we the only family who lives on land?"

"As far as I know. Most mer guardin' a gate are scared of losin' their fins so they stick close to Natatoria. But Jack is a different lot. The Council likes for him to keep tabs of what's goin' on up there."

I laughed under my breath and tried to keep from squirming in my seat. How could we be the only family who lived on land? Was that why Uncle Alaster wanted our gate so badly? Colin had said someone noticed we were getting too friendly. Was he purposely spreading rumors to get us kicked out? To get our fins taken from us?

I gulped, suddenly weighted with the responsibility. The King could, in all honesty, frown on Tatch's friendship with Ash. I could lose Tahoe.

"But it be nothin' to worry about." Badger scratched his beard. "Azor's off his nutter. No one's goin' to be so daft to do that again. But still, let the plonker blather with his gammy and fake like you be on his side."

I'd assumed something completely different—like a band of rebel mers threatened to overtake the palace and start a new reign or something. That would make more sense after Azor's speech, spoken to mermen who never left Natatoria. A javelin couldn't compete with a torpedo or a gun. Mind-wiping would be our only defense against humans.

"Yeah, sure." I stared at the painting of Badger's old ship, anxious to change the subject. I liked things better when I didn't know the truth. "Do you know were my dad went?"

"No, lad." He shrugged. "I haven't got a baldy."

I assumed "baldy" meant he didn't know. "So you're good friends?"

"Aye." Badger sat up to pour himself another stout. "I suspect if I weren't one of the bottom feeders, he'd a took me with him."

I squinted, working hard to follow his Irish slang.

Badger sighed and bowed his head. "Son, there be some right ole hoors who don't be trustin' us turned folk. They say if left alone, we'd be goin' back to the mainland just to tell our friends the secret."

"What? That's crazy."

"I agree. And because of it, we be treated like the womenfolk, forced to have the coppers keep an eye on us gits."

I laughed. Chaperones were a far cry from actual cops, mostly intrusive and annoying. But the whole idea of keeping everyone under lock and key over an event that happened such a long time ago seemed senseless. We blended into society perfectly fine without any suspicion. "Well, I trust ya, Badge," I offered eagerly.

"I know, Son." He raised his glass to me. "Fer that, I'm truly grateful. And fer Jack too. He never be lookin' down his nose at me."

I tapped my glass against his and took a swig of my juice. "So, if you could guess what they're doing, what would you say?"

"Maybe rescuing someone. Or fixin' a slip up. Who knows?"

I slumped in my chair, suddenly aware of our responsibility. We were in a big test tube, being watched to see who we'd stay loyal to. Tatch was going to blow everything when she chose to become human.

Badge looked at me with pity in his eyes. "Man, you look shook. Why aren't ya with yer pals doin' the ri-ra?"

"Oh," I scuffed my foot on the ground, my stomach sick, unsure what ri-ra meant. "I don't know. They're a little—"

"I know they be a bunch of quare hawks, but you need to be gettin' yerself a bird."

I began to realize, once Badge had a few drinks, his Irish slang came out indiscriminately. This time I didn't dare ask what a quare hawk or a bird meant.

"Oye." He shook his head and pounded his mug on the table. "Don't be a Fecky the Ninth! A girl, lad! Or don't ya be likin' girls?"

Ash came to mind. Though I wouldn't pursue a relationship with her considering my heritage, she'd been the first girl I'd ever noticed as being pretty. Back when we were kids, the three of us would sit for hours on the beach at Fannette Island, shooting the breeze. Even at fourteen, she'd talk about her passion for swimming, politics, and keeping Tahoe free from pollution. I'd hang on her every word, amazed at the depth of her understanding and confidence of what she wanted out of life.

I thought all girls would be like that until I met the other mermaids in Natatoria. They were flighty and only concerned with the latest girly trinket or palace gossip. Quite a disappointment.

"Yeah, of course I do. Geez, I've never heard them called *birds* before!"

"Aye," Badge mumbled something indecipherable under his breath.

"We're home," I heard Sandy sing-song from the front door porthole.

I sighed, hoping Sandy would subtly explain Badger's Irish humor to me. "We? Who ya brin' with ya?" Badge snipped.

From behind the curtain, Sandy and the redheaded girl who distracted me yesterday stepped into the living space. I shot to my feet.

"Well, look who's here," Badge said, getting to his feet as well. "How's my lil' gingernut?"

"Uncle Badger," she said playfully and walked forward to give him a hug.

"You be looking flah today."

"Thank you," the girl said gracefully, smoothing her skirt with her hands.

Badge whirled around, grabbed Sandy into an embrace, and leaned her backwards, planting a kiss on her lips. "Missed ya, love."

I looked away and noticed the redheaded girl move aside to keep from getting knocked over, cheeks flushed. Our eyes met for a second and she smiled sheepishly. Adrenaline zinged through my veins.

Sandy came up for air and righted herself. "I guess I should leave more often," she said. "I didn't know Fin would be keeping you company. Let me get everyone some treats." She disappeared into the kitchen with a dripping wet bag in her hands.

Awkwardly I stood and waited for Badge to suggest something, watching the redheaded girl look everywhere but at me.

"Well, sit yerselves down." Badge led us to the couch and forced us to sit together by placing his meaty hands on our shoulders and pushing down. "Lily, this here is Fin. He be a sound lad, so you should get to know him. And Fin, you'd be right to mind yer manners with my niece."

"Uh, hi," I said and offered my hand.

She took it and smiled; her green eyes sparkled at me under thick black lashes. "Hello."

My stomach did flip-flops when the soft skin of her hand brushed against mine.

"So, we were talkin' about the courtin' room in the palace and wondered what the kids were doin' there. I was quizzin' Fin on why he don't attend."

Lily scrunched up her face. "Oh, it's 'cause it's so boring, Uncle. The girls stay on one side of the room and the boys, the other. With the chaperones floating about you can barely get close enough to talk without someone tapping you on the shoulder, making you stay six inches apart."

In awe, I watched her lips move. The perfect pink crescents framed white straight teeth and produced a source of melodic eloquence I'd only experienced with Ash.

Badger slammed his cup down again, knocking me out of my daydream. "Janey Mack! Why do they all got their knickers in a bunch over kids talkin'? How they expectin' folk to be attending the festival if they don't let you at least mingle? If I were a chappy, ya all would be getting' promised tomorra'."

"Uncle." Lily rolled her eyes. "How anyone can think we'd just start making out because we were alone in the same room with a boy is absurd. We know the promise is a lifetime bond and, contrary to popular belief, mermaids do have self-control. Besides, have you seen the mermen? There definitely isn't anyone there I really want to—" she looked down and blushed, "—court."

She flicked a glance at me. I swallowed hard, lost for words.

"Ya got a level head on yer shoulders like yer ma and aunt," Badge interjected.

Lily smiled. "Thanks." She perched her hands on her knees. "So, I don't think I've even seen you at the palace. Are you visiting?"

"Uh." My mouth became dry. "Yeah, I guess so. We—my family—spend most of our time in Tahoe, guarding the gate."

"Oh?" Recognition flashed across her face. "That's it. You must be Colin's cousin. Right?"

I looked away, unsure if our relation would harm my chances of getting to know her further or not. "Yes?" I eventually croaked out. "Are you friends?"

"Yeah, actually. He's always talking about taking over the gate and I haven't seen him around lately, so—"

I ran my hand through my hair. "Yeah, he's there now 'cause my dad had to go on a mission for the King."

"Oh, wow." Lily's eyes grew wide in understanding for a second. "I see."

I looked away and Sandy came back in the room with a tray of cheese and crackers, along with fresh strawberries, grapes, and cut up wedges of apple with peanut butter. "Lily and I went into town today and picked up some fresh fruit."

Badger grunted in approval.

"Oh, my gosh!" Lily suddenly exclaimed, "I can see now why you spend so much time on land, Fin! The town was amazing. People were everywhere. Girls and guys holding hands and kissing right in public, and Sandy made me wear a dress and shoes. Shoes! Can you believe it?" She propped her barefoot up on the table and giggled with pride. "Look. I've even got a blister!"

Badger laughed. "Only me niece would think a wound received on land is a badge of honor. Now this be a wound." He pointed to a large scar on his thigh. Sandy punched him in the arm and gave him the evil eye, while sitting on the arm of his chair. "I was teasin'." Badge rubbed his arm and tried to act hurt until Sandy wove her hands into his hair.

Lily swooned, oblivious to their incessant flirting, and continued. "And we ate homemade pizza which was amazing and chocolate ice cream. And the animals—I've heard about dogs, but never seen one in real life before. This little white fluffy one was so adorable. I wanted to take him home with me."

"You've never been on land?" I asked, eyebrows knitted together.

"Well, we went once when I was younger, but not where people were around and definitely not to a—what did you call that, Auntie? A farm?"

"A farmers' market," Sandy corrected.

"Yes, with the farmers selling their fruits and vegetables in a park. I can't wait to try an avocado and a tomato. But you say you live on land in Tahoe all the time? How do you get to do that?"

"Uh, we've got a pool in our basement." I licked my lips, amazed at how naïve she was to the world above her. I guess if you always stayed in Natatoria, you wouldn't know what life on land was like. "We also have a sailing business and take people on cruises around the lake."

"You take humans on rides in your boat? No way!" Her eyes bulged from their sockets. "How did you get permission to do that?"

"Lily," Sandy interrupted, "remember, you have to keep our

adventure a secret. We don't want anyone to know that I go on land as often as I do."

"Of course. But I can talk to Fin about it. Right?"

Sandy chuckled and curled up into a tighter ball on Badger's lap as he rubbed her shoulders. "Yes. Fin's safe."

Lily looked at me with a glimmer of wonder and touched her lips. "I wish I lived on land and my parents had a gate instead of sea bed cultivation. I can't believe you get to be like a human every day."

I shrugged. "It's kinda cool, I guess. People, for the most part, are like us except they don't promise for life and there's crime and stuff. But, it's not all that bad. One day I hope to guard the Tahoe gate myself. I like the vibe there."

Lily sank back in her seat and curled her legs underneath her body. With a dreamy look, she bit her lip. "Wow. I wish I could live in a real house in a town like you and have a dog. Maybe one day." She hit me with a look that zinged an electrical current down my torso and into my legs.

"Yeah," I choked out, trying to sound like her suggestion didn't affect me like it did, "I think you'd like it."

Badger and Sandy, lost in each other's eyes, hummed in agreement.

17

ASH

The time flew by faster than I expected, and the fact that it was April 1st and the day before my big meet and Senior Ball was no joke. Nightmares of being crowned Senior Ball Queen in my underwear or trying to swim my race in JELL-O riddled my dreams.

I yawned at the cafeteria table, resting my chin against my palm while Georgia filled in the quiet with her random observations. Callahan, who'd become a regular at our table had a pre-game baseball meeting, putting a damper on my spirits. The way he'd blended right in as if he'd always been there and easily opened me up in our conversations left me awestruck. And again, we'd talked the night before until 1AM.

Georgia pushed the hair off her forehead with a freshly manicured fingernail. "So, I'm all set for tonight's up-do practice. I picked up this amazing hair paste and I can't wait to try it out."

"Sounds good." I sucked the last drop of milk from my carton but continued to make an obnoxious gurgling noise, remembering something Callahan said the night before—about wanting to have a son so he could teach him to snowboard.

Georgia reached over and stole the noisemaker from my hands. "Seriously, could you be any more blasé about this?"

I leaned back in my chair and folded my arms. "I'm not. I'm just thinking."

The warning bell rang and she moaned. "All ready? Come on. Let's go."

I scuffed my feet slowly behind her, still lost in a multitude of worries and thoughts. Once the school day finally ended, I headed to my locker to deposit my books before practice. In one swift turn, I plowed right into Callahan.

"Hey," he said, steadying me by my shoulders, holding me there, "where's the fire?"

"Oh, hi." I looked up into his big brown eyes beneath the shadow of his STHS baseball hat. "Do you have a game today?"

My legs wobbled as he rubbed his warm hands further down my arms.

His eyes softened. "Yeah. Can you come?"

My lips curled up as I imagined myself in the stands, my presence his good luck charm. "Is it here?"

"It's in Minden."

"Oh." I frowned. Swim practice would be at least an hour, then afterward Georgia expected me to do make-over night. Not to mention Minden was at least forty-five minutes away and I didn't have a car. "Why couldn't it be a home game?" I mumbled.

"You've got plans?" Disappointment darkened his face.

"Sort of. Sorry."

"That's too bad. Maybe next time."

We stood extra close as the hall emptied out, everyone rushing off to get to his or her Friday night plans or the locker rooms. My eyes darted to his perfect lips and my heart took off in a gallop, wondering if he'd make a move.

"Callahan. We're late. Let's go!" someone called down the hall, breaking his concentration.

Darn it.

"I'll call you tonight," he said and pulled me into a hug, kissing the top of my head.

I breathed in his scent, tempted to stretch up and kiss his neck. Instead I ran my hand over his muscled chest on top of his jersey as he held me close. "Of course."

He released me, was down the hall, and around the corner before I knew it. I leaned up against my locker to regain my composure. Maybe I could break plans with Georgia, beg Mom for a ride, and catch the tail end of the game.

Tardy for practice, I ran across the pool deck and took a spot next to Georgia in the sea of bodies laying, eyes closed, on the cement wearing their street clothes. They were listening to coach run through a visualization exercise. Normally we had practice the day before a meet, but today, for some reason, Coach cancelled it.

"Where were you?" Georgia whispered, jabbing me with her big toe.

"Sh-h-h." I pushed her away and checked to make sure Coach didn't see us talking.

I closed my eyes, already versed in the routine. We were supposed to be timing our race, but no matter how hard I tried, my thoughts reverted back to Saturday night. Twirling on the dimly lit dance floor and gazing up into the eyes of the one I adored, hoping to coax a kiss. Instead of brown eyes, blue ones, clear as a sunny day in Tahoe, looked back at me. Fin's as he held me close.

A pang of dread hit my stomach. His family still hadn't returned—each day making me crazy with worry. What could possibly have happened that they'd abandon their business? Another man with white hair and beard who frequented the building, told my mom Captain Jack's was closed indefinitely. Was Tatchi and Fin never coming home?

I felt sick. And Colin, though breathtakingly gorgeous, the vibe I'd gotten from our two interactions made my internal warning bells sound off. I didn't entirely trust myself around him to ask what happened.

Without them in my life I felt empty.

Startled at the sudden rustling of feet and backpacks scuffing across the pavement, I opened my eyes. I'd missed Coach Madsen's dismissal.

"Good work, everyone," she barked out. "I want each of you to eat a dinner loaded with carbs tonight and practice the visualization before you go to bed, early! I'll see you all at eight o'clock sharp. Eat breakfast!"

Georgia stood over me with one hand clutching her gym bag and the other on her hip. "Come on, let's go."

I rose to my feet and grabbed my things in the process. She looped her arm within mine, pulling me toward the gym doors faster than I wanted to walk.

:::

We arrived at her house and Georgia promptly whisked me upstairs to her room. The attached bathroom (that I totally drooled over) resembled a hair salon with oodles of products strewn across the counter. In her room, hair magazines were scattered across her bed and she plopped me down in front of them.

"Pick a style you like."

I thumbed through a few pages, but the busyness of her room distracted me. Every inch of her walls contained a pin-up of either a hot movie star or boy band, half of which I'd never heard of. The rest of her childhood collections were stored on shelves that hung a foot below the ceiling: dusty birthday figurines, ballerinas in boxes and teddy bears galore.

I focused back on the pages and finally found a girl with hair similar to mine. Loose ringlets fell gracefully around the model's shoulders with a few tendrils pulled up and piled on her head. "What about this one?"

Georgia turned from the mirror with a lipstick tube in hand. Her bright red lips parted into a smile. "That's awesome. Let's try it."

She coaxed me into the bathroom, forcing me to sit on the porcelain throne.

"So," she said while sucking on a lollypop, curling iron in hand, "have you kissed him yet?"

"What?" I bit my lip as my cheeks heated up. Not only had I never been kissed, but the thought of finding some dark corner at school to make-out in made me nauseous. The last thing I wanted was Georgia to know the embarrassing truth about my lack of experience. "We haven't really had the opportunity."

"Seriously? Well, I'd be making the opportunity, girlfriend," she said sexily. "And quick 'cause you don't want to lose this fish. Besides, I hear he's an *ah-maz-ing* kisser."

The thought of him kissing other girls and knowing they'd bragged about it made my chest hurt. "Really? Who said that?" I asked, shifting in my seat.

"Just the talk. Hold still."

I looked down at the magazine in my hands, desperate for something to get the conversation off of me. On the front was a picture of a familiar face, Zac Efron. She had a poster of him in her room. "He's kinda cute."

"Kinda?" She flapped her hand back and forth in front of her face. "He's like the most gorgeous actor ever."

I smiled. The bait worked. With each comment, I hummed and hawed as I felt her spray and press each piece of my hair carefully with a curling iron. But the whereabouts of Fin's family consumed my thoughts. Sadness crept in as I hoped I worried for nothing and they'd come home—and soon.

"You hate it, don't you?" Georgia chewed on her fingernail after handing me the mirror.

I came to my senses and looked at my reflection, shocked at what I saw. "Oh, wow." I stood up and turned to the side, using the hand mirror to see the back. She'd perfectly replicated the hair style in the picture.

Georgia blew out a gust of air. "Whew. I was worried. You looked so sad."

"No, sorry. I'm distracted, that's all."

She crinkled up her eyes and sighed. "Not the race again?"

"Well, yeah," I lied.

She turned her finger in a circle to signal me to spin around and sit back down. "Don't. It's going to be fine. Stop thinking about it or you'll psych yourself out."

"I know."

"Close your eyes," she demanded, make-up brush in hand.

In rapt concentration, Georgia quietly painted a masterpiece on my face, letting out little "oohs" and "aahs" every once in a while. The sweep of the feathery brush and her warm breath eased my conflicted heart as she blew off the excess make-up. After what seemed like multitudes of brush strokes, she finally handed me the mirror. I expected to see myself completely vamped out, but the girl looking back at me was stunning.

"He's gonna kiss you when he sees you," Georgia cooed and danced out of the bathroom. "I'm starved. Ready for pizza?"

I turned away with a blush, inspecting the fake eyelashes. "Yeah, sure."

With each mention of kissing, the butterflies already in my stomach started doing crazy aerial stunts. I hoped some food would make them knock it off for a while, but with the continued thoughts of Fin, they'd just start up again with a renewed vigor. Why I kept thinking about him and not Callahan stumped me. Maybe my feelings stemmed from me wanting to prove I was worthy of Fin's attention. With one look, he'd have to finally realize I'd grown up into a beautiful young woman.

When Mom picked me up a little after nine, I expected her to rave about my make-over. Instead, I got a lecture about how girls my age were trying to grow up too quickly and make-up should enhance one's natural beauty. Crushed, I remained silent the entire way home.

Without even saying hello, I strode past my family and went to my room, slamming the door. I threw myself on my bed and burst into tears. *Why did she have to ruin everything?* A soft knock interrupted my pity party.

"Can I come in?" Dad asked through the door.

I looked down at my pillow case. Charcoal smudges lined the fabric. "Um…" I jumped up and studied my reflection in the mirror over my dresser. Georgia's handy work had turned into black trails down my cheeks. I did my best to wipe away the evidence.

"Yeah, Dad. Come in."

He turned the knob and peaked around the door. "Everything okay?"

"I don't know." I sat on my bed and rubbed my toes into the carpet.

He joined me and put his arm over my shoulder. "More sister drama, Mom troubles, guy issues, or is it nerves about the meet tomorrow?"

I fidgeted with my newly painted nails. "Mom hurt my feelings."

He grunted, partly in acknowledgement, partly in concern. "Does she know?"

"She should know." I scoffed. "She insulted me in the car. Basically called me a tramp."

"Is that what you thought I meant?" Mom asked, appearing from around the corner.

The waterworks started, leaving me humiliated. I hated to cry, but in front of my parents for something as stupid as too much make-up left me feeling wretched. "Sort of."

Mom walked over and put her arm around my other side. "Honey. I was only trying to tell you that you're naturally beautiful, inside and out. You don't need to put on a lot of make-up to impress anyone or get a boy's attention. I'm sorry if that hurt your feelings."

I leaned into her shoulder and hugged her back.

She pushed a wayward curl behind my ear. "It's hard for me to see you looking so grown up. You'll be lovely tomorrow night."

"Thanks." I looked away. She could retract what she said in the car, but I knew her first impression—lovely wasn't a word she used.

I scratched my eyelid and loosened a lash. Embarrassed, I darted from my room toward the bathroom, praying Lucy wasn't hogging it. "I'm going to wash my face."

"Well, my work here is done," I heard Dad say behind me.

I closed the door and leaned up against it. In the mirror, conflict etched its worrisome talons down my smeared skin. First with Mom's hurtful comments, and second from the turmoil of my continued drive-by thoughts about Fin. What did I expect to happen tomorrow? Did I want things to go further with Callahan? Or was I holding back because I still harbored feelings for Fin?

With an angry tug, I pulled off my other eyelash. The skin underneath stung, making it painfully obvious I'd done something wrong. I stood with two black rows of fake hair stuck on my fingertips. I didn't do the girly thing well.

But still I floundered, with more than what to do with the eyelashes. Life felt so unsure, especially knowing Callahan would be expecting a kiss from me tomorrow. Why was I so willing to kiss Fin, or even Colin, but scared to death with Callahan?

The warm wash cloth felt good over my face and a little moisturizer brought back the natural glow to my skin. But Mom's comment still rang loud and clear. Was I really trying to grow up too soon? Maybe she was right. The excessive make-up was a little over the top.

With a flick of the lashes into the trash, I went back to my room to wait for Callahan's call. I hoped my sheep flannel jammies would infuse my psyche somehow and help put me to sleep later. From the window, Tatchi's house caught my attention. All the lights were on inside.

Without hesitation, I picked up the phone and dialed. Someone had to pick-up and when they did, I would make them give me answers. I'd had enough.

18

FIN

The day couldn't have ended better. I rushed home to find Mom in the kitchen cooking dinner.

"Mom!" I briskly walked toward her and held out a golden cup filled with rubies. "Here."

"What is this?" she asked with knitted brows, dusting her hands on her apron.

I smiled proudly. Only after a few weeks of training, I'd managed to defeat Badger in the first round and then took out the subsequent fighters with ease. "I won the tournament today."

She blinked back at me, confusion crossing her face.

"This was the prize," I said, lifting my eyebrows to convince her. "And I want you to buy back your diamonds with it."

Mom gulped as she looked at me, then back at the cup. A tear spilt down her cheek—not the reaction I'd expected. I could count on one hand the times I'd seen her cry.

Needing a distraction, I tipped the cup to the side, ready to spill out the contents. "You better hold out your hands."

She dropped her dish towel as the blood red stones piled into her trembling hands. Once the last gem fell, her hands formed a ball over them like they were a life saving rope.

"Fin, I can't take these—"

I put my free hand on top of hers. "This isn't an April Fools joke. And if you don't use them to buy your diamonds back, I'll be upset. Just think of it as my gift to the family—that I paid for the stove and air bubble. And that's what we'll tell Dad when he comes home."

Her voice hiccupped. "This is too generous."

"What else am I going to do with them? Save for college?" I laughed under my breath and thought of the solitary ruby I'd put aside for the future in my sling pack. "It's what I want to do."

She put the stones in her apron pocket and enfolded me in a hug. "Thank you, Fin," she whispered in my ear. I puffed out my chest. Dad would be proud.

: : :

Still on a high from the tournament win and Mom's surprise, I rushed off to collect Tatch at the palace.

"You're late," she said, punching me in the arm and swimming ahead, this time decorated from head to fin in blue.

"Sorry. I had things to do." I raced to catch up with her.

"Nothing can be more important than saving me from the palace and Azor's claws, so it better be good," she said with a sneer.

I smiled evilly and watched her smirk vanish as I filled her in on what really happened with the win and the rubies.

She rolled her eyes. "Okay, fine. I guess that's kinda important, but next time, please come get me first. I can't stand being there any longer than I have to."

"Yeah, sure."

"Today was exceptionally grueling." She slowed her pace, lengthened her neck and stuck her nose in the air, wiggling her tail in small precise movements. "We learned how to swim proper, like a merlady," she said, complete with an English accent.

I laughed. "What?"

"It seems the only thing mermatrons care about is beauty—not education or any type of *real* accomplishment. Their only goal is to teach us how to be a pretty thing for the mermen to enjoy—oh—and to make merlings with. That's it. And amazingly enough, the maids all seem cool with it, anxious to be paired to the one their parents have picked out for them."

"Really." At the mention of merbabies, I checked out. I wondered instead how Lily felt about beauty school and who her parents had planned to match her up with. "Are all the mermaids there?"

"I think so. But are you even listening to me? It's primitive and wrong!"

"Yeah," I said nonchalantly. All I wanted to do was deliver her safely home and get to Badger's. I hoped Lily might stop by again.

"Oooh!" Tatch spun around and put her blue tinted face inches from mine. "The girls are slaves for you boys! To keep as trinkets and baby makers!"

I backed away. "I know. But what can we do about it? No one seems to care the customs are ancient. I mean, once someone promises, they end up living happily ever after—pretty or not."

Tatch groaned and threw her hands upwards. "Boys! You all think the same!"

She took off and disappeared over the ridge. I let her go since our house was just on the other side. Finally free, I darted the other way toward Badger's house.

a

Badger walked to the porthole and motioned for me to come inside.

"Aye, look who be washin' himself up on me shore. Welcome, lad." He clapped me on the back once I phased into legs and directed me toward the living room. "Have a seat."

My stomach pinched when I spotted Lily sitting on the couch, wearing a pink dress that accentuated the curves God gave her. I tried not to gawk.

"Hi, Fin," she said.

"Hey." My heart rate increased as I walked over to join her. "How's it going?"

She smiled, flashing her white teeth. "Great."

Badger relaxed back in his usual lounge chair and kicked up his feet. "We's just be talkin' about the weather on land. Lily here's never seen snow before.”

“You haven’t?” I raised my eyebrows. It didn’t take long to get over the wonder of the messy stuff; being buried in drifts six months out of the year tended to make it more of a hassle than a phenomenon.

“No.” She looked down and played with the beads on her skirt. “There aren’t too many gates in snowy places, and yours is a little unique and unfortunately not open to the public.”

“Oh, right.” I paused. “Well, sometimes we get as much as fifteen feet in one dump. I’m sure you could visit next winter, when we’re back there. We could go ice skating.”

Her face lightened. “Ice skating? I would love to try that. Is it hard to do?”

“Blarney!” Badger interrupted. “In my country, we don’t entertain such silly sports. Now Gaelic football, that’s the—”

“Badger,” Sandy called from the kitchen. “Would you come here for a moment?”

He pressed his furry eyebrows together. “Ya need me, doll?” It appeared helping Sandy with chores didn’t rank high on his list when he had a captive audience listening to him *yammer about the good ole days.*

“Yes, please,” she replied.

“Hold that there thought, you two,” Badger said, hoisting himself from his chair. “Coming, love.”

Once alone, Lily looked up at me through her eyelashes and my heart roared in my chest. The desire to grab her cheeks and bring her lips crashing to mine rocketed through my shaking limbs.

To leave two single mers of the opposite sex alone was against Natatorian law. I used to think the temptation to kiss a mermaid was a total myth, never having the opportunity until this moment. But as if someone had just said, “don’t think of elephants” all I could think about was kissing her. I stood up and began to pace, suddenly interested in the trophies on the mantel piece.

"So, do you go to the school at the palace too?" I asked.

"Yes. All mermaids are required to attend school until they are promised."

I ran my hand along the rough-hewn wood and closed my eyes, trying to focus. "My sister comes home every day colored from head to fin. Is that all they do there?"

"No." Lily giggled, a light tinkling melody that warmed me. "The matrons have taken a liking to her ever since she's arrived. They've swarmed on her like a shark in a feeding frenzy. It's because she doesn't have a prospect of a merman yet. They're all trying to get her to pick one of their sons. It's all about promising up."

I turned around, careful to avoid staring at her lips. "Really? How's that? We aren't royalty or anything."

"Well, your family is one of the few allowed to live on land." Out of the corner of my eye, I saw her tilt her head down and watch me from behind her red hair. "Most families arrange promisings for their merchildren, but you and your sister get to choose."

I gulped. Her presence stirred something in me I'd never felt with another mermaid, beyond simple hormones. Most were content to stay underwater and be pretty playthings, unaware a world lived above them. Her adventurous side made her far more attractive than anything else, connecting us somehow, like the whispers of our souls wanting to be united. "Do you get to choose?"

Her face remained downward. "They'll choose, but I get to have the final say."

She looked up at me and my breathing increased. At that moment, everything about her called to me to seal the deal. My feet moved on their own accord toward her wonting gaze.

"I didn't know Fin was here," Sandy said suddenly, slicing through my intentions. I froze mid step.

"Aye," Badger said, eyeing me curiously and giving a wink. "I gave them a moment to be talkin', right?"

"Yes," I choked out while Lily remained silent.

"You shouldn't leave them alone, Badge," she whispered, then turned and gave us both a chastising once over. "You know the rules. The temptation is—" She stopped and raised her eyebrows.

He gave his own eyebrow waggle in return. "They be good kids." He wrapped his beefy hands around her slender waist. "Nothing of the sort would've happened."

She stared at us, knowing she stopped us from doing what we wanted. Badger, having set the whole thing up, looked away like he knew nothing.

"It's actually getting late. You ready to go, Lily?"

She sighed and threw me a sad smile. "Yes, Aunt Sandy."

Within minutes they were gone and I caught myself staring senselessly at the empty porthole.

"She's a pretty, wee thing," Badger said, cutting the silence.

"Yeah," I mumbled, confused at my lack of self-control.

"Proud of you, lad. You did right fine today."

I snapped around to look at him, questioning. He couldn't have meant my near accidental promising.

Badger bobbed his eyebrows. "With the tourney."

"Oh . . . thanks." I watched him stuff his pipe with tobacco. "Hey, where'd you learn to fight like that anyway?"

"Funny you'd ask. I learned from Jack, of course. Surprised me when you showed up to the practice field, green as a June bug."

My jaw went slack as my brain bounced out of its infatuated state. My dad was an expert fighter? I assumed back in the day when he'd come home roughed up, he was just messing around, not actually training someone. "My dad taught you everything you know?"

"Well, the mer way to fight. The army was much different back in the day when I arrived as a new merman—back when he led things."

"He was part of Azor's army?"

"No, lad," he guffawed. "He be runnin' the joint."

My jaw fell the rest of the way open, but no words came out. Dad never mentioned he was captain of the army either. Why didn't he ever offer to train me? Was I that inadequate? Was that why he didn't take me on the mission? My head reeled.

"He didn't tell ya?" Badge asked, noting my shock. He scrubbed at his beard. "Son, don't take it too hard. Yer da' is a humble and peaceful man. I'm sure he wanted you to make your own path in life. I rightly would have done the same for me son, if I had one."

The punch to my gut didn't decrease with his words, though what he said made sense. But the disappointment of finding out secondhand about the truth behind our gate, the mer expectations, and my father's past didn't hurt any less.

"On a good note, I think Lily fancies you. She'd make ya a great wife."

With Lily gone, reality returned and the notion of promising didn't seem as important. Dad had some explaining to do when he came home. "Yeah."

Badger blew more smoke circles. "I hate to be kickin' ya out, but when Sandy returns we'd like to have a quiet evening together."

I stood up. "Sure."

"Don't be disheartened. Jack woulda been right proud of you today. You were a true merman out there on that field."

I gulped and tried to imagine Dad's response. Would he have been proud? I thought I knew him well. Now I wasn't so sure. "Yeah, Badge. I'll see you tomorrow."

Wounded and full of questions, I dove into the porthole and swam home.

19

ASH

Oddly, the phone rang and rang, without even an answering machine picking up. I redialed, figuring maybe someone was on the other line, but the same thing happened.

Who calls someone at ten o'clock at night?

If someone called that late here, I'd assume there was an emergency. And there was. I needed to know where my best friend was and when she was coming home—right now. Good things were finally happening in my life and I couldn't enjoy them not knowing her whereabouts.

I clicked the off button and slumped back against my pillows, my plan a total failure. If it wasn't for the fact that I'd be a wreck for the meet if I didn't get to sleep soon, I would have walked over in my jammies and knocked on the door. Instead, I picked up a book off my nightstand and flipped it open, looking for a distraction. Maybe reading would be the trick to ease and tire my racing mind.

Next thing I knew, the sun shone through the curtains and Mom was shaking my shoulder. "Come on, sleepy head. You overslept."

I sat up with an adrenaline jolt. "Holy crawfish!"

Her eyes met mine. "I have breakfast ready. Just get dressed."

I nodded and flew to the bathroom to take care of pressing matters, like peeing and brushing my teeth. A shower would have been nice, but had to wait until after the meet. I put on my black team sweats over my suit, bunched all my curls into a ponytail holder, and ran downstairs, gym bag packed and ready to go on my arm. Mom handed me a plate of pancakes and scrambled eggs as we headed for the car.

"Oh, please tell me you packed me some snacks?" I asked with a mouth full of food as we backed out of the garage.

"Nuts, trail mix, protein bars, Red Vines, and water."

My shoulders relaxed. "Thank you."

Though mom wasn't the doting type, organization and remembering details was definitely her forte. We pulled into the parking lot and parked in the loading zone. My heart thumped harder when I saw people going into the pool area with green "SVA" windbreakers that stood for Squaw Valley Academy.

"Aren't you staying?" I asked, suddenly feeling like this was my first meet and I wanted my mommy to walk inside with me.

"It doesn't start for another hour. I need to go home, wake up Lucy, and get the family together. We're all coming to watch you today."

"Oh." I blinked back at her with shock and awe. "But what about the store?"

"We have Jaime covering."

"You do?"

"I need to go." Mom motioned for me to close the door. "Get in there and warm-up. I'll see ya in a few. You're going to do great." She smiled.

I closed the door and walked into the pool area with an extra bounce in my step.

"Where have you been?" Georgia said from behind me. I whirled around and she gasped. "What happened to your eyes?"

I reached up and wiped the inner corners, worried I had sleepy seeds from the night. "Nothing, why?"

"They're puffy. Did you cry last night or something? Did Callahan break things off with you?"

"No!" I looked away, caught, remembering he didn't call.

"Well, whatever happened, when you get home today, put a cold teabag on each eye for at least an hour. I can work magic, but you need to prep the canvas or your dance pictures are going to look horrible."

Great.

"Yeah, sure." I turned and headed toward the locker room, hoping Callahan wasn't getting cold feet on me. If he was, my worrying about it couldn't have been happening at a worse time. I had a race to win.

The energy and hubbub from the crowd added to my nerves and chased me after warm-up to a secluded spot on the shaded lawn where I could hide in my sleeping bag. Within the wings of emo and indie band music floating into my head through my earbuds, I waited for the race and played solitaire.

Georgia knew not to bother me and an hour later, she lightly knocked on my hooded head. "Time to go."

I nodded, grabbed my necessary stuff, and headed toward the blocks. I'd already decided to keep my eyes low and avoid contact with anyone, especially my rival, Meredith.

I chanted my zone pep talk as I sat in the seats behind lane four. But from the corner of my eye, I saw Meredith next to me and heard her teammates wish her luck. Just her very presence bombarded my confidence.

"You okay, honey?"

I looked up to see Mom, relief flooding me. "I'm nervous."

"Would you like to pray real quick?"

I nodded.

She bent down and whispered in my ear. "Dear Lord, calm Ashlyn's nerves and help her swim her very best. Amen."

Peace filled my spirit. "Thanks, Mom."

She smiled as I stood and patted me on my butt, like she'd done before every race since I started swimming at age six. "Go get 'em, Lanski."

"*. . . in lane three, Hamusek. In lane four, Lanski. In lane . . .*"

The announcer's voice sent my heart hammering. I slipped on my goggles and stepped up onto the block. The timer stood next to me, stop clock in hand.

I glanced over at the stands to find my family. Gran waved and nudged Lucy, who conveniently yawned. To my complete surprise, someone with a familiar blue baseball cap and STHS jersey sat next to Dad—Callahan! They both grinned and nodded at me. Dad gave the big thumbs-up. My mouth fell open, my nerves on overload.

"Swimmers, take your mark."

I snapped my head around toward the starter and leaned over. The gun popped. I was airborne. The second I hit the water, a million things flashed through my mind: Senior Ball, Fin, the make-up incident, the last time I saw Tatchi, the weirdo at her house, Meredith's face when she'd hit the wall before me last time. I couldn't stop the barrage which gave Meredith time to get a half a body-length ahead.

I panicked and took an extra breath.

Dear Lord, help me.

Something settled within and I found my rhythm in the current. Up and over my hips followed my butterfly stroke, the crowd's roar filling my ears at each breath. Coach's voice rang out clear over everyone else.

"Go, Lanski, go!"

Courage surged through my veins as I finished another lap. I'd caught up and we were neck and neck, flying through the water like dolphins.

I need this. I want this.

One more lap to go. I raced with all my heart, kicking with burning legs and aching lungs. I refused to lose time by taking unnecessary breaths, gaining a tiny lead.

This is it.

Both of us slammed into the wall. I popped my head out of the water to scan the board. The quiet hush covered the stadium like a blanket of fog.

"And first place goes to . . . my, this is unusual."

With heavy breaths, I felt my pulse continue to hammer on. Who won already? They never took this long to call a race.

"Ladies and gentlemen," the announcer said, sounding baffled, *"this is a first . . ."*

Two matching times popped up on the board next to our names.

". . . a new record and a tie!"

My eyes bugged out of their sockets, imagining my name on the record board in the gym hallway. Meredith turned and moved toward the lane rope, holding out her hand.

"Good race, Ashlyn."

I shook it. "Yeah. Good race."

"Lanski!" Coach called out with a huge grin. "Great race! I knew you had it in you!"

She put her hand down and pulled me out of the water. Her rapid-fire pats on my back sent splatters of water all over her clothing.

"You did awesome!" Georgia handed me my swim jacket before accosting me with a hug. "And broke a record!"

I stood there, shaking from the evaporated adrenaline in my body and took a deep breath. "I guess this is better than second, right?"

"Heck yeah!" Georgia said, jumping up and down. "You broke a record!"

I looked around, still in shock, when the stroke-and-turn judge asked me to move aside. The next race was starting.

Then I saw him. Callahan walked toward me, escorted by my whole family. Our eyes met and he smiled, weakening my knees. He looked amazingly sexy and oh so kissable in his baseball hat.

One big event down. One more to go.

I held my breath, ready for the onslaught, wondering what kind of impression my family left on him and why he didn't call the night before. I'd soon find out.

20

FIN

"Before you start today, I need two volunteers," Azor called out over the assembled group of mermen.

I yawned and looked off to the side, bored out of my mind. Whenever Azor called for volunteers, it meant some type of grunt work for an elder mer. He scanned the crowd with a straight face. Usually someone wanting his favor raised their hand, but with his foul mood and crappy assignments, no one did today.

Actually, after all Badger and I discussed, I planned to quit Azor's army. During the last few weeks, I'd technically honed my fin fighting skills like Dad asked me to do and I had no purpose here anymore. Sunlight exploration was more up my alley and could be useful knowledge when we returned to Tahoe. I'd sell Azor on the idea and move onto bigger and better things.

"Thank you, Kieran, for volunteering. That leaves one more. Anyone?"

Come on with it already.

"Fine then," he waved his finger over the group and landed on me, "Finley, I'd like you and Kieran to report to Mrs. Crabtree's house. She has some rocks to move."

"What—?"

Azor shot his beady eyes at me. "Excuse me? Were you saying something, Finley?"

"With all due respect, I'd like to be transferred. Someone else should go in my place."

Badger grunted while smashing his eyelids together.

Azor's dark lifeless eyes sparked with deviousness. "Transferred? Interesting. Well, since you've proven you're able to fight at least, I agree. You can be in charge of maintenance now and Grommet will partner with Badger in your place," —he signaled to Grommet who watched attentively— "dismissed."

"What?" My jaw dropped as the group scattered, everyone eyeing me with relief and curiosity. With stars in his eyes, Grommet swam up alongside us as Badge gave me a deflated look, shaking his head.

"Badger!" I called out.

He whirled around, disappointment eroding deep grooves into his face. "Son, you've heard the captain. Get to yer new assignment."

"What? This is crazy. He can't force me!"

I knew I sounded like a child, but I couldn't help it. If Dad were here, none of this would have happened. Azor was taking out his frustration on me because my sister refused him. I couldn't be a gofer for the elder mers. Badger needed to stick up for me and make Azor see reason.

Badger narrowed his eyes. "That he can and that he has. So, you better go. We'll talk later."

He patted Grommet on the back and together they swam away to our corner of the practice grounds. Kieran hovered off to the side and watched me like a lit stick of dynamite.

"Come on," I grunted and swam ahead as Kieran followed behind at a distance.

As soon as we were out of Azor's sight, Kieran caught up to me and filled the silence with useless nonsense about his inventions. I didn't pay close attention, still angered at the rotten assignment, confused why I had to listen to Azor in the first place. Why couldn't I just leave? Of course, deserting an assignment probably didn't look good on my record and I did want Tahoe some day.

Once arriving at Mrs. Crabtree's, I changed my mind. No matter where we moved her decorative rocks, she complained. After an entire day of repositioning the stones in her front yard, she ended up liking them best in their original location. I knew there was no way I could handle this until Dad returned. Azor had to see reason.

I picked up Tatch at the palace without a word and swam ahead. Today, she looked almost normal with only a few streaks of purple in her hair.

"Fin, I've figured it out," she called behind me.

I looked over my shoulder and sighed. Didn't she see I was pissed? Would it be too much for her to be quiet for once? "I don't feel like playing games today."

"Rough day at the office?" Tatch giggled. When I didn't respond, she caught up to me and nudged me in the ribs. "Lighten up, Mr. Prickleback. All I wanted to say was I figured out how to get the mermatrons off my back."

I lifted my right eyebrow when her silence went on too long. "I'm too hungry and tired to guess."

"You're no fun," she said with an upturned lip. "Fine. It was really so simple. Rumor has it they all want me to promise to their sons, so I announced that I'd finally chosen."

"You've chosen? Who?"

"Dorian." Her face brightened.

Dorian? Sandy's cousin? Stunned, I waited for her to laugh and tell me she was kidding.

"Oh come off it. I'm not *really* going to go through with it. He's got his sights on a human girl anyway. It's just a way for both of us to get the pressure off, you know?"

The mention of Dorian picking a human girl over a mermaid brought Ashlyn to mind. Though I'd never bring her into this world willingly, there were so many times when I was tempted, like the day we left. But after meeting Lily, I started to feel like I could be happy with a pure-born mermaid.

Tatch thumped her fist into my shoulder. "Didn't you hear me?"

"That's a great idea."

"Geez, take all the fun out of it, why don't you." She gave me a dirty look then swam up through the porthole into the house.

I clenched my jaw a few times and looked up at the house. Yesterday had been my best day since we'd been trapped in Natatoria and today, my worst. I didn't want Mom to know about my altercation with Azor so I plastered on a fake grin and went inside. Crap day or not, my stomach was about to turn inside out and start digesting itself.

21

ASH

I paced the length of my room in my sling-backs, trying to get a better handle on walking. My hair was perfectly styled, make-up done to my mother's standards, dress altered to fit me like a glove, and my ride fashionably late. And to top everything off, all I wanted to do was vomit.

"They're here!" Lucy called up the stairs in a breathless frenzy. "Hurry up, Ashlyn!"

I craned my neck to look out the window as the limo and three cars filled with parents pulled up into the driveway. At the sight, my pulse thumped wildly through my veins. Callahan got out first and took my breath away wearing a magnificent black suit.

His shoulders rose and fell. I wanted to call to him and wave, but stood faltering in my self-confidence as the rest filed out: two of Callahan's friends: Dustin and Evan, and their dates: Shannon from the swim team and Kylie, who happened to be a close friend to Brooke.

What if I make a complete idiot of myself tonight?

I wasn't as prepared as I'd hoped to be, especially with Kylie being in the limo with us. Visions of her prying the crown from my head on the ride home flashed through my mind. For my safety, I hoped the student body voted someone else Queen.

I smoothed my sweaty hands on the bedspread and proceeded toward the stairs. The parents' chattering voices swooped up the stairwell. I hesitated, wishing for a place to hide.

Dad turned the corner and looked up at me, his comforting eyes sparkling with pride. "Ashlyn, you look breathtaking."

I willed away the tears as I walked down the steps to take his outstretched hand. He kissed me on the cheek before escorting me into the living room. The occupants hushed.

Callahan's dark chocolate colored eyes met mine and his smile wrapped me with warmth, melting away my nerves. I joined him by the fireplace and Mom handed me the green orchid boutonniere. The noise returned as parents voiced compliments and snapped photos, lessening the attention on my entrance

"Hi," he said with a rickety voice. "You look really beautiful."

"Thank you. You look great, too."

My hands shook, trying to pin the darn flower onto his lapel and not stab him by accident. Mom noticed and took over. I gratefully moved out of her way.

He opened the plastic case containing a red rose corsage and took my hand. His touch sent electricity down my arm, energizing my skin as he slid the elastic over my wrist and slyly interlacing his fingers with mine. I squeezed his hand back and smiled.

The chaotic photo shoot slowly turned more organized as couples were paired up and commanded to smile, look over here, get closer together, move further apart. When I thought I couldn't take another blinding flash, Georgia pulled me close for a best friends shot. Reluctantly, I let go of Callahan's hand.

She giggled and pressed her cheek into mine. "Isn't this awesome?" she asked through the teeth of her smile as her mom aimed the camera.

I grunted an acknowledgement and noticed my feet had already begun to hurt. Behind Georgia's mom, Kylie stood with a straight-face, solitary hand on her hip. I questioned why she'd agreed to ride with us. Was she here to ruin my evening with Callahan on purpose?

After the last flash, I pulled away. "Shouldn't we be leaving soon?"

Georgia looked at her cell phone and gasped, grabbing onto

Jeremy's arm. "Time to go."

To my relief, Callahan's hand found mine again and we locked eyes for a brief minute. Though we'd spent a lot of effort to make the evening so exquisite, all I wanted to do was go somewhere, just the two of us, and talk. In his eyes, I read he wanted the same thing. But the tide of dresses and suits swept us out the door toward the limo.

"Oh, wait," Gran called behind me and I turned. She draped the white fur over my shoulders. "Have fun, Dear." Her soft hand wrapped around mine briefly and I smiled as she kissed me on the cheek.

"Thank you, Gran."

For a moment her eyes twinkled. She joined the line of parents on the porch as they called out well wishes. I waved and got into the luxurious limo, anxious to experience my first ride.

Georgia got in on the other side and snuggled in next to Jeremy. Then the iPhone party began: photos, texting, videos—you name it. Georgia's gleeful banter kept the limo relatively warm in spite of Kylie's insipid chill. Kylie ended up moving to the other end of the limo with Evan, engrossed with the screen of her cell phone. Shannon, on the other hand, cooed and posed under Dustin's arm. I watched the comedic interaction, distracted by Callahan's gentle fingers entwining and playing with mine, his breath tickling my ear. The driver watched through his rear view mirror with a shake of his head.

"Ready to go?" he asked gruffly.

Callahan nodded and we were off. I leaned deeper into his shoulder and Georgia eventually stopped talking and turned on the radio.

"You look awesome," he whispered again, tucking me under his arm.

I looked down at my corsage. Delicate flowers made of gems lay hidden in the greenery. "Thank you."

"Geez, Ash—you seriously need a Facebook account. I can't tag you on anything," Georgia whined, her fingers moving over the touch screen.

"Yeah, well . . ." I sighed. She already knew my parents were techno-tards.

"Do you want to drive around for a little bit?" the driver asked through the window between the front seat and us. "Or go straight to the country club?"

We glanced around at one another, no one voicing an opinion.

I shrugged and finally said, "Sure, why not?"

Kylie cleared her throat. "If we're late, the line for pictures will be out the door. We should go now. I *am* on the committee after all." She batted her eyelashes at Evan for support.

Georgia chimed in. "Do we really need to go to the country club now? Can't we at least drive around for thirty minutes and get our money's worth? We've only got the limo until eleven—pictures can wait."

"That sounds good to me," Shannon said.

Callahan and Dustin agreed. Evan remained silent, which angered Kylie further.

"Fine. Whatever." She tossed her hair over her shoulder, side swiping Evan in the face. "I was just thinking of everyone else since I do have *privileges*, so you'll just have to enjoy the line."

Privileges?

She began texting, I'm sure to tattle to someone that we were holding her hostage. When her phone buzzed with a return exchange, she cackled and looked straight at me. The others might have finally noticed her visual assault, but another limo zipped by, its occupants hanging out of the sunroof, causing a major ruckus.

Georgia laughed and began to open our own sunroof. I grabbed her knee. "You'll mess up your hair."

Kylie snorted and looked at her phone. We both glared at her.

"I'm laughing at my text message."

Sure you are. I was glad her acidity finally crossed into someone else's territory.

I took a deep breath to calm my nerves, but my heart wouldn't stop pounding for what lay ahead. Deep down, though incredibly sweet, I wished Callahan hadn't nominated me, especially now with Kylie in our limo. Who in their right mind would agree to this arrangement? Evan was clearly not thinking. He should have never made his date share a limo with Callahan, her best friend's ex, and me, her best friend's competition for Senior Ball Queen. Ridiculous.

Instead, I ignored her and focused my gaze out the window at the lake, breathing in Callahan's glorious scent. I wasn't going to give her the satisfaction of letting her know she bothered me. Callahan responded the way I needed, unaware of my internal battle, and wrapped his arms around me, causing my heart to beat faster for good reasons.

22

ASH

When we arrived, Kylie jumped from the limo with Evan in tow, and proceeded past the swarm of people—never to return. I guessed that's what "privileges" meant. More like a line-cutting pass.

Shifting my weight again to ease the ache in my arches, I looked down the never-ending line of overly-dressed students that snaked around the building. In the short fifteen minutes, we'd only moved a couple of feet.

"Cassie just texted and said we are in the right spot for pictures and once we get through the doors, it's only twenty minutes more," Georgia said, craning her neck.

I looked for this mysterious door as well, hoping to get off my feet soon. "Are you sure you want to wait?"

Georgia hit me on the arm. "Of course, silly."

I sighed as my tummy rumbled, noticing some of the girls' dates had come back with hors d'oeuvres. With the swim meet and the nervous rush to get ready in time, I'd completely forgotten to have lunch. My mouth watered.

"You hungry?" Callahan asked, noticing my eyes glass over at the sight of crackers and cheese.

I nodded, feeling a little weak in the knees. I'd even eat a green olive if offered at this point.

"Come on," he gestured toward Dustin and Jeremy. "Let's go."

The guys left in search of food, conveniently leaving us alone.

"So why do you think Kylie laughed when I called you Senior Ball Queen in the limo earlier?" Georgia asked softly, pulling Shannon and me into a tight circle.

"Who knows," I mumbled, feeling the title a bit presumptuous and inappropriate. "Maybe she already knows I lost."

"She can't," Shannon said with wide green eyes fringed with glitter eyeliner. "Only the teachers on the committee know. They count the votes, right?"

I shrugged. This was all new to me. "Who cares. I'm not going to win anyway."

"Oh yes you are," Georgia said with a stamp of her foot. "Everyone I know said they voted for you and I know everyone."

But would they tell her the truth? "Still, Brooke is so popular—"

Georgia put her hands on her hips. "—and treats everyone like crap. I think the student body is sick of her superiority complex and wants someone who deserves to be Queen. Like you." She straightened up and cupped her hands over her mouth. "How many of you think Ashlyn would make the best Senior Ball Queen ever?"

The line turned at her voice and, to my surprise, erupted in a cheer.

I ducked down and brought my hand to my forehead. "Shut-up, Georgia. Please."

Callahan came up behind me and put his arm around my waist. "What's going on?"

"Food!" I exclaimed quickly before anyone else could fill him in. "Thank you." I force fed a mini croissant slathered in some white creamy sauce into Georgia's mouth to silence her. She smirked knowingly as I winked.

After thirty minutes more, we finally made it to the red carpet for The Night at the Oscars, complete with a life-sized golden replica of Oscar himself. The paparazzi photographer and posing with the golden statue made for a fun photo shoot. And to no one's dismay, Kylie missed out on the group shot.

Afterward, the six of us proceeded to the dining area and looked for our table number amidst the swarm of people. Callahan noticed his table number on his ticket said twenty-one and mine, twenty-three. Twenty-one happened to be Kylie's table.

"Oh." He licked his lips. "I had to buy an extra ticket for you and I must have gotten the table wrong. Kylie is on the committee. Let's ask her to straighten this out," he said, glancing in her direction.

"Oh, this is awkward," Kylie said after looking at our differing tickets. "But there's nothing I can do now. We've only got enough room for one at our table. Callahan, you could sit here next to Evan and rejoin Ashlyn once the dancing starts after dinner."

A pit formed in my stomach at her suggestion. How could he not check the tickets? I noted the jackets resting on the backs of most of the chairs, unsure of the owners. Next to the empty seat was a silver beaded bag I could only assume belonged to Brooke.

"I'll find Ashlyn a chair and squeeze her in," Georgia exclaimed and began to scan nearby tables for one to steal.

"No!" Kylie called out with a panic stricken face. "We can only have eight people at a table. Country club rules."

I looked around and noticed others had successfully added additional chairs, all the way up to ten in some cases.

"That's okay," Callahan said, gripping my hand tighter. "I'll find a seat where I can be with Ashlyn."

"Well, okay." Kylie put on her fake smile. "Good luck."

We turned away and looked for a number twenty-three in the centerpieces of popcorn boxes, fake movie reels, and glittery stars.

"Don't worry. There's always an overflow table," Callahan said just to me.

I finally relaxed my shoulders. How convenient for the mix-up to put Callahan in with Brooke and her hornets' nest of friends. My heart warmed that he'd rejected the idea and insisted we be together, even if he didn't have a seat.

"Oh, cool!" Georgia exclaimed after looking at her phone. She waved at Cassie standing on the other side of the room. "Cassie just texted me. There is an extra seat at table twenty-three after all."

Callahan and I exchanged relieved glances. "See? It all worked out," he said.

The group assembled around the table.

"I'm so glad you're finally here," Cassie said, looking a bit distressed. "People were trying to steal our chairs."

"Thanks," I said as Callahan pulled out my chair for me to sit.

As we settled in, I noticed more students filtered into the room and floundered to find their seats like we did. Across one wall, a replica of the HOLLYWOOD sign stood and on the other were famous black and white pictures of actors and actresses. But my attention was at the center of the room where the buffet tables sat with covered chaffing dishes.

Shortly thereafter, but not soon enough, Mrs. Kiefer finally dismissed our table to the buffet. The choices were palatable: grilled chicken, tortellini salad, green salad, diced red potatoes and wheat rolls. With a snug dress that left little to no room for stomach expansion, I stuck with the tortellini.

When the music started, my heart sped up, but not for obvious reasons. The last dance I'd attended had been freshman year and ended horribly when Ricky Anderson, my date, tripped me on the dance floor and I ended up in the ER. I vowed then to never return to a dance floor from sheer embarrassment, until Callahan asked me to be his date.

Callahan turned to me with a knee-melting smile. "Would you like to dance?"

His gentle brown eyes made saying "no" impossible and I nodded, completely captured by his enticing lips. He pulled me to the middle of the floor for a slow dance, drawing me into his arms. I leaned into his chest as we swayed in a small circle. My heart fluttered when he pulled me closer, his hands holding the small of my back. Everything was finally perfect, the way I'd pictured this night since he'd asked me a week ago.

"This is magical," I whispered in his ear.

He hummed back in agreement. My throat hitched remembering Georgia's suggestion. This was the moment she talked about, but on the inside, I was a bundle of nerves, out of my element. Last thing I wanted to do was kiss Callahan right here in front of everyone. We circled around again and I felt him shift, as if to coax me to look up. I didn't dare move, keeping my cheek glued to his shoulder.

"Are you having fun?" he asked, his warm breath tickling my ear.

"Yes." *No. Maybe.* I felt too light-headed to be sure.

He brushed his hand over my hair and wrapped his fingers under my chin. My pulse hammered through my body as he guided my face upwards. Behind his blazing brown eyes, I saw his desire shimmer. He glanced at my lips and back again. With a smile, he leaned in toward me.

I trembled, closing my eyes as he tipped my chin upward. *This is it.*

Expecting warm lips to touch mine, a bright light flashed over my eyelids instead. I popped them open and turned, Callahan's lips making contact with my cheek. With lipstick smeared faces, Jeremy and Georgia froze, wide-eyed and embarrassed, caught in the direct line of a chaperone's flashlight. Then, the unforgiving light illuminated yet another couple whose display apparently was objectionable. I put my head back on his shoulder to avoid the probing beacon, my mind racing, embarrassed I'd messed up the kiss.

The next song sped things up and resulted in people bumping into us, followed up with snide remarks to take our slow dance somewhere else. We broke apart and danced more appropriately for the music selection, but when Callahan moved behind me and took ahold of my hips, I wasn't about to rub my butt up against him.

"I need a rest," I said, pointing to my feet once the third song started.

Callahan nodded and we headed to sit at our table alone.

"Sorry about the ticket mix-up," he said after a few minutes.

I bit my lip as he took my hand, and brushed his lips over my fingers. "I've been meaning to ask you something."

My breath increased anticipating what he was going to ask. "What?"

"I—" his eyes darted away for a moment as if he were gathering his courage. "Would you be my girlfriend?"

Callahan's girlfriend? Me?

I smiled and nodded. "Yes."

He leaned forward, about to kiss me again, when Georgia ran up to the table with Jeremy behind her, oblivious to the situation. My shoulders went slack. Would the moment ever be right?

"Come on," she said breathlessly, grabbing both my hands. "I love this song!"

Knowing *the moment* with Callahan was over, I let her pull me to the dance floor, shooting him a sad look. He shrugged and motioned for me to go on ahead anyway. Once on the dance floor, I let loose a little and closed my eyes to avoid watching the couples booty grind next to us, but the DJ stopped the song early.

"What?" Georgia exclaimed, as the lights in the room grew brighter.

The tawdry couples moaned at the interruption and finally broke apart. I exhaled and rolled my eyes.

"Attention everyone," Principle Tanner said into the microphone after she tapped the top, making the lame thumping noise. "It's time to announce our royal court."

Georgia grabbed my hand and squealed. "This is it. This is your big moment!"

The tortellini rolled over in my stomach and I gulped down the bile. No matter what the results, I didn't feel prepared. I clutched her hand for dear life, hoping I'd be happy with whatever happened.

23

FIN

After dinner, I contemplated going out for a swim to ease my frustration. After Tatch and Mom started giggling in the back room over some vampire book mom had smuggled into Natatoria, I bolted.

"I'm going over to Badger's," I called out before disappearing into the inky black waters.

The crystal ball bounced cerulean shards of light, signaling the land above was experiencing a full moon. The buildings looked like upside down candles, red lava glowing from the gel-covered domes from below. Speckled circles of light came from the windows of the homes, littering the coral canyon around the palace, mer families settling in for the night. The peacefulness of the scene should have been breathtaking, but Natatoria was the last place I wanted to be.

Within a few short minutes, I arrived at the cave leading to the Tahoe gate instead of Badger's. Saying goodbye to Dad on this spot just a week ago, it felt like ages had passed. My heart pounded as I scanned the surroundings before ducking inside. My eyes adjusted to the dark of the room.

I hesitated before pressing the button to open the gate into Tahoe. Underage mer needed permission to leave Natatoria and had to be supervised by an adult male. Grounding or community chores would be the consequences of the offense. Of course, that was already my lot in life. But I couldn't stand it anymore. I had to take the chance. I needed to breathe fresh air and bask in the light of the moon if only for a few minutes.

The icy water sent a chill up my spine as I swam through Tessie's mouth into the frigid current. I laughed that my heart hammered even though I knew the waters would be empty. The fact that Uncle Alaster or Colin left the gate entrance unguarded didn't surprise me. And I'm sure Dad didn't tell his brother about the movement meter he'd installed that would register higher readings if someone had opened the mouth of the cave. In the old days, Dad and I used to put soft rocks under the doorway so if someone did sneak into Tahoe unnoticed, we'd know and watch for them.

Gate guarding should have been more about keeping humans from finding the entrance and not keeping mers out—most of them deathly afraid of getting caught to even try. But everyone knew we took our job seriously and didn't test the boundaries.

Alaster or Colin could have been somewhere else in the lake, monitoring water vibrations with their tails. But my guess was they were living it up in the basement, eating and drinking everything they could find, and enjoying the oversized TV—the lazy bums. Any mer could come and go right under their noses, and they'd never know—something I planned to capitalize on until Dad returned.

I swam the 1,600 feet with ease and carefully surfaced to make sure no one saw me before taking in a deep breath of crisp air. A fresh blanket of snow glimmered on the bank from the moonlight, illuminating the entire cascade of mountains like a silver crown. Lily's face came to mind as I imagined her reaction to such an amazing spectacle.

Everything inside me wanted to swim to shore and roll around in the powder, making merfish angels or something so I could cup the earth in my hands. But my visit had to be inconspicuous. Getting caught by my lame relatives, or worse, humans, would ruin this opportunity.

I floated on my back and admired the night's sky. Stars pebbled the heavens and I vowed to never take the beauty for granted once we were back home, guarding the gate like it should be.

Light shone from every window in our house, though I knew they wouldn't be scooting around on their fins upstairs. If mers didn't keep their tails wet, their scales would dry out. Any sort of dehydration interfered with our natural ability to regulate our internal temperature, thus putting us at risk of a coma or even death. *So much for them being incognito.*

Headlights shot out over the lake and I ducked down. The vehicle—a stretch limo—pulled down our street and headed toward our house. I squinted in concern. Who would be visiting at this time of night? Then the car turned and parked in front of Ashlyn's house instead. I swam to a nearby rock to investigate.

A guy my age, dressed in a suit, assisted a female out of the vehicle. She looked regal with a long green dress and red curls trailing down her back.

Ashlyn.

I watched as she turned, her alabaster skin hitting the moonlight just right, stabbing me in the chest with her beauty. She walked up to the back porch, hand-in-hand with this punk and my stomach twisted, but I couldn't look away. They stood together, too close for my liking, whispering things I could barely pick up. She had a good time. He did, too. There was a pause and they continued to gaze into one another's eyes. Blood hammered in my veins and I clenched my jaw. When he tilted her chin up with his hand and Ashlyn closed her eyes, leaning into him, my stomach lurched. I couldn't take it anymore.

A kiss for a Natatorian was the most intimate act two merfolk could do; once a mer's lips touched another's, they were promised to each other for life as mates. Through their breath, their souls intertwined, binding them together spiritually, emotionally, and physically. This is the main reason why mermaids weren't allowed out of the kingdom alone. One kiss would drive a man insane. His soul, seared from the loss of the mermaid herself, would never allow him peace until he found her again.

But for me, watching Ashlyn kiss someone else, merman or not, drove me crazy. I dove into the water to try to shake the jealousy. This whole time, I'd done my best to keep my distance and not get too close. Harboring feelings for a human was risky. But watching her with the other guy made me realize I'd only wanted her to be with me all along.

I groaned and raced toward the gate back into Natatoria. If I was with Dad on the secret mission, I would have avoided seeing her with someone else. But instead, I got an eyeful of her future and all I wanted to do was rip things apart with my bare hands.

"Good, you're home," Mom said, catching me off guard as I came out from behind the curtain. A sunbeam transported in from the other side of the globe allowed me to phase into legs. "Did you have a nice time with Badger?"

My eyes hit the floor. I could never successfully lie to Mom. "I ended up just going for a swim."

She walked closer to me and put her hand on my shoulder. "Everything okay, Son?"

I nodded. "Just a little homesick, that's all." *And heartsick too.*

"Oh, I see. There are a few more cookies in the kitchen if you'd like some. They always seem to cheer you up." She smiled and leaned her head to the side to try to find my gaze. I turned up the edges of my lips to appease her.

She bought the façade and went back to work on her needlepoint.

I stood for a moment, head low. Cookies wouldn't fix what ailed me this time. Now, a few Guinnesses might have put a dent in my pain, but I didn't think Badger would share, and being intoxicated might lead me to doing something very rash, like returning to the surface to get Ashlyn's attention. Instead, I went to my room, sat on my hammock, and put my head in my hands, searching for answers.

24

ASH

Callahan escorted me to the porch and my heart never pounded more excitedly. Well, except a few hours ago when the results of Senior Ball Queen were announced.

"Sorry about tonight," Callahan said sheepishly.

"For?"

"Everything." He looked away, guilt covering his face.

I chuckled and squeezed his hand tighter. "I'm not. I got to leave with the Senior Ball King. What more could I ask for?"

He peered down at me and wrapped his hands around my waist, knocking my breath away with his closeness. "I wanted *you* to be my Queen."

I squealed on the inside, far happier to have his vote above anyone else's, and put my arms around his shoulders, gazing back into his eyes. "Who says I have to have majority vote to be yours?"

"True." He raised his left eyebrow.

His reaction zinged my chest and I giggled at how brazen I'd become.

"You were really great with everything I had to do tonight, too." Callahan's gaze darted away again. "I don't know if I could have handled things if the vote had gone another way."

I leaned my head over, forcing him to look at me and smiled once his baby browns met mine. "If it weren't for the fact that you just asked me to be your girlfriend, then I might not have handled your Kingly duties very well either."

He flashed a coy smile. My breath quickened as he brought me closer. *Finally, an uninterrupted moment.* I tilted my lips toward his, parting them slightly as he leaned in. I shut my eyes.

A loud splash down by the lake drew my attention away, causing me to turn at the last second. Once again, Callahan planted a kiss on my cheek.

"Did you hear that?" I asked, peering over his shoulder. My heart still thundered at a sprinting pace, leaving me breathless and shaky, especially after I realized what I'd done.

"What?" He turned and looked for the interruption, dropping his hands from my waist

I let go of his shoulders and readjusted my corsage on my wrist. *How could I have let this happen again?* "Sorry, where were we?"

Callahan put his hand on my chin and caressed my cheek with his thumb, his eyes filled with concern. With his other hand, he brushed a wisp of hair away from my face.

"Maybe we're taking things too fast," he said solemnly.

I gulped back the rejection, begging with my eyes for him to kiss me again. "No, I'm sorry."

He straightened the corners of his lips; disappointment crossed his face. "We'll have a better chance another time. I need to relieve the driver and get home. My parents won't be happy if I end up owing overtime."

"Right." I stared at the ground, my cheeks flushed from screwing up the perfect ending to our crazy night.

Callahan caught my hands and forced me to look at his tender eyes. "I had a very nice time tonight."

I sighed as he pulled me into a hug, kissing me on my temple. The warmth of his body, encased against mine, temporarily calmed the rollercoaster in my stomach. "I did, too."

I wanted to say something else to fix it or just grab his face and lay one on his lips, but my cowardice wouldn't let me. Instead, I pulled out my set of keys and unlocked the door.

"You're such a sweet girl," he said before heading down the walkway toward the limo. "Have good dreams tonight, Ashlyn,"

"Good night," I whispered and shut the door.

My head reeled as I removed the bothersome heels and tip-toed barefoot through the dark house toward the stairs. What the heck just happened?

I purposefully avoided going to the after-party just so we'd get a quiet moment together. Why did I look away? Why didn't I just kiss him when I had the chance? Would he go now to the party without me? I dreaded waiting for his phone call tomorrow. I bet he'd break up with me in the morning because of my lack of experience.

And then the stupid dance. Why was I so disappointed when Principle Tanner called Brooke's name instead of mine? Did I really want to be Queen or was I just jealous of Brooke getting his attention? I struggled watching her fawn all over him for pictures and the dance reserved for royalty. Georgia had me so convinced I'd win, like the swim race earlier. Was the vote even close? How badly did I lose? And why was Brooke so smug even after people booed her? The audience's reaction didn't jive with the results. Thank goodness Kylie and Evan were more excited about the after-party at Justin's house than rubbing the defeat in my face.

I took off my dress and carefully wrapped up the fur in the garment bag Gran left for me on the bed and slid into my jammies. With an empty stomach and a full brain, I curled up on the window seat and peered into the dark night. Tatchi's house was lit up like a Christmas tree and Fin's Jeep sat like a statue. Every time I'd attempted to go over there to talk to Colin, I chickened out.

Why couldn't she just come home already?

25

FIN

I woke up sick: sick to my stomach, sick of Natatoria, sick of waiting for Dad to come home, sick of Tatch's complaining, and sick of the rules. And when I showed up for practice at the field, all I got was another laundry list of stupid stuff elder mers wanted me to do . . . like moving decorative rocks.

All I needed was one excuse and someone was losing an appendage.

26

ASH

"Get up, Ashlyn," Mom demanded from down the hall. "Hurry or we'll be late for church."

I pried my stubborn eyelids open and removed a wayward fake lash, but didn't leave the sanctuary of my bed. Church was the last place I wanted to go. More than likely, Callahan would be there, along with other kids from my school. I didn't want to face him yet, still dying of embarrassment from the flubbed up kiss.

Within minutes, Mom opened the door and picked up the dirty laundry off the floor. "Didn't you hear me? You need to get ready."

"I'm not going," I said plainly.

"And why not?" Her tone told me she wasn't in the mood for theatrics or sob stories.

"I have cramps," I lied, knowing my period could get me out of anything since she had horrific cramps herself.

"Oh," she said with a softer tone. "I didn't realize. Did you start early?"

A flicker of dread flashed across my body. Did she keep track of my cycle? I wasn't supposed to start until next weekend.

"Must have been all the stress," I mumbled into my pillow, curling into a ball and moaning for affect.

"I'll bring up the Midol," she said quietly and closed the door.

I asked God for forgiveness for my deception, knowing He'd understand. If Dad had come to wake me instead, he'd have accepted my need for solitude, but chances were, he'd already left for the fire station.

Shortly after Mom brought the pills and a heating pad, the family got into the car and left. I exhaled at the sudden quiet. Three peaceful hours all to myself. What would I do first?

I closed my eyes and tried to sleep longer but couldn't shake the anxiety. If Callahan noticed I wasn't at church, he'd probably call. I wasn't ready to talk to him yet.

I pulled on jeans and my team jacket, deciding a walk far away from my phone would calm my nerves. The cool breeze off the lake tickled the inside of my nose as I sloshed down the soupy path to the water. Memories of playing on the trail with Tatchi before we were old enough to take *The Sea Star*, our four-seater row boat, to Fannette Island, prompted a desire to visit our secret spot.

Inside the shed, the blue boat leaned against the wall closest to the door. I heaved it down the dock, then grabbed two paddles and looked at the life vests. A big hairy spider had made its home on the edges of the fabric, wigging me out. I shrugged and left the eight-legged beast alone. It wasn't as if I didn't know how to swim.

The paddles glided the boat across the calm deserted waters. Out in the bay, the clarity allowed me to see down into the eerie depths. I bit my lip thinking about the source of the splash the night before. Was Tessie the one making noise, distracting me from kissing Callahan? I giggled, before the embarrassment hit me again. *As if.*

Fannette Island was closed to tourism this time of year due to the frigid weather. I made sure the coast was clear before I snuck over to "our" spot. Underneath the ponderosa pines and white firs, I scooped the dirt away from the line of rocks we'd arranged as kids. Somewhere under the sand, a plastic Folgers coffee-can slept with childhood treasures deep inside. We'd counted twenty steps from the spot to the water. Now, the steps were more like fifteen. The landscape had changed, but I still remembered where we'd hidden it.

The sandy loam made digging the earth easier and I finally hit something hard. With my fingers, I traced the edge of the circular object under the dirt and lifted the can from the ground. The outside wording had faded, but when I pried the duct tape free, the inside was dry as a bone.

For a moment, I just peered into the container, afraid to stir the contents. We were supposed to open this together before we left for college. Before she left without saying a word. *Oh, Tatchi.* My insides ached. I felt more like a thief than a discoverer.

Inside were the two friendship rings I'd made from a broken gold chain, a paperclip, and fake stones all hot glued together—a blue stone for me and a yellow one for her. Tangled in the loose chain was a necklace charm of a mermaid she'd given me for my birthday one year, something we liked to pretend when we swam in the bay. A picture of us with the inscription "best friends forever" written with liquid paper reminded me how we loved to play with Mom's office supplies at Gran's shop. I put my friendship ring on and held the picture to my chest.

Two envelopes with our names written in glitter pen caught my eye. I stopped before taking mine out and breaking the candle wax seal. A thread of guilt for opening it early wrapped around my heart.

Dear Ash,

You are my bestest friend in the whole world. Swimming, reading books, pretending to be rescued by handsome princes, and riding bikes with you is my favorite things ever. I hope we live next door to each other when we grow up and have lots of babies who grow up and like to play together. When you read this, I want you to remember the time we took Fin's underwear and put it up the flagpole. ha-ha. Or the time we tricked Fin into tasting the whipped cream pie and smashed it in his face. That was hilarious. Okay, I can't think of anything else to say, so good-bye.

Love your BFF, Tatiana aka Tatchi aka Super Spy #2

Ps. If you aren't Ash, you're stealing. Rebury it or else.

I held the note to my chest, laughing and crying at the same time. We'd had such a fun childhood together—so many good memories. And now this. Silence.

I sat overlooking the water, flipping the mermaid charm in my fingers, contemplating a life without my best friend. As the wind blew through the trees, the aged wood protested—aching with me. Did something bad happen? Did her parents find out about her plans for college and move away? What if she never came home? Would I have to go to college alone? The thought killed me.

My butt fell asleep after sitting on the cold ground. I put everything away except the picture and reburied the can.

Dejected, I pushed off shore and began the slow process of rowing back. The urge to cry burned in my throat. This wasn't fair. Who just picks up and leaves their things, abandons their business, and doesn't tell anyone why for weeks? Was this the insanity of living with an alcoholic? I pulled out the picture and studied it—our happy faces, our innocent joy. How could we be *best friends forever* now?

A ski boat zoomed by, the curious onlookers prying into my business. I turned away but had to grab the sides as their stupid waves rocked the boat too hard. An oar slipped into the water. I went to grab it, dropping the picture, too.

"NO!" I cried and reached over the ledge to retrieve both items.

Another wave knocked the boat just right and I toppled over into the water. The icy current ravaged my skin like sharp needles, jabbing relentlessly into my body. Everything ached except one part of my thigh where it burned instead.

I tried to swim but my leg wouldn't work. Something red colored the water around me. A huge tear in my pant leg revealed the source. *Lucky there aren't any sharks.* I laughed at myself.

Horrified I was able to make jokes at a time like this, I turned around to reach for the boat. I slapped empty water. *Where was it?* Panic began to take over. And then I saw it. The wind had pushed the boat out of reach. With each passing second, it moved further away. I tried to paddle, but my muscles seized with the cold.

Forcing myself to calm down, I rolled over and floated on my back. But as I watched the blue sky above and felt the icy water below, reality sunk in. If I didn't get out of the water soon, hypothermia would set in. I was about to drown.

"Help!" I screamed, hoping the people who'd just cruised by and caused the accident actually saw me fall in. "Help . . ."

Salty, hot tears burned my cheeks and slid down my face into the water.

This was it. The best swimmer on our swim team had met her match. I was going to join the underwater grave of mobsters in cement boots at the bottom of the lake. Cold seeped into my bones, numbing my hands and toes. Uncontrollable shivers overtook my strength. The desire to keep my eyes open became harder to fight.

My face submerged.

I opened my eyes one more time, my last breath bubbling out of my mouth. The light from the sun twinkled in the water as the darkness pulled me downward. My lungs burned for air, air impossible for me to swim to.

A bright light barreled toward me under the water. It couldn't be good, but I couldn't bring myself to care. It's what everyone sees at the end.

"I've got you," I heard in my mind. The voice sounded faintly like Fin's.

I smiled. Of course my last thoughts would be lying cradled in the warm and safe arms of my unending crush: Fin. What an amazing way to go.

27

FIN

I could have swam in circles of joy when Mr. Gumboot requested smooth rocks for his fence surrounding his algae garden. With pleasure, I insisted on retrieving them and left Kiernan to help arrange the existing collection. With a quick flap of my fin, I secretly slipped back into Tahoe for a little extra curricular rock-hunting adventure. Sure, I was pushing the limits, but hey, Mr. Gumboot asked and my explicit instructions were to please the elder mers. And where else would I find smooth granite stones?

I returned to the lake with a grin and swam to the shoreline, careful to stay far enough underwater so no one would see me. Of course, Uncle Alaster and Colin were nowhere in sight either. Scanning the bottom, I laughed at the bountiful selection. How would I choose? Heck, it might take me all day to find the perfect stones.

Hours later, when I finally stopped procrastinating, I found some that were satisfactory. I lugged them back to the gate. That's when I realized the opening through Tessie's mouth wasn't very large.

Annoyed, I returned to grab some smaller ones to take back with me when a scream from the surface grabbed my attention. One I'd know anywhere. Ashlyn's scream. Without a thought, I dropped the stones and with a powerful flick of my tail, I shot through the lake like a cannon, only slowing to listen.

The voice came from somewhere in the bay. Without a care for who might see me, I raced underwater. I found her lifeless body, slipping under the waves.

In one swift motion, I cradled her fragile frame and burst onto the shore, phasing as soon as my skin found the sunlight. Holding her against my body, I turned up my internal heater to warm her blue-tinted skin.

"Ashlyn, open your eyes," I said and rocked her, watching the water steam off her skin, but she wasn't breathing. I pulled her tighter into me, giving her a gentle shake. "Come on. Wake up."

She lay there, lifeless in my arms, the minutes ticking by, her life ebbing away. I panicked. The mer power behind my breath would save her, but our lips touching would seal me to her forever; our souls would intertwine. She'd want for me always and become immune to my powers to erase her memories.

"Ashlyn, please wake up."

She wasn't responding. Death's fingers were wrapping around her soul. I couldn't wait any longer for a miracle. I couldn't let her die. A world without Ashlyn in it, even if she wasn't mine, would be a travesty.

I pressed my lips onto hers and exhaled. The heat from my immortal kiss warmed her from the inside out, pinking up her skin. With the next breath, something inside broke free, flowing into her and making me care deeper than I'd ever cared for anyone. She had to live. Then she coughed, a tiny sweet cough that melted my fears. She'd survived. Barely.

I clutched her to my chest and patted her back, helping the water escape from her lungs. With a quick glance, I scanned the tree line for onlookers and didn't see anyone. I was naked, holding a drenched-to-the-bone girl. Quite an awkward situation. I kneeled down, holding her against my body with one hand, and took out my shorts with the other. Thank goodness for Velcro.

Ashlyn began to shiver and lulled her head around on the crook of my arm.

"Shhh. . ." I whispered, tucking her back into my side once I was clothed. "You're safe. Just stay with me. Fight."

Her words garbled off her tongue, recalling the events prior to her falling into the water.

"I fell . . . fire . . . it's burning." She feebly reached down toward her leg and that's when I saw the blood. Blood everywhere.

"Oh, no."

I inspected the wound. A clean slice ran right across the side of her thigh. She needed medical attention quickly. Gently, I tore the rest of her pant leg off and tied it above the wound to stop the bleeding. I removed her sopping wet jacket and shrugged into it. I turned up my internal body heat to see if I could dry it out and put it back on her. I looked down. My choice of board shorts and ill-fitting girl's swim team jacket looked—interesting.

I trudged up the hill to the Rangers station and braced for the reaction as I walked through the door. My entrance caught the tall, lanky, slightly-graying man on duty by surprise. He glanced at me, then at Ashlyn, and then at my wardrobe malfunction.

"Uh—" Theories to what really happened danced across his face—most of them dark.

"She's hurt. We need to call nine-one-one."

He kept staring at the water mixed with blood dripping on the floor, a deer in the head-lights.

I sighed.

"Forget you ever saw me and the next five minutes," I spoke in my native tongue and waved my hand over his face.

The Ranger's eyes went glassy as he sat down, the mer playing tricks with his mind. I rushed inside and found a first aid kit, a cot, and blankets. I put Ashlyn's coat back on her, dressed her wound, and wrapped her up in the blanket, tight like a burrito. I knew I should take off the rest of her wet clothing, but I couldn't do it, not wanting to violate her in any way or injure her leg further. She was shivering uncontrollably now, which was a good sign but difficult to watch.

I palmed through the Ranger's things and found some pants and a shirt. Not my size, but I put them on anyway. On the radio, I called for help.

"We have a young woman, unconscious. At the Fannett Island Ranger Station. She fell into the lake. Please send an ambulance."

"Yes, sir," someone crackled on the other end of the line. "Right away."

I went back to Ashlyn, smoothed her damp hair, and kissed her temple. "I'm sorry. I have to go. You'll be okay. Help is on the way."

"Fin?" Ashlyn's eyes fluttered open. She took two deep breaths and stopped shivering for a moment.

Time froze. Everything inside me ached to kiss her for real, to finish what I'd started. My blood would heal her leg and we could run away somewhere and live together, under the waves in peace and solitude.

She managed a smile. "I knew you'd come."

My throat hitched. Could she actually be awake? Should I screw everything and take her with me? Her voice was nothing but a whisper, but then her eyes rolled back and she started shivering again. She wasn't lucid; she couldn't be. And since I couldn't erase anything further from her mind anyhow, I had to take off before she woke up again.

Each time I'd mind-wiped her in the past tortured me so deeply—to watch her fade underneath a blanket of confusion. She'd never remember this moment anyway, but her sweet voice and leaving her here was going to haunt me forever. I hoped since she didn't know what had happened, she'd be unaffected.

The Ranger's groan interrupted our moment. Dude was coming back around and I had to get out of there. The choice to leave her with the clueless Ranger took every bit of energy I had.

Just outside of the door I heard him say. "Oh, sweet Mary.

Where'd you come from?" and then, to my relief, he called for the ambulance again, oblivious to the fact that one was already en route.

I groaned and headed back to the lake.

28

ASH

"Ashlyn, please wake up, sweetie."

My mom's voice bounced inside my tired brain. Everything ached. Beyond my closed eyelids was a bright light, too bright for me to want to look at.

"Ohhh," I moaned.

I brought my hand to shield the nuisance and found something taped across my skin, hindering me. Beeps and other whooshing noises coupled with the antiseptic smell were more hints we weren't at home.

"Mom?" I groggily choked out and opened my right eye a crack.

"Oh, my heavens." She grabbed ahold of my tethered hand. "Yes, honey, I'm here."

I looked around the strange space, apparently a hospital room. My weighted body felt detached as I attempted to sit up. "What happened?"

"Just lie still," Mom said and put her hand on my shoulder. "You . . . apparently had an accident and fell into the lake. The Ranger found you before it was too late and brought you to the Forest Ranger Station. They were able to warm you up and stop the bleeding until the ambulance could arrive."

"Bleeding?" I reached down to my leg and felt a mountain of gauze.

"Yes." Her hand trembled. "You're going to be okay though. They've patched you up. You're good as new."

"New?" I mumbled. I felt nothing of the sort. Thrown out of a moving car and run over was a better description.

"Look who's awake," a blonde nurse in pink, *Hello Kitty* patterned scrubs said as she pulled back the curtain and walked into the room. Before I could answer, she popped a thermometer in my mouth and replaced the bag of fluids running down a tube into the back of my hand. She checked my temp reading, wrote something in my chart, and smiled. "Very good. How do you feel?"

"Tired."

"I bet. You've been through a lot, but the fast work from the Ranger gave you the best chance for recovery."

"Ranger?"

Fuzz lined my brain and impeded any memory beyond my excursion to the island. The past came in short movie clips: the coffee can of treasures, rowing back to shore, the bitter wind, the picture floating into the water. I never wanted to be that cold again. For the first time ever, water terrified me. With a vacant expression, I looked toward Mom.

"You fell into the lake, sweetie, and cut your leg pretty badly."

My hand went to my mouth to hide my embarrassment. Then I froze. The warmth of my lips felt different—tingly somehow.

"I remember," I mumbled, part in acknowledgement and part to make sure I hadn't been dreaming.

"Where did you manage to fall in, honey?"

My gaze met hers. Worry stamped unforgiving grooves into her skin, creating small fissures. Gray hair mixed with brown lined her temples like weeds in a pristine lawn. What if something bad had happened to me?

I glanced down and played with the tape on my hand. "I don't know . . ."

My nurse gave Mom a reassuring look. "Well, you're almost back to normal. I'll give your doctor an update. Maybe you can go home today. How's that?"

Mom sighed, the kind that sounded like a huge boulder had been lifted from her chest. I willed the nurse to stay, but she squeezed my blanketed foot and walked out the door instead.

Mom kept looking at me with her deep blue eyes, her powerlessness threatening to choke me. I almost burst into a monologue of a million sorrys when my nurse came back in the room. I held my breath.

"I almost forgot your lunch." She put a cafeteria tray on my bedside table.

"Thanks," I mumbled and decided to wait on spilling the truth of what happened. My stomach hurt from hunger and I lifted the lid covering the plate. Palatable fragrances of macaroni and cheese, and steamed broccoli hit my nose. At least the food looked better than the bland cafeteria crud they fed us at school.

"I'm... I'm going to go call your father," Mom said and left the room.

I nodded, wanting to be alone. My guilt would keep me company.

While I ate the first couple of noodles, my brain fought to remember the details of what happened to me after I fell into the water. A Ranger dragged me out of the lake? How could that be? I'd been so far off shore. The memory was there, murky like the bloody water I'd almost drowned in. Blood. That's right, lots of blood. I'd heard a voice. A male's voice . . . like Fin's. Only melodic. And a light—a beautiful light. An angel?

A knock at the door interrupted my brainstorm.

"Uh, sorry to intrude. I just got off work and wanted to stop by."

I smiled at the graying gentleman in front of me. He wore a button down shirt and dark green slacks. A gold park emblem on his lapel tipped me off.

I set down my fork. "You're the guy? The one who saved me?"

"Well . . . not really, Miss. Someone brought you into the back room of the station without my knowledge . . . and left. I called the ambulance once I saw your condition. I wanted you to know. They deserve the credit."

Apparently, I wasn't the only one with amnesia.

"Oh?" His version of the scene ran through my head and I pressed my lips together. They tingled again. "Thank you."

"Don't mention it. Just wanted to make sure you were okay. Good day." He tipped his hat and left.

Mom passed him on her way back in the room.

"Was that the—?"

"Yeah." I shoved a peach into my mouth, unsure how to explain what his role was in my daring rescue. "He's the Ranger."

"I wanted to thank him." She darted back to the door and scanned the hall. "Sir? Sir!"

"Mom!" I called out, hoping to stop her before she made a fool of herself. I tried to get out of bed, but my leg protested in pain, forbidding any sudden movements. "He doesn't want the attention, Mom!"

She didn't come back—her voice echoing down the hall. I slapped my forehead.

What a mess.

29

FIN

With my blood pummeling through my veins, I slipped back into Natatoria unnoticed. A group of mermaids, tittering and giggling, swam past moments later chaperoned by an annoyed merman displaying the gold Natatorian insignia strapped to his bicep. He gave me a glare that might suggest he'd seen me return, until one of the mermaids told him to be nice while she winked at me.

I wanted to laugh. Suddenly, they seemed as appealing as an old woman. Ashlyn was the only one I wanted to look at and be with for eternity—petting her soft white skin, gazing into her enchanting green eyes. Thoughts of tangling my hands in her red curls and bringing her lips to mine grappled with my being. How could I have left her with that incompetent Ranger? Was she okay? Did she make it to the hospital in time? I knew she was still alive, at least.

Wracked with grief, I hurried home to find it empty. Mom and Tatch were still at the palace, but would be home soon enough. Maybe I could tell them what happened. After all, Dad had kissed Mom under similar circumstances.

Ashlyn's sweet lips and tender body in my arms wrapped around my mind. With one kiss, everything had changed. All I wanted was her—forever. I had to be with her or I'd go mad.

I phased into legs and sprawled out on the couch, wishing for a TV show to pass the time. With a groan, I pounded my fist on the granite arm of the couch. A searing ache of longing replaced the initial high when I'd promised myself to her. Now our distance rubbed salt into my soul. *Why didn't I just heal her with my blood?*

Then I'd know she was all right.

When I heard Mom and Tatch talking outside, I got up and hid in my room.

"Fin, are you here?" Mom asked after entering the house. She sounded distressed.

"Yeah, in my room."

I clenched my jaw. There was no way I could handle another minute without knowing if Ashlyn was okay or not. I had to get back on land before the sun set and double check. I marched into the living room, ready to spill my guts.

I stopped short. Azor, Colin and Uncle Alaster were standing in my living room, each of them exuding their own flavor of a condemning stare. The one I wanted to wipe off with my fist, though, was Colin's ugly little smirk.

"Finley, we need to talk," Azor said calmly, motioning for me to sit down.

I darted my eyes to Mom, then Tatch, who both were a little pale. My heart began to hammer but I remained composed, taking my seat. Yes, I'd left my post without permission, but no one saw me leave Natatoria.

Crap!

Then I remembered. I forgot to deliver the rocks. Kiernan must have told Azor I didn't return. If only I had gone back, then he could have been my alibi.

Azor ran his hand through his obsidian hair and frowned. "Where were you today?"

Great. Here we go. "At Mr. Gumboot's place."

He raised an eyebrow. "The whole time?"

"No. He wasn't happy with his selection of rocks, so I left to find him some new ones. Good customer service is key, you know." I smirked.

"You never returned." Azor's eyes fell into slits.

"I couldn't find any that where smooth like he wanted. The work day was over, so I went home." I leaned back and rested my ankle on my leg. Neither Alaster, nor Azor would be able to do so, forced to sit ladylike in their archaic man-skirts.

Azor leaned forward. "You were seen today, outside of Natatoria."

A laugh exited my lips. "Oh, really? By whom?"

Uncle Alaster sat up and placed a digital camera encased in a watertight container on the coffee table. "Colin was able to recover this—" The blood drained from my face as I eyed the proof. "—and mind-wiped the owner, but I'm not sure if anyone else saw."

My glare landed on Colin's overly happy, beady eyes. "And you're sure it's me?"

"Quite sure, Cousin. I, of course, was running a charter when you chose to jettison out of the gate, creating five-foot waves. My cruisers panicked and thought an earthquake had erupted along the fault line, causing a tsunami. I had to mind-wipe the entire group and confiscate this camera."

Every cell in my body wanted to pummel the little snitch.

"Five-foot waves? I highly doubt that."

"Tomorrow the lake is going to be swarming with boats and divers. I can't wait to see what they say on the evening news."

"Colin, you little—" I lunged for him, but Azor held me back.

"That's enough, Finley. Unfortunately, you'll need to be sanctioned. This is serious. A trial will be set after we assess the damage. You'll need to come with me to a holding cell."

"What? And Colin mind-wiping an entire group of people isn't grounds for sanctioning, too? What about the gate? And even now, who's guarding it?" I glanced over at Tatiana's anxious eyes and then towards Mom. She wouldn't look at me. I threw my hands into the air. "This is insane!"

Azor ignored me. "Alaster, I'm hoping you and Colin will be able to contain any rumors. And keep a better eye on the gate."

"Of course, Captain." Alaster bowed his head.

Out of the corner of my eye, Colin moved to snatch up the only known evidence of my infraction off the table; I countered to stop him. What was on the camera anyway? I didn't surface the water until I reached Ashlyn's body. No one was around.

Tatch caught the nonverbal exchange.

"Don't you want the camera, Azor?" she asked with a silkened voice. "For evidence?"

"We should return it as quickly as we can to its owner," Alaster shot back. "Before his subconscious forces him to remember what really happened when he can't find it."

Azor glanced towards Alaster, then at the clear box in Colin's hand with disgust, apparently undecided on what to do. His naïveté had to have left him unsure how to work the foreign gadget. As a rule, human technology was looked at as being something useless to the mers and thus to be avoided. Azor strictly followed those guidelines.

"Azor," my sister purred as she slithered closer to Colin and plucked the box right out of his hand. "Let's look at the pictures first." The case opened with a hiss.

She clicked the buttons with a stoic disposition, then her shoulders softened.

"Maybe you should look, Azor?"

She got up and perched herself on the arm of the chair Azor sat in. She demonstrated the gadget with one hand and wrapped her other hand around his shoulder. "See? There's no fuss."

Azor tightened his eyes for a fraction of a second as each picture flashed on the screen. "Yes, I see what you mean." He ran his hand through his hair again. "Still, Alaster is right. The camera should be returned. Colin?"

Tatiana held out the contraption with a coquettish smile. Colin took the camera and threw it into the box, unconcerned with damaging the device. Azor, unaware, gazed headily into Tatiana's eyes.

I gasped. "So there's no damaging pictures?"

Alaster coughed and grabbed his son by the arm. "Come, Colin. We have a gate to guard and rumors to squelch."

They left through the porthole before I could raise a larger stink.

Azor snapped out of Tatiana's bewitching stare and looked angrily at me. "Yes, the pictures seem to have discounted Colin's claim you were seen as a merman by humans, but your unauthorized exit must be discussed. You better hope they don't find any other evidence against you."

"Wait. Let me get this straight. I leave unauthorized through an unguarded gate, and I alone get in trouble?"

"You didn't have permission to leave, Finley. As far as your uncle's post is concerned, that's my business."

"I was getting rocks!" I yelled. "Because it's my *job* to make the elder mers happy. I only left for a minute!"

Azor turned and scowled. "You just can't leave and get rocks."

"This is utterly ridiculous!" I pounded my fist on the chair, breaking off a piece.

Tatiana batted her eyelashes at Azor. "Aren't you overreacting?"

"No, Tatiana. Finley has broken the law," he said plainly, then turned to me. "Be prepared to answer when the Council asks what you were doing. How you managed to create a wake while retrieving rocks is beyond me, but a solid explanation might reduce the time of your punishment."

Unlikely. "You'd better stop rumors here in Natatoria too. Once it gets around the gate's unguarded, other mers might stop by for a visit," I said with a sneer.

Azor glared. "Don't test me, Finley. The other mers respect our rules and you need to be reminded why we don't break them." Azor motioned for me to get to my feet. "We must go."

Mom kept eyeing me with worry. "When can I visit my son?"

"Mag—excuse me—Mrs. Helton, not until after the trial next week."

The withering glance of my torn mother ate at the lining of my stomach. How could I have been so careless? Colin tricked me into revealing what happened and I fell for it—hook, line, and sinker. By blaming me, Alaster completely avoided a reprimand. Without Dad's help to smooth matters behind the scenes, I doubted I'd get a fair trial. I could kiss Tahoe goodbye for my future now.

Azor made me go behind the curtain and phase first.

"*Sorry,*" Tatiana said, once she exited the porthole behind us. She and Mom floated, clinging to one another, in the current under the eve of the porch. "*What were you doing out there anyway?*"

"*Nothing,*" —besides promising myself to the girl of my dreams, risking the family's livelihood and putting everyone in jeopardy— "*You wouldn't believe me if I told you.*"

"*Better not have been nothing. I just flirted with Azor. Ugh.*"

I withheld a nervous laugh. "*Something personal. I'll tell you later.*"

"*Oh-kay,*" she said disparagingly.

If we had more time, she might have pulled out the truth. "*Take care of Mom. Who knows how this will turn out.*"

"*It'll be fine. I'm going to see you before the trial somehow.*"

Our eyes met. "*Don't you dare do anything rash.*"

"*We'll see.*"

"Finley, let's go," Azor said, noticing I'd stalled.

Azor and I crossed the bluff and the girls disappeared out of view, leaving me with my guilt. I had no idea what the punishment would be for leaving without permission. If Alaster or Colin testified, it would be my word against theirs, considering they had no proof. Maybe I could mention the fact that they weren't monitoring the gate. There was no way I was going to take the fall for everything.

As we swam closer, I noticed a few changes to his grandiose living quarters—more gilded surfaces and additional spires. The magnificent coral garden stood out, rumored to be directly from Fiji to accent his statue of a bare-chested mermaid—a custom he wanted reinstated.

A new room protruded off to the side, which he bragged he had built specifically for his hunting trophies. But in the back, behind a barnacle-encrusted stone fence loomed the ravenous creatures no one ever wanted to contend with—great white sharks.

From the Pacific Ocean, the sharks swam in and out of the Pacific gate as they pleased, only allowed in one small corner of Natatoria and blocked by floor-to-ceiling rock spires so they couldn't have a feasting frenzy on the mers. The windows of the jail cells off the back of his house were within this gated area.

No one had ever escaped and lived to tell about it. I was trapped until Azor let me out.

30

✺

ASH

My eyelids slowly opened, registering my surroundings. The clock on the wall said it was only one in the afternoon, but it felt later. Mom and a male's voice spoke outside the doorway, probably Dr. Peet. From the anxiety in her pitch, I figured my condition had worsened. I turned up the volume of the TV with the remote and flipped through the lowly thirteen channels. My choices were *Bonanza*, soap operas, *Let's Make A Deal,* or daytime reality TV.

Before I'd fallen asleep from the pain meds thirty minutes ago, the nurse said my white blood cell count was higher than they liked and they wanted to monitor me for infection. I wasn't sure if that meant here, or at home.

My dream fluttered back into my mind. A huge hourglass protruded out in the middle of our dining room table. Within the sand, bits and pieces of blue wood were showing through. Only I knew what was underneath. I struggled to move the gigantic thing out of sight of my inquisitive family—without success. Once more grains fell away, *The Sea Star* would show everyone what I'd done today.

My attention jerked to an interruption on the TV; warning of unusual activity in Emerald Bay.

"*. . . mysterious waves over six-feet tall accosted the shore shortly after eleven thirty this morning, damaging small boats in the harbor. Seismologists say there wasn't any activity on the fault line, leaving them baffled as to how the occurrence happened. Locals blame Tessie for the disturbance, others the full moon. Officials are asking, until* *further notice, for extreme care to be taken near the water until divers can determine the cause."*

I wanted to laugh until I heard, *"In other news, a local high school girl was swept out into the bay after a rogue wave hit the beach . . ."*

I dropped the remote.

"I saw the whole thing," a guy in a dirty shirt said, his missing tooth creating a lisp. *"The girl got washed into the lake by this crazy wave over there and then some guy jumped in and saved her."*

Did someone else have an accident besides me? I wasn't close enough to shore to have someone dive in and save me. All I remembered was the bright light underwater. My lips prickled again at the memory.

The camera cut to the lake and panned across the water, Fannette Island in the background. A pit formed in my stomach as I anticipated seeing the empty blue boat bobbing along. Then the Ranger came into view, the same one from earlier.

"Ranger Prescott, people are touting that you're the hero today. Did you jump in and fish this girl from the lake?"

He cleared his throat and looked down. *"I didn't rescue anyone, ma'am. I found her in my station, bundled up and almost frozen to death. I did what any citizen would have done and called nine-one-one."*

His words hacked through the fluff lining my brain. This story *was* about me. I started to break out in a sweat as the woman continued to ask him probing questions about my injuries and if I'd said anything. He didn't have much to say. The others she interviewed blamed the waves and, surprisingly, not my stupidity. Did no one truly see me fall? What about the jet boat riders?

"Ashlyn!" Dad said breathlessly, as if he'd run all the way here.

His voice made me jump. I pawed at the covers to find the remote, shutting off the TV. He walked briskly over and hugged me hard.

"Thank God you're all right. I got here as soon as I could." He kissed the top of my head and held me, letting out a sigh. "If anything ever happened to you, I don't know what I'd do."

"I'm okay, Dad. Really."

He didn't move, just kept his arms around me. His sniffle set guilt careening through my body. Why did I do something so stupid? We stayed that way for several minutes. I finally melted into his shoulder.

He composed himself and stood by my bed, still wearing his fire-station T-shirt. "You worried us. How are you feeling?"

"Okay, I guess." I pushed my hair out of my eyes. My chest clenched watching him suffer, the "what ifs" playing horror films within his eyes. "I didn't mean to get anyone upset."

"Just—" He put his hand on my shoulder and squeezed—torture running wicked grooves across his forehead and eyes. He sighed again, sounding tired, defeated. "We need you to be more careful. Mom said you weren't feeling well, so you didn't go to church today. What were you doing down by the water?"

I worked to catch my breath as the truth smoldered on my tongue. I wanted to come clean, but knew their reaction would be fierce once they realized what I'd done. Could the consequences be punishment enough? My injury grounded me from swimming for a few weeks and the scar would forever mark my thigh. "I—I needed some fresh air."

"How did you fall in?"

I nervously chuckled. "A wave, I think."

The timing of the huge waves couldn't have worked more perfectly to my advantage. But as far as I could remember, other than the ones from a jet boat that knocked my oar into the water, nothing unusual happened.

Dad didn't appreciate my jocularity and frowned. "You don't remember where you were or how you ended up in the lake?"

"No." I held my breath, the treacherous sand falling faster and faster.

He shook his head. "Hmmm."

My mind slowly whirled, thick with pain meds, searching for an alibi to his next set of questions. *What if someone saw me? Or worse, what if my rescuer comes clean? Maybe I could stage a break-in to make it look like someone stole the boat.*

Mom came from around the curtain and interrupted my thoughts. She slid her hand into his and kissed Dad. "Good, I'm glad you're here."

I faked a smile. In private, they'd compare notes of what happened and bust that hourglass wide open. Should I just come clean and take the heat?

"They're keeping her tonight," Mom said, as if I wasn't in the room. "There's an infection somewhere. And her quad muscle is injured pretty badly so she'll need to stay off her feet. She's not allowed to swim for several months either. Then there's physical therapy, too."

"What?" I'd figured weeks, but not months. That would be the rest of senior year. I slouched back in the pillows and turned my face towards the window as the tears welled up in my eyes. A knock at the door cut the dreary silence.

"Come in," Mom said softly.

Callahan walked in with a beautiful bouquet of gerbera daisies and yellow lilies. "Sorry to interrupt." He nervously held out the arrangement, his gaze darting between my parents and me. "I heard about what happened and wanted to bring you these."

I wiped away the tears and tried to smile, taking the flowers from him. "They're so lovely. Thank you." I put them to my nose, inhaled the sweet fragrance, and swooned. No one had ever brought me flowers before.

Realizing his arrival was poorly timed, he looked at me with questioning eyes, then shifted his weight from side to side, as if preparing to bolt out the door. "Sorry. I should have called first."

"Sit, son," Dad said and motioned to the chair next to me. "We were just leaving."

Mom blinked as Dad pulled her towards the door, her eyes filled with frustration. Now that the initial grief and shock had worn off, I'd have to answer to why I'd lied and left the house. "We'll talk later."

Once they shut the door, I exhaled the breath I'd been holding. "Parents. They won't stop smothering me. I've insisted I'm fine."

Callahan looked concerned. "What happened?"

Gazing at his curious expression made me realize I'd be retelling this story for a very long time. Maybe missing some school might not be a bad thing after all. The rumor mill could drum up the tale just fine in my absence. And really, my brief story didn't make sense with all its incongruous edges.

"Other than falling into the lake, I'm not sure. Someone must have saved me, I guess. All I remember is waking up here."

"Weird." Callahan squished his eyebrows together in a cute, confused way. "Did a wave knock you in?"

"I don't quite remember—"

Technically this wasn't a lie; a wave *did* knock me in. Just not from shore. I ached to confess to ease my battered conscience.

"I'm just glad you're okay. When I found out, I freaked."

I played with my fingernails. He did care after all, proving my breakup theory wrong. But now I was more confused. His comment should have made my heart soar like a bird, but surprisingly it didn't. My gaga feelings had evaporated; I no longer saw him as the most adorable boy in school that tripped up my tongue and made me blush.

He took my hand, startling me. "So, when do you get out of here?"

"Tomorrow, I think."

He traced my knuckles with his thumb, giving me goose bumps across my arms. "If I'd been there, I would have jumped in and tried to save you. Even though you're a better swimmer than me."

His confession made me grin. "Then we both would have drowned. It's pretty cold," I said and laughed under my breath. "Now I know what the victims of the *Titanic* felt like."

He stopped massaging my hand, and stared.

"Sorry," I mumbled. "I think the drugs are messing with my head."

He shook his head. "I'm just glad someone saved you."

My lips pulled up at the corners, but not because of his concern. "So am I."

I had a good guess who saved me and he wasn't of this world. Only an angel could have braved the freezing water and delivered me to safety right under the Ranger's nose.

My lips tingled again.

31

FIN

The lifeless eyes of the curious sharks moseyed past the window, spelling my doom. As I sat in my cell on an uncomfortable rock, I kicked myself again for allowing Colin to trick me into confessing. If I'd only pretended I didn't know a thing, they'd be the ones rotting in jail, not me. My life was in King Phaleon's hands now.

Dad, the best negotiator I knew, wouldn't have allowed Azor to hold me, especially since I wasn't a danger to other mers. House arrest would have been more fitting than these dingy closet-sized quarters, void of a functional bed or chair. A caged animal in a zoo.

Azor had locked me inside and said, "Be ready to tell the truth when I come for you." Who knew how long that would take? The light never changed, as if it were night 24/7.

I tried my best to piece together a good defense. But all I could think about was Ashlyn. The sweet taste of her lips, the softness of her skin, the delicate shape of her body—all of it haunting me. My parents had warned me at a young age, once your soul entwines with another, it's all over until you can be together and make your commitment official to the public. I see why they insisted I wait. My soul, lit with a burning passion, wanted nothing but for me to figure out a way to be with her forever.

The decision became easy. I'd run away. Living in the water at night as a merman would be far easier than trying to survive the elements on land as a human, lacking money and a place to stay. And mer to human conversion was dangerous to do alone anyway.

Of course, I'd need to tell Ash something creative about why we couldn't be together at night and why I didn't live next door anymore. Then we had the mark of the promising to contend with—the matching symbol of our bond etched on our ring fingers like a tattoo. I studied the skin, noticing mine was already starting to show. Would Ash notice as hers filled in on her finger too?

She'd need to learn the truth, and I had to do it in a way that didn't scare her like the last time. When she saw us by accident a few summers ago, she screamed bloody murder—her voice permanently etched in my mind. I'd been forced to mind-wipe her back then, but now I didn't have that option.

And if the time to convert became necessary, careful consideration would be taken first. I'd never ask her to change for me. Getting married and living on land as undercover mers for the time being, like my parents did, might be the best.

I groaned and took another deep breath of salt water. For my latest meal, one of Azor's goons gave me a live sunfish in a cage and conveniently forgot the utensils. Was I supposed to tear the poor thing apart with my teeth? A deep fiery red, the fish darted around inside, looking for an exit. Identifying with his fate, I let him go. I didn't have much of an appetite anyway.

"Be careful, Freddy," I called out, watching him swim through the bars into the shark infested waters, headed towards freedom. He looked back for a moment as if to say "thank you" and slipped out of sight. I wished he could deliver a message.

Tell her I love her and we'll be together soon.

I returned to my lowly spot on the floor and recreated the triangular peg board game with the fifteen golf tees, using shells as my placeholders to pass the time. Every once in a while, a crab would skitter by and try to hide under my tail. I'd shoo the nasty thing away. After a few days of this, I'd go stark raving mad.

Tatch said she'd visit so I stared at the outer stone door through the bars, hoping she'd enter. If somehow she could flirt again and gain access, I'd be forever in her debt. I doubted Azor would ever allow it. Solitary confinement was part of my punishment.

I scratched at my scales, trying to remove the nasty, slimy film that had grown over the top. Trapped in my mer form for what I suspected was over twenty-four hours with no way to switch was like depriving a caffeine addict their morning brew. Everything ached, including my soul.

"You've got a visitor," Goon One said through the little slot in the stone door. I got up and tried to look like being caged wasn't affecting my psyche.

Maybe Tatch found a way to see me.

When he pried open the heavy door, for a brief second, I could see Azor in his living quarters with some of his men crowded around a table. Then Badger came into view.

"Aye, Blanchard. Good to see ya," he said and wrapped his arm around the brawny goon's neck. They briefly pounded one another on the back.

My shoulders slumped, relieved to see a friendly face, even if he was here to chew me out. At that point, I didn't care. I needed the company.

"You here to see this lousy lot?" Blanchard asked with a guttural laugh.

"Aye. And talk sense into him." Badger laughed with him which bristled my dorsal fin. "Kids."

I turned away and folded my arms over my chest.

"Lad," Badger said with a "tsk" after the door shut. "Whatcha doin' here?"

I leaned my head against the wall and studied the starfish lining the ceiling. "Why do you care?"

Badger lowered his voice. "I just be smoothin' over ole Blanchard so I could have a private word."

I let my arms fall free and glanced over at him. He'd pushed his hairy eyebrows into a line, a concerned look covering his face. I believed him and moved closer to the bars.

He shook his head. "What did ya do?"

I closed my eyes. Though I knew Badge would never rat me out, rotting in the cell for a day convinced me no one could know what happened, especially since I planned to run away. The only person I truly trusted was Dad.

"I left Natatoria without permission."

"Ya what? What in the devil's name possessed you to leave without permission?"

I looked down. "Rocks."

Badger pressed his eyes into slits. "Yer locked up like a convict because of rocks?"

"Yup."

"Oye," Badger said and scrubbed his hand over his face. "You know better than to be leaving without an escort. Who be needin' rocks?"

"I was trying to be helpful. It's fine, Badge. I'll explain my stupidity to the King and plea for more community service, until my dad returns of course."

Badge held up his hand to stop me. "No! This is serious. They're real strict about the young'uns leavin' the gates. Who'd be standin' up with ya at the trial?"

I blinked back at him. "No one?"

"Ya can't be havin' no one."

"What's the big deal?"

He let out a groan. "The deal is, you be a loose torpedo, not mindin' the rules. So, yer gonna need someone to keep watch on ya, put their neck out and swear they'll make ya mind. Though I'm just a bottom feeder, maybe they'll let me vouch for ya."

"No, Badge." I pursed my lips.

"What do ya mean no?"

"I—I don't seem to be able to stay out of trouble and I don't want your reputation tarnished."

Badger tilted his head and studied me quizzically. "What else happened up above?"

I lifted my chin. "Nothing important."

He grunted. "Well, until ye get someone to stand up for ye, I think you'll be here a right long time."

My jaw fell. "What? Is that why you're here?"

"You don't have another male family member who'd do it and you surely don't have anything valuable they want, so, yeah. I'd be here to bail yer mangy arse out."

My head spun, my hopes smashing in front of me. Azor might as well have pulled my beating heart from my chest. This ensured I wouldn't be able to see Ash any time soon without getting Badger into serious trouble. I wanted to yell and rip the bars apart, but I remained sullenly calm and simply replied. "Fine, Badger. I promise I'll behave."

"It'll be all right, lad," Badge said with a smile. "Let me go tell Azor I'm standin' in for yer da'. Maybe they'll let ya out early before the trial to go home instead of stayin' in this shite hole."

I grimaced. Azor wouldn't dream of letting me out early. I didn't even think they'd let Badger stand in for me, being a beta-mer and all. I flipped my tail, stirring up the sand and a lowly crab into a forced whirlpool.

32

ASH

"Gran's letting you stay in her room," Mom said from the front seat. I sat in the back with my bandaged leg stretched out.

"She is?"

Mom looked at me through the rearview mirror and raised her eyebrows. "You're not going to be able to go up and down the stairs."

"Oh, right," I chuckled and turned to watch the sparkling water zip by. The pain pills were doing a number on me, making things speed up and my stomach topsy-turvy. "Wish we could have taken the wheelchair home."

"Hmmm," Mom mumbled and turned on some easy-listening jazz.

On the floorboard, the flower vases clinked together in time with the balloons bobbing on the ceiling. Mom drove faster than normal or at least it seemed she did. After Callahan left, Georgia and some others from the swim team came by. And with them, oodles of gifts showed up as well. I felt like a coward for lying and not coming clean. Would they do the same if they knew I'd purposefully put myself in harm's way?

I leaned back and took a deep breath. "Where's Gran? She never came to visit."

"She did, but you were asleep. She's at the store right now. We're short-handed."

"Oh." I noted the animosity in her voice. Heaven forbid they close down for a day. She'd probably rather have changed places with Gran. I preferred Mom anyway. Driving with Gran *was* putting your life in your hands.

Earlier at the hospital, Mom asked again if my memory returned. I warred with myself as the "not yet" slipped easier off my tongue than the truth. I vowed to confess after the hysteria wore off and Mom was a little less frantic.

We pulled up to the house and parked out front. I assumed this was so she could make an easy get-away to the store after delivering me. As I waited for her to come around and assist me, I looked at my second story window. It had only been a day, but things looked different, almost as if I didn't belong there anymore.

Mom opened the car door and gave me a hard look before handing me my crutches. "You are to take it easy."

I sighed. "Yes."

With all the medication pumping through my veins, how could I even fathom anything other than sleep? I struggled to get to my feet, my head spinning.

"Ashlyn! You're home!" Lucy ran up to the car and wrapped her arms around my neck as I teetered on one foot. "I was so worried."

"I'm fine," I said and warmed at her kindness. Apparently twelve-year-olds were germ breeders; anyone under fourteen couldn't visit unless they were actually a patient.

"Can I help carry anything?"

I did a double-take before pointing at my bounty inside. She rounded them all up and hauled them into the house with a smile on her face. I stood like a flamingo and gawked.

Gran's room had a stale smell to it mixed with potpourri and sickly sweet perfume, but I didn't mind. The bed was comfortable and she had a TV, which I planned to use liberally. I untucked the blankets so I could drape them over my leg easier; the excess pillows became a foot rest.

Lucy perched herself on the chair with wide eyes. "What happened? Mom said you can't remember anything. Do you have amnesia? I read about someone with that once in school. Are you staying home all week? Where's your cut? Do you have stitches?"

"Whoa," I spluttered out, head swimming with questions. "You'll need to slow down. I can barely keep up."

Lucy laughed. "Sorry."

"Yeah, I'm staying home all week so my leg will heal. It's pretty nasty. Want to see it?"

"Ewww, no." Lucy squirmed.

I smiled at my creative diversion from answering her about my supposed *amnesia*. "I'm just glad to be home. My nurses woke me every three hours to check my temperature, blood pressure, and heart rate. I couldn't get any sleep."

"Crazy," she said, blowing her bangs out of her eyes. "Did Callahan come and see you?"

"Yes and he brought me flowers."

"Oooh! He did?" Lucy squealed and got up to find the arrangement.

I watched her with wonderment. Who was this delightful girl? I would have fallen into the lake years ago if I'd known she'd be nice to me afterward. Having a real conversation for once was refreshing.

"Did he kiss you?" she asked abruptly.

"What?"

"After the dance."

I felt my cheeks warm up. "Oh. Not yet."

Lucy shot me a smirk with half-lidded eyes. "Yeah, right."

I shook my head and laid back on Gran's bounty of pillows as Lucy read my cards out loud. The popcorn ceiling reminded me more of cottage cheese sprinkled with glitter—like stars. I imagined my angel up in the clouds and wished to see him again.

"You're kinda famous, you know."

I rolled my eyes and turned towards her, propping my leg up on pillows. "Famous?"

"Yeah. You were on TV and Laura Jane says you could probably write a book about what happened and make a lot of money."

"Oh she did, did she?" I tried not to laugh at her best friend's ridiculous observation.

I finally realized why she was being so nice to me. My accident must have raised her social standing at school, giving the kids something to fawn all over her with.

"Do you remember how you got to the Ranger station?"

I chewed on my fingernail. "No."

"Well, we went and talked to that Ranger guy. He didn't know anything either. That's weird, don't you think?"

"You went alone?"

"No, I went with Laura Jane." Lucy got comfortable at the foot of the bed, clutching the stuffed teddy bear with a bandaged leg Shannon had brought me. "It was her idea. Her mom drove us over there so we could get an interview with him for the school paper."

"Wow. That's—"

"—impressive," Lucy said, finishing my statement. "I know. She's going to be a journalist someday."

"I bet she wants to interview me, too," I muttered under my breath.

"Oh, would you?" Lucy's eyes shone.

I blinked, realizing I'd opened myself right up, practically volunteering. I couldn't say "no" now that we suddenly had a pleasurable sisterly relationship. "Sure. If she wants."

Lucy smiled from ear to ear. "Awesome!"

"Lucy!" Mom barked from down the hall. "Ashlyn needs to rest."

"Fine," Lucy called back with a grimace. She walked closer to me and whispered, "I'll have Laura Jane come over later, okay?"

I forced a smile. "If I'm feeling okay."

She perked up and skipped out of the room, closing the door behind her.

I pushed away the worry they'd want to do the interview anytime soon, snuggled under the covers, and reveled in the silence. No beeps or annoying nurses to bother me. Sleep came easily.

Then he returned. All glowy and warm. I felt his strong arms tenderly wrap around my body, breaching the surface of the water as he carried me to safety. His melodic voice told me to fight, to stay alive. I would have done anything to stay there in his blazing hot arms. If only he'd fly us up into the clouds of heaven. His lips touched mine and golden heat tickled my skin. Something within my heart released, like a bird soaring toward freedom. Only there did I feel complete. Like his kiss was the key that popped open the lock in my heart, setting me free.

33

FIN

A groan coming from behind the door startled me from my sleep. Somehow, I'd fallen over and the crabs were jockeying for position under my back. As I sat up, they scattered to the holes in the walls. I shivered and moved away from the floor.

"Stupid crabs."

"Hold your breath."

I swiveled around and went to the bars at Tatch's telepathic voice. As the outer door began to slowly open, black ink spilt into the water.

"Don't breathe!" she said with a forced whisper.

On the floor behind her, Blanchard lay knocked out cold from octopus ink.

"What did you do?" I asked silently as she rushed to the cage.

"I have to get you out of here before you pass out." Her hands shook as she flipped through the ring of keys, inserting one in after the other. Finally she found the right one and popped the lock open.

"Come on!" She grabbed my hand and pulled me down the hall to the interior of Azor's house. Through the thick clouds, I could make out a few other mermen laying in the same sprawled-out way as blackness tainted the water above their heads. I couldn't see Azor anywhere, though.

I knew Tatchi was smart, but to use octopus ink to incapacitate all the mermen so she could help me escape was brilliant. Mermaids for some reason were immune to its effects. Unable to hold my breath any longer, I let a small sip of water through my gills and felt my thoughts grow fuzzy. Tatch responded with a gasp and pulled me harder.

Once we exited out the front doors, I sucked in a huge breath to clear my head. "What did you do?"

Tatiana exhaled, but continued to pull my arm so we moved farther away from Azor's compound. "I'll explain everything after we get out of here."

I allowed her to drag me along since the tiny bit of ink I did inhale affected my ability to reason and swim. But once we turned away from the direction of our house and towards the far rock wall where the Tahoe gate loomed, I flared out my fins to stop.

"No!" she screamed, continuing to pull. "We have to leave! Now!"

I yanked my hand back. "I just got in royal trouble for leaving unchaperoned and I'm not about to drag you into this with me. If we escape to Tahoe, we aren't ever coming back."

"I know that. And if we don't leave now, we may never get another chance."

I pushed my hands into my temples to force away the headache from the ink. "But what about Mom?"

Tatch fidgeted and avoided eye contact. "She wants to stay and wait for Dad."

I clenched my jaw. "We can't just leave her. We promised Dad we'd watch out for her."

Tatch's face pressed into a scowl as she pointed her finger in my face. "Look. You know as well as I do they aren't going to give you a slap on the wrist and say 'never do it again.' You'll be forced to stay here. Forced to serve the elder mers for who knows how long. Forced to choose someone here to promise. Do you want that?"

Ashlyn's sweet water-drenched face shimmered in my mind. My soul was trying to claw its way out of my chest to take ahold of my fin and make me leave Natatoria now. But without Mom coming with us, it didn't feel right.

"Fine," Tatiana said after I didn't respond and my eyes met hers. "You can go back and lock yourself up if you want. I'll just leave without you."

"Wait." I grabbed her wrist.

"I'm done with this place, Fin. Don't you see I can't stay? First with all the crap at the palace and then with you getting locked up. Now Uncle Alaster is saying he had to mind-wipe a whole bunch of people, stop divers who were getting too close to the gate, and deal with the press. I guess there was a news story about the waves you caused and people are frantic for answers. It's very serious. The King may just banish you and take your fins for all the trouble you've caused. Then where will you be?"

I scrubbed my hand over my head and wished for a crystal ball to see the future. Was this the way to bolt? The ink would be evaporating soon and the guards would wake up. I needed to make a decision

"Where will you go?" I finally asked.

"To Fannette Island tonight. Then tomorrow, I'll take the Jeep and head towards the Pacific. There I can start searching for Dad. Something's wrong. I can sense it."

I should have been livid she was thinking of taking my Jeep but the thought of her trying to find Dad alone didn't sit right. Helping her sounded better than going back to my cell. Plus Dad would fight for us and stand up against our injustices. Besides, I needed to see Ash.

"Do you have the spare key?"

Tatch's lips widened into a huge grin as she nodded her head.

"I know I'm going to regret this, but let's go."

"Yes!" Tatiana swam ahead of me.

Inside the meeting room between Natatoria and Lake Tahoe, we pressed the button and waited for Uncle Alaster or Colin to bust us. Tatch held a small vial of octopus ink ready to throw if they happened to come through the mouth of the cave—but no one came.

We looked at one another with growing grins and swam through the gate to the other side. Once we figured the waters were safe, we hightailed it for Fannette Island.

"Yes!" Tatch squealed as she swam in circles and blew bubbles with her arms spread wide.

"Careful," I said playfully. "You might create waves."

"Ha-ha. Very funny big brother. And anyway, why did you have to swim so fast you absently made waves on your rock collecting trip?"

Too mentally exhausted to share and afraid of her reaction, I stayed tight-lipped. She'd flip once she knew her friendship with Ash was forever changed. Telling the full story after we'd both had a decent night's sleep, far away from things she could throw at me, would be better.

"That good?" she asked after I didn't answer.

"I'll tell you everything tomorrow. I just want to get to the island before we get caught."

She giggled. "Sure thing."

We surfaced the water together, but Tatch flipped her head back, making a huge arch of water with her hair. She laughed as the droplets rained down on her face.

"I'm finally home," she squealed and I couldn't agree with her more.

Brenda Pandos

34

ASH

I felt absolutely horrible in the morning. Whatever drugs they'd put in my IV were far better than the stuff I took every four hours during the night. After a fitful night of sleep, I finally stumbled to the kitchen to eat breakfast.

My parents bustled around, competing for counter space as they made lunches to take to work. I ate my Mini Wheats in silence only to catch Mom's fretful glance every once in a while—silent questioning of my stability, I assumed.

"You know, Ashlyn. We eventually need to talk about what happened," she said abruptly.

Dad stopped and shot her a puzzled look. "Karen. It was an accident. If Ashlyn doesn't remember what happened, the doctor said there's nothing we can do to force her."

"Yes. I understand that, but the fact that she lied to stay home from church and then left the house without leaving a note bothers me."

I stopped eating and stared at the last few unappetizing Wheats floating in the milk. The silence weighted heavily on my guilt-torn chest. I hated living this lie. "I'm sorry. It won't ever happen again."

Mom moved a little closer. "Did something happen at the dance?"

"No." I forced a Wheat under the milk with my spoon. "I didn't get picked for Queen, so I wasn't ready to see anyone yet."

"Oh." Her eyes softened. She cast an anxious glimpse at Dad, who took pity as well.

"I wanted to go for a walk to clear my head. That's all."

"There's no need to apologize again," Dad calmly interrupted. "It all worked out and could have been much worse. Luckily, the Fire Chief recognized you when they arrived at the scene. We're not mad at you, Ash."

I swallowed back my tears. "I know. But I really *am* sorry."

They watched me with compassion in their eyes and I wanted to crawl into a hole. Here was my opportunity to come clean and I wasn't doing it. My heart started to pound as I finally opened my mouth to confess.

With a cheery smile, Gran came bustling into the kitchen. "And she's obviously got a guardian angel. God's not finished with her yet, is He?" She rubbed her hand over my shoulders and squeezed. "Oh, and Jack, you forgot to put the boat back in the shed."

The spoon fell out of my hand and hit the milk with a clattering splash.

"I didn't take out a boat," Dad said.

"What?" Mom darted to the sliding glass door. "Where?"

"I think it's *The Sea Star*." Gran pointed towards the dock. "Right there. Shouldn't it be locked up in the shed 'til summer?"

Dad looked out the kitchen window too. "Yes, it should. I wonder how it got out there." He turned toward me, the empathy replaced by a straight face.

"I'm not feeling so well," I said, shooting a guilty smile.

He watched as I made my escape.

They continued to talk about who might have borrowed the boat as I hobbled back to Gran's room, heart pounding. I turned on *The Price is Right* and hid under the covers, dreading the conversation I knew would be coming, hoping everyone would just leave. Would he confront me before he left for work or later tonight?

I pinched my eyes shut and listened, waiting. After what seemed like forever, the house finally quieted down. My mind whirred with a million questions as I limped outside on crutches to the dock. Who found the boat and returned it? Did they see me? Did they know what happened? Where was it? Would they tell my parents?

And there *The Sea Star* floated, pristine and tethered to the dock as if nothing ever happened. I touched the jagged piece of metal and shivered. Could the angel have possibly brought the boat back as well?

Growing excitement tickled my belly as I scanned the tree line, thinking he could actually be here—watching me. Ever since the accident, my dreams were filled with nothing but him. All I wanted was to talk to him, ask him what happened.

"Thank you," I whispered, holding my hand out towards the horizon, "wherever you are."

My body fluttered with warmth until I remembered the biting frigid water and the fear in my parents' eyes. I shook my head, unable to wrap my mind around what was real and what wasn't.

Just beyond the beach, a group of men walked to the back door of Tatchi and Fin's house. The stiff way they moved reminded me of Secret Service Agents except they were all wearing skirts. Who were they? And what were they doing? I took a seat on the bench and tried to melt into the surroundings so they wouldn't notice me staring.

"Ashlyn?"

I jumped at my father's voice. "Dad?" With wide eyes, I watched him walk down towards me on the dock.

"Should you be out here?"

The tears came from nowhere. "I can't take it anymore with the boat, and the guilt. I have to tell you the truth about what happened."

A pensive look crossed his face as he joined me on the bench. "Okay."

I discretely wiped my nose on my sleeve. "I didn't get swept out by a wave like everyone thinks. It's all my fault what happened. I took the boat to Fannette Island because I thought it would somehow bring Tatchi back. We have a treasure box buried there from when we were kids but when I was paddling home, I accidentally tipped the boat and fell in. Someone saved me and I honestly don't know who. But now the boat is back. And I've been trying to figure out what this all means."

Dad took a deep breath and put his hand on my knee. "Well, that explains where the boat went."

I gasped. "You already knew?"

"About the boat missing? Yes. But not that you'd taken it to Fannette Island and fell out. It makes sense being the Fannette Island Ranger Station is miles from our house. The reaction you had to the boat reappearing did seem suspicious this morning."

I blinked back in astonishment. "Does Mom know?"

"It would probably be best if you told her."

"Me?"

He pursed his lips together and nodded.

I wanted to die. Telling Mom was the last thing I wanted to do.

"I know you'll make this right, Ashlyn."

His words came crushing down on me and the last thing I wanted was to disappoint him. "Oh, Dad," I wailed and threw my arms around his neck, "I'm so sorry, you don't even know."

He patted my back. "Mom will be mad, but it's better to tell her the truth than have her find out otherwise."

"I didn't mean to lie. Everything was so fuzzy at first and then when I remembered—" I pulled away and looked at him with my tear streaked face. "Wait. Why are you still home? Aren't you supposed to be at work?"

"I don't need to be in until nine."

"Oh."

"Feel better?" He smiled warmly with knowing eyes.

I shook my head.

"Good. This was a hard lesson to learn, but always remember; the truth will set you free."

"Thank you, Dad." I hugged him again. *And does it ever.*

35

FIN

"Crap," Tatiana said as we crouched in the bushes next to our former house. "What are we going to do now?"

I rubbed my hand across my forehead as the early morning sun sparkled against the snow patches scattered across the ground. The Jeep wasn't in the driveway where I'd parked it. But that was the least of my worries. Azor and a few of his men just walked inside, obviously looking for me and quite possibly my sister as well. Without the Jeep, we were stuck.

"The first thing we need to do is get some clothes. Right now we look like we should be in Hawaii, not in the middle of an extraordinarily cold spring in Tahoe."

"Oh, good idea," Tatch said as she wriggled her bare toes in the snow. "I do have Mom's credit card."

"You what? Never mind." I creased my brow. "I was thinking more along the lines of borrowing instead of buying. We can't go walking into American Eagle Outfitters looking like this anyway."

Tatch bit her lip. "I wonder if anyone is home at Ash's. I could borrow something of hers and get you an outfit from her dad's closet."

Ashlyn's name sent an anxious tingle up my spine. If only she was home. What I wouldn't give to accidentally run into her. But I didn't trust myself from grabbing her and kissing her madly if I did. More than likely, she would still be at the hospital, giving us an opportune time to break in.

"Earth to Fin." Tatch snapped in front of my eyes. "What is it with you when I mention her name anyway?"

"Nothing. Yeah, that's actually a good idea."

I glanced over at the house and stopped breathing. Ash was limping on crutches up the path from the dock, her father by her side. The world stood still for a moment as the sun filtered through her curly red hair. She was better than I thought and already at home.

Tatch's gasp broke the spell. "Oh my starfish! What happened?"

I grabbed her arm as she lurched forward. "No! You can't go!"

"But don't you see her?" Tatch flailed under my grasp. "She's injured or something."

Everything inside me wanted to run to the dock, scoop Ash up off her feet, and carry her the rest of the way. "We can't reveal ourselves to her. She'll have too many questions."

"Fish sticks! That's ridiculous," she said in admonishment and yanked her arm back. "You can just wipe her mind afterward. I have to know."

She looked up at me with such earnest concern that I nearly caved, but now that Ash was promised to me, the incantation wouldn't work. "I can't—don't want to do that to her anymore. It's not right."

"Oh, geez, Fin. That's never stopped you in the past," Tatiana whimpered, watching the two of them disappear inside. I felt her pain and tried not to show it. "Why not?"

I sighed, wondering if now would be a good time to tell Tatch the truth. "I just don't think it's right to do that anymore."

The night before, on the way to Fannette Island, we happened upon *The Sea Star*, floating abandoned right off shore. I tried not to make a big deal about it, but Tatch insisted we return it to Ash's family dock at least. Seeing her now flooded me with relief, but the brevity sliced right through my soul, leaving a longing to hold her I couldn't quench yet. Staying hidden and convincing Tatiana to do the same took all my strength.

At the same time, Colin pulled up to the house in the Jeep. We ducked down behind a bush just in time. Tatch elbowed me as I mumbled a few curt words. But when Colin stepped out wearing my "silence is golden but duct tape is silver" T-shirt, she was the one holding me back.

"I could kick his ass," I growled.

"Shhh! If they hear us, it'll be all over."

Another man exited on the passenger side and turned around—Chauncey, Azor's right-hand man. "Colin, pull the car into the garage. If Fin is around, I'm sure he's got his own set of keys."

"Oh, right," Colin said and got back into the Jeep. I cringed when he ground the gears.

Within minutes, our get-away vehicle was locked up tight in the fortress guarded by bored mermen anxious to drag me back to my tomb.

"Now what?" Tatch whispered.

I looked over at Ash's house and spotted her dad's truck driving away. He was the last to leave the house this morning. Ash was home alone.

::::

Against my better judgment I stood on Ash's front porch, my pulse pounding in my veins. I tried to remain somewhat hidden by the trellis so none of Azor's goons would see me as I prayed everything would go over smoothly with her. If she didn't respond right, Tatch and I would have a whole bunch of explaining to do.

The door slowly opened and her honeysuckle scent hit me like a wrecking ball. At the sight of her, my mouth went dry. All I wanted to do was kiss her right then and there.

"Fin?" Ashlyn gasped as she blinked back at me in disbelief.

"Hi." I tried to sway her with a charming smile. "This is really embarrassing, but I need a little help."

At first she didn't respond. Then her gaze slowly panned down my torso towards my feet and back up again. "You're—why don't you have shoes on? Or clothes for that matter?"

"It's a long story. Can I come in?" I pretended I was cold and faked a shiver.

She motioned for me to come inside, shuddering from the gust of chilly air herself. I graciously stepped around her and walked over to the couch as she stood at the doorway. When she didn't move, I patted the couch cushion next to me. Robotically, she closed the door and limped over to the couch to sit down. Her location put her back conveniently towards the stairs.

"What happened to your leg?" I asked to fill the stony silence.

"Oh," she said and stopped. Her eyes darted to her leg, then back to my naked knees and bare chest. "I had an accident."

"Are you all right?"

"Yeah, I'm—" She swallowed as the confusion visibly flashed across her face. "Are you in trouble or something?"

"Oh, of course not," I said with a laugh. "My good for nothing cousin is pulling a joke on me. I was in the hot tub and he locked me out of the house to be funny. I thought I saw you earlier, so I came over here instead. Could I possibly borrow a shirt? I have a feeling he's not going to let me in anytime soon."

"Oh."

Ashlyn furrowed her brow and shimmied forward to stand up when I spotted Tatch darting up the stairs.

"That looks really painful. Are you sure you're okay?" I quickly asked, getting to my feet to help her.

Our hands touched as I cradled her elbow, pulling her up and close to my side—away from the direct view of the stairs. Her breath trembled as we stood by one another.

"Yeah, I'm fine," she said softly. Her eyelashes obscured the deep green eyes peering down at the floor.

Our faces were inches apart and everything in me wanted to press my mouth to hers. She stood there, her lips terribly inviting. I had to do something before my body took over and our entire plan unraveled.

"Was it a car accident?"

"Oh . . . no." She swallowed, her cheeks flushing an adorable shade of pink. "I fell out of the boat into the water."

"What were you doing on the lake in this weather?" I asked and then wanted to take it back, sounding more like a parent than a concerned friend.

She crinkled her nose. "Worried about Tatchi actually." Then, like a spark hitting a dry patch of brush, anger ignited in her eyes and she pushed me away. "Where is she anyway?"

I tried to bring her closer to me again, but she stepped backwards.

"Doesn't she have access to a phone or even a postage stamp to let me know what happened to her?"

"I—" My brain went blank, leaving me mute. There wasn't an excuse good enough to assure her we didn't purposefully abandon her.

She laughed callously. "You two just disappear over night without a word and have no concern that I might be worried sick about you? Is she at the house right now?"

Instead of heading towards the stairs to get me clothes, she began to hop towards the door on one foot. "She's going to get a piece of my mind when I see her. No word this entire time! And then you have the audacity to show up here, unannounced, because you need clothes? Seriously? You have some nerve. Funny you'd have time to come home, joke around with your family when I almost got myself killed because of you two!" She waved her hands frantically. "But oh no. You two are living it up with your relatives like nothing ever happened."

She fumbled to open the door but her hands shook too violently to get the lock open.

"Whoa," I said, holding my hands up in surrender. I should have known that after the initial surprise of seeing me again wore off, she'd lash out. "We've had a death in the family and had to leave abruptly. And Tatiana isn't even here. She's still back . . . East."

"Pschtt," she said venomously. "I'd contact my best friend before I did anything else. I find this whole story a little fishy."

"They're Amish. It's complicated."

She let out a forced laugh and opened the door. "Get out, Fin. Go back to your weird Amish cousin and beg for him to let you inside. You can freeze for all I care."

When I didn't move she yelled, "GET OUT!"

"Okay."

I walked past her and turned once I got outside. She slammed the door in my face. Not only was my heart breaking that I'd hurt her so deeply, I didn't think Tatch made it out in time.

I stood on the porch calling Ash's name for several minutes and then finally left to hide in the bushes again.

36

ASH

I leaned against the door as tears poured down my cheeks. I could hear Fin calling my name, but I didn't care. I wasn't ever going to speak to him or Tatchi again. Part of me wanted to crumble to the floor and cry my eyes out, but I knew I'd never be able to get up without help.

Instead, I limped to Gran's room and curled into the fetal position. Hopefully, the two pills I took would numb the emotional pain whirling in my heart. My best friend never had any intention of going away to college with me. How could I not see she was never going to break free from her family? I rubbed my chest. It felt like they'd stabbed me with two knives and twisted in opposite directions.

I closed my eyes and drifted off to the sound of squirrels running across the roof. Minutes later, a rustle in my room woke me up. I rolled over and groaned, twisting myself in the sheets again.

"Sorry, dear," Gran said softly, "I didn't mean to wake you."

"No," I said, shifting to a sitting position. I glanced over at the clock, amazed to find I'd slept three hours. "I should probably get up."

She walked toward me with a grimace and pushed my hair from my puffy eyes. "How are you feeling?"

I exhaled as the fog cleared and my sweet dreams dissipated. Remembering Fin's visit reopened the wound in my chest. I needed to talk about something good, or I'd start crying again. "Gran, do you believe in angels?"

She smiled. Her entire face lit up. "Why of course I do. Who else is going to help God perform all those miracles?"

I felt the corners of my lips lift. "Do you think we can see them sometimes?"

"I do. The Bible does say to be hospitable to strangers because you might be entertaining an angel instead."

A small memory about that verse tickled my mind. Sometimes, when we drove as a family, Dad would give a bum all the change from the car ashtray. Mom worried Dad was encouraging their behavior, giving them money to buy booze or drugs. He'd look back at her and remind her about this verse.

I looked away and bit the side of my cheek. "It's not a coincidence the boat magically showed up."

Gran sat down next to me on the bed and watched me with gentle eyes. I took a deep breath and confessed what happened.

"I see," she said after I finished, no judgment in her tone.

"But what I do remember about the person who saved me, in a dreamy sort of way, they might not have been entirely human. Even in the freezing water, he was very warm and glowed a little. I'm pretty sure he flew me out of the water into the air."

Gran studied me for a moment with pensive eyes. "Have I ever told you my angel experience?"

I shook my head.

"Well, when I was newly married to your grandpa, I got very sick. My heart would start beating fast for no reason and the doctors didn't know what was wrong with me. It got to the point where it happened all the time. In fact, one time it raced so hard and wouldn't stop, they had to hospitalize me. I remember shivering uncontrollably because the blood wasn't circulating through my body like it should. But there was this one mysterious warm spot right on my arm"—she touched me in the crook of my elbow—"as if something unseen was holding me.

"You see, one of my biggest fears was I'd die and Grandpa Frank would remarry. I couldn't bear it." Gran's eyes glistened as she swallowed hard. "But I finally got to a place where I thought death was near, so I gave his life to God to worry about because if I were gone, he'd need someone to take care of him. Instantly, my heart slowed and it's never raced since. And in the end, I was the one who outlived him, the lucky devil.

"So, yes. I do believe in angels, because mine was there, touching my arm during the worst episode."

I looked down at the bed sheet folded over my lap. "Did your angel ever come back?"

"He's around, somewhere. But more importantly, I feel the presence of God and there are no accidents, sweetie. You have a very special purpose in life and I'm glad your angel, or whoever, was there to save you. I don't know what we'd do without you." Another tear trailed down her cheek.

Dread slugged around in my throat, stopping my words. "I'll never do anything so stupid again," I finally choked out.

"That's a good thing, but you should tell your folks and ask for forgiveness. They love you, Ashlyn, more than you realize." She gave me a reassuring smile.

I took a deep breath and nodded. "I know, Gran. I will."

She reached over and hugged me tightly. When she let go, it was as if all was forgiven and forgotten. "Can I get you anything? Lunch? I made some of that tortilla soup you like."

My tummy rumbled at the thought of food. "Yeah, that sounds good."

She looked at me one more time with forgiving eyes before leaving the room. Once she closed the door, my gaze drifted to the window, to the sunlight dancing on the lake.

37

FIN

"What was that all about?" Tatiana demanded, out of breath while throwing a pile of clothes towards me.

I caught them before they hit the wet ground, but not before Ash's lingering scent on Tatch's borrowed clothing seized my chest with longing and guilt. "Nothing. It's okay."

"Okay? I heard her yelling for you to 'get out'. Did you mind-wipe her afterward?"

"Not exactly." I tried to remain nonchalant as I inspected the outfit Tatch got for me. The navy blue Tahoe Fire T-shirt would be fine, but the jeans were definitely too big.

"What do you mean not exactly?"

I took a deep breath and pulled on the jeans. Telling the truth was easier than hiding what happened. Problem was she'd be just as mad as Ash, if not worse. "I can't."

She blinked back at me with confusion, and then her face fell with shock. "NO! You didn't!"

I swallowed hard. "It's not what you think."

Tatch's legs began to wobble. I grabbed her before she fell on the ground and pulled her toward me so our eyes were level with one another. "We have other things to worry about. You need to buy me some shoes."

She blinked back wide-eyed, her hands covering her mouth. "You kissed her? You've promised yourself to her? 'Cause that can be the only reason why your powers wouldn't work on her. Tell me!"

She pounded her free fist into my chest. The confession that I'd kissed Ash wouldn't come out of my mouth. I looked blankly back. She finally stopped protesting and her eyes glazed over.

"For the love of the kraken! This is huge, Fin." She pulled her arms free and folded them over her chest. Then another wave of anger flashed in her eyes. "Why? WHY? We were going to go away to college. Now she's doomed to join the mermaid world I'm trying to escape. I can't believe you did this to me. YOU! My own brother!"

She let out an animalistic groan, threw her hands up, and stormed away from me.

"Wait, Tatch! It wasn't like that. I had no intention of promising myself to her. She was drowning. Look at her leg. That happened right before—why she couldn't swim. I had to give her mouth to mouth or she would have died. That's why I made the waves. To get to her in time. That's why I can't tell anyone what happened. Why the boat was floating free in the bay."

She turned around, tears streaming down her cheeks. "You what?"

"I came to Tahoe to collect rocks for Mr. Gumboot, then I heard her scream. She fell from the boat and sliced open her leg. By the time I got to her, she was already underwater, bleeding to death. I couldn't let her die."

Tatch listened with a frown. The severity of what happened seemed to soften her, but the disappointment still remained visible on her face and rubbed acid into my conflicted soul. "So now what? Are you going to change her too?"

"She doesn't remember what happened."

"What do you mean?"

"She was unconscious. I'm hoping there's something we can do to reverse it," I lied, desperate to earn back her trust, knowing my promise to Ash, something I would fight with everything I had to keep, was irreversible until death.

Tatiana exploded into cutting laughter. "Really? That's funny.

There's no cure and you know it. Poseidon!"

I looked down at the ground, terribly conflicted. Dad would know the best thing to do. But for now, I needed shoes.

"Can't we discuss this later?" I asked, pointing to my feet.

She looked down and grimaced. "Yeah, I guess so," she said as she sniffled, heading down the lakeside trail towards the strip mall on the pier.

Since she took the news so hard, I followed in silence, letting her mull things over. I had my own demons to tame. Ashlyn's angry words wouldn't stop echoing through my head as I walked, holding my pants with my hand. Going to her house was a bad move; I regretted ever trying to smooth things over. But more importantly, I wanted to tell her the truth.

"I need a belt," I finally said.

"You should have told me before you volunteered to go to her house. That might have been smarter," she said over her shoulder. "So what did she say when she saw you?"

I sighed, still noting the hurt in her voice. "I made up a story that Colin had locked me out of the house while I was in the hot tub to explain why I was wearing board shorts. But after a few minutes, she flipped out because she's been worried about us this entire time. Then she thought we just didn't care about her anymore and we were ignoring her."

Tatch moaned. "We have to fix this. You have to fix this. I can't just leave her there, upset without knowing what's really going on."

"Even if she was talking to me, what would I say?"

Tatch massaged her temples. "I don't know. This sucks."

"Tell me about it."

As we came closer to town, I wondered how far I should walk with her. Shoeless and coatless, I stood out like the stripe on the back of a skunk. "I think I should wait here."

Tatch turned around. "Really?"

"Well—" I pointed at my feet again.

She shrugged. "Right. Shoes and a belt?"

"And socks too. Oh, and a sweatshirt."

I watched her disappear around the corner of the local strip mall and hoped she wouldn't be long.

I sat on a nearby granite boulder and turned towards the lake. The sun lit up the water like diamonds as the waves lapped the beach. The air blew across my skin and made me feel alive. The difference between Natatoria and Tahoe showed how unbearable underwater living had been on my psyche. No matter what happened, living there permanently could never be an option for me, or Ash—once she, or rather if she, accepted me and we were finally able to be together.

At the pier parking, I spotted my Jeep again, parked next to Captain Jack's. The *Empress* was about to leave the pier. I could only assume they were collecting or dropping off more mermen for the search. If so, this entire lake would be crawling with mer life soon.

If only the lake fed into a river that led to the ocean that wasn't knee deep in places or intersected with dams. We'd have to figure another way to get across the state.

I waited as the Jeep sat unattended—top down—begging for me to take it away from Colin's grimy hands. *If only I had the key. What's taking Tatch so long?*

I snuck over for a closer look when Colin came out of the store and got into the driver's side. I ducked as he pulled the Jeep out and drove past.

What an idiot! Driving in this weather with the top down?

My fists curled into a ball, I wanted to punch him in the face for everything. I returned to wait for Tatch and paced to keep my nerves calm.

"Here ya go!" Tatch threw a bag my way.

"Dang, what took you so long? I could have stolen the Jeep back."

I pawed through the items inside. She'd gone a little overboard: shoes, socks, a belt, pants and a jacket.

"The Jeep was here?" She looked over towards Captain Jack's. "Well, no worries. I figured out another plan." She fanned out a set of tickets in her hand.

I looked closer and let out a groan. "The bus?"

"Yup. We'll leave tomorrow at seven and get to San Francisco by five. It's perfect."

"Perfect?" I ripped the tags off my new clothes. "If you say so."

She smiled. "Once we find Dad, we'll be able to come back to Tahoe and I'll smooth everything over with Ash. Then we'll all go to college and no one will need to turn anyone into a mermaid."

"And you'll stay a mermaid?"

"Mom said I could go to college."

"In Tahoe."

"She'll change her mind once I tell her about the scholarship."

I laughed under my breath at her "happily ever after story," unwilling to argue. "If you say so."

"I know so. This is going to work!"

38

ASH

A large pile of school books, notes from each teacher, and a card signed by the entire swim team lay in front of me on the bed, courtesy of Georgia. Mom had suggested I start on my homework but I could barely concentrate to read the mystery novel she'd picked up from the library yesterday. How could I fathom school work?

"Everyone is asking how you're doing," Georgia said while sitting on the nearby chair. Her leg was propped over her knee and bounced to some unheard beat.

"I'm healing." *Sort of.*

The bitter ache of Fin's visit and realization I'd lost my best friend kept me on the rocky precipice of tears. All I needed was one good reason and they'd fall from behind the paper thin dam.

"Well, good because we really need you to come back and swim in the finals."

I gulped. Finals. I hadn't told her I wouldn't be able to swim at all and even if a miracle happened, I wouldn't be as fast. Once Florida Atlantic University found out about my injury, I was sure they'd pull my swim scholarship.

"Where are you going to college?" I asked abruptly, my conversation filter a little off its axis.

"UCLA. Where else?" She laughed. "How about you?"

"I don't know for sure anymore. This accident has changed everything."

My somber mood made Georgia unusually antsy. Normally, her upbeat spirit and spunk would lighten any room, but my crappy attitude smothered everything. All I wanted was for her to leave so I could curl up in bed and watch soaps.

"Did Callahan visit?"

My stomach clenched. We'd talked a few times on the phone and he asked to come by but I kept making excuses why he couldn't. I didn't need anyone else feeling sorry for me, nor did I have the energy to entertain.

"No. My mom wants me to rest. I think you're allowed 'cause you were bringing me my homework."

"Oh," she said and chewed on her fingernail. "Did you hear Brooke and Kylie were suspended?"

"No. Why?"

"No one knows. Something happened at the dance apparently."

"*Senior Ball Queen gets suspended.* That would make for good school PR." I faked a smile.

The dance seemed like ages ago, back when my problems were laughable.

"It reeks of conspiracy, don't you think? Remember how everyone reacted when the vote was announced? And the mix up with the tables? Well, maybe they'll crown someone new."

"Better not be me," I laughed caustically. "I think I've had enough attention for the time being. It's all a huge joke anyway."

"Aw," she said in disappointment, pouting her lip, "it's not."

I swallowed down two more pain pills with some water and pulled the covers up to my chin. "Life is a big pu pu platter for me right now and the last thing I'm worried about is some stupid popularity contest. I'll be lucky if I can keep up my grades at this rate. My mom thinks I can take pain pills and do homework when I can barely concentrate on a TV show."

"I think someone needs a sash and a crown right about now."

"Have you been listening to me? I'm going to lose my scholarship. I don't know when I can go back to school. I'm going to be so far behind, I might not even graduate!"

Georgia clammed up and pressed her lips together.

I took a deep breath and closed my eyes. "Sorry. I'm just super frustrated."

"I was just trying to cheer you up."

"I know. So what else is going on at school?"

At the invitation, Georgia shrugged off what I'd just said and prattled on. I lay back into the pillows and listened with half-lidded eyes. The distraction was appreciated, though Fin kept barging into my thoughts. Luckily, the pills started to buffer my physical pain and my emotional ones as well.

After about a half-hour Mom came into my room and ushered Georgia out. She continued to talk as they walked down the hall, adapting to a new audience. Exhausted, I pushed everything off the bed, closed my eyes, and drifted easily off to sleep.

:::

When I opened my eyes again, the house was quiet. The red numbers on the clock flashed 12:03AM. I turned on the light and lay back, wide awake. A little index card that had been folded in half stood precariously on my nightstand. The words "Dinner is in the fridge. Love, Mom" were scrawled across the front. I warmed at her thoughtfulness, wondering if Dad or Gran had told her the truth yet. An opportunity to mention anything about the boat had eluded me since I'd slept most of the time when she was home. Once someone did, I knew she'd make me fend for my own food and ground me for life.

Gingerly, I hobbled to the kitchen as my stomach growled. They'd had their regular pasta night and my mouth watered at the garlicky smell still lingering in the kitchen. I found the plate in the fridge and popped it into the microwave. Within seconds, the steaming hot goodness was ready for devouring.

The pills were definitely working to my disadvantage as the

creepy trees beyond the lit porch played tricks with my mind. My imagination flipped through a sundry of bad guys, like a vampire or a zombie, who could appear and scare the heck out of me.

I tried to hurry and eat, when I heard a noise. At first it sounded like people talking but quickly escalated into an argument. I stood up and turned off the porch light to get a better look. Even under the full moon, I couldn't see anyone.

My adrenaline pulsed as my clammy hand fogged up the glass. Then a girl's angry voice registered over the other male voices. Could no one hear this? Was this girl in danger on the beach?

I opened the door and slipped outside to listen better.

"Get your hands off her!" Fin yelled. His voice temporarily stopped my heart.

Without a thought, I limped down the path and headed towards the beach.

"Finley, it's time to head back. You're in enough trouble as it is," a guy said, his voice slightly deeper and huskier.

"I don't have to go anywhere with you. We chose to leave Natatoria of our own free will and I have that right," Fin barked back.

Natatoria?

"You're still underage for a few more months," another masculine voice said.

"Get your hands off of me," Tatiana said plain as day. The smack following made the others laugh.

I pushed through the pain to walk faster.

"I like a spunky girl," the husky voice said. "Take her down."

"No!" I yelled as soon as I approached the edge of the shoreline. But I wasn't prepared for what I'd see.

Several feet off shore, a group of shirtless men with hulking muscles waded waist deep in at least six-foot deep water. Colin, the car-thieving cousin held Tatchi, and another held Fin against their wills.

"Ashlyn, no!" Fin yelled and struggled to free himself from the gnarly bearded guy who had him restrained by his arms. Fin flailed and something like a large fish tail flipped out of the water.

I gasped.

"Great. See what you've done? Brought the attention of your neighbor," the husky voiced guy said, apparently the leader, wading empty handed off to the side. His jet black hair glistened in the moonlight as he turned toward me. He reminded me of a slimy snake. "Blanchard, take care of her."

I scrambled backwards and fell flat on my butt into a pile of melting snow. Pain flared up the side of my leg and I pressed my hand on my thigh, worried I tore out some stitches.

Like an oversized seal, he came out of the water and dragged a giant fin where his legs should have been. Frozen in shock, I watched the fish-man raise the palm of his hand towards me. I pinched my eyes shut and flinched. Instead of some act of violence, a melodic sound flowed from his mouth, making my insides feel warm and tingly, taking away the alarm. I opened my eyes and stared back blankly as the weird language mesmerized me.

Blanchard stopped after a minute and studied me. Still stunned, I didn't move. Then he smiled and swiveled around on his belly, and plunged himself headfirst into the water.

The guy with dark hair nodded appreciatively. "Okay, now that that's handled, let's go home," he said. "Do not let either of them get away this time."

Fin shot me a agonizing look before his handler pulled him unwillingly underwater.

"No!" Tatiana screamed as she disappeared, too, the liquid silencing her cry.

I waited for a moment to hear "You're on candid camera," but the water became eerily silent.

Wake up, Ashlyn. You're just having a bad dream.

When I didn't wake up, the reality hit me that Fin and Tatchi were pulled underwater and never came back up, I screamed out their names into the night.

"Ashlyn!" Dad called from the house. "Ashlyn!"

I looked up through watery eyes at my father's distorted image, running down the path towards me. I couldn't stop sobbing.

"Fin . . . Tatchi . . . They were here . . . They're in trouble!" I yelled out between broken gasps.

"Ashlyn, honey," Dad said, fear in his voice as he glanced at my bloodied pajama's. "It's okay. You're going to be just fine." He lifted me off the ground and cradled me in his arms. I rested my head against his chest and closed my eyes, wanting the insanity to stop.

"Ashlyn?" my mother called from the doorway. "Oh, no! What happened?"

"She was outside on the beach," Dad said softly as he carried me past her into the house. "I think it's PTS. Karen, get me a blanket."

Dad laid me on the couch and covered me up before he redressed my wound. I tried to make sense of what happened but nothing coherent formed in my brain, let alone would come out of my mouth. I just felt dread washing over me like I should have done more—dove in after them to stop the abduction at least. Where did they all go? Were the bad fish-men taking them away to that place? To Natatoria? But the biggest shock, the thing that kept echoing over and over in my mind was: forget Tessie, mermaids were real and lived in our lake.

I was surely going crazy.

39

FIN

Tatch's scream both in my head and in the water shot adrenaline straight into my muscles. I wasn't about to be taken home like a captured fugitive. This is the moment Badger had groomed me for—the moment to prove who I was and what I could do.

I popped my shoulder back into Chauncey's arm and felt him momentarily loosen his grip. With a quick flip of my tail, I slid out of his grasp and circled around, piercing a barb filled with poison into his chest. He groaned and tried to hit me with his spear, but the direct shot took affect quickly and pumped into his body. I snagged his spear as he slipped into a daze and floated in the current.

Tatch took advantage of the attack and bit Colin in the arm. He yelled and released her. "You filthy little—"

I smacked Colin across the face with my tail before he could finish. "Don't you dare insult my sister." Before he could recover, I spun around and hit him again. "And that's for taking my Jeep without permission."

Colin shook his head and held his bleeding nose. I prepared to whack him again for wearing my clothes when Blanchard got between us with a spear, pointed directly at my chest.

"Enough," Azor yelled.

Tatch floated behind me, nails bared. "Stay back," she said, followed with a hiss.

I held my spear and pointed it towards anyone who moved.

"Don't do anything stupid," Azor replied, keeping his distance and his cool.

"Where are we going to go?" Tatch asked.

"I don't know yet. Just watch my back."

We mad-dogged Azor and his goons, and waited for someone to make a move. I had no idea how long this stand-off would last or how we'd escape and hide without being seen, but we had to try. We weren't letting them take us back to Natatoria without a fight.

"Like I said earlier, we don't mean anyone any harm," I said and slowly swam away from the group. "All we want is to leave peaceably and I suggest you don't follow us."

"Or you'll what?" Azor asked mockingly. "You can't possibly think you'll be able to hide in the lake tonight. You can run, but we'll find you. You'll be returning to Natatoria—both of you. It's your choice whether or not it's *peaceable*."

"I'll never go anywhere with you!" Tatch growled at Azor.

The group let out a collective "oooh." He turned and silenced them with a glare.

For the most part, Azor was right. But there was one place we could hide that no one would consider looking—the upstairs bathtub of our house. We could escape through the hatch and crawl upstairs while everyone combed the lake. We'd avoid the game of cat-and-mouse and in the early morning we could take the Jeep right from under their noses. With the contrived plan I smiled, until I realized Uncle Alaster wasn't part of the apprehending party.

"Fin, watch out!"

I swirled around just in time to see my Uncle's tail barbs headed straight for my face. Then the world suddenly went black.

∷

"Just like his father," I heard a deep male voice say.

I slowly pried open my eyes and winced at the pain radiating from my cheek. King Phaleon stood just beyond the bars, staring at me coolly. Though I'd never seen him up close in person, he bore a striking resemblance to the large statue outside of the palace and he wore a crown. Azor was perched smugly on his left, showing me off as if I were a prized stag. His happiness made me wish I'd stabbed him with the spear when I had the chance earlier.

"Aren't you going to say something, son?" the King asked gruffly, his piercing gaze practically pinning me to the floor.

Though flustered in his presence, I fought his contempt and tried to sit upright. The world felt very unstable, slanting at a bit of an odd angle. "This whole thing has been a misunderstanding," I said with a hoarse voice.

"Aye." He shook his head, suddenly amused, as if what I'd said was humorous. "But what should I do with you now?"

I waited, as he appeared to be contemplating a punishment. I'd learned from Dad that the best way of surviving an unsavory predicament was to keep my mouth shut. After a few moments of stifling silence, a coy smile spread across his mouth, pulling up the large white beard that hung from his face.

"On your wrist you'll find a new ornament to your attire—" I looked down and found a gold bracelet with the Natatorian symbol stamped across the top. "If for some reason you can't manage to keep yourself within the boundaries of Natatoria, poison will be injected into your skin and render you unconscious."

I looked at the bracelet more closely and felt a sense of panic set in. I'd seen other merman with these before, but I just thought they were employees of the King or something.

"Don't be alarmed. As long as you don't try to disable the device or leave, you should be just fine. After your promising ceremony, I'll have it removed."

"Promising ceremony?"

He smiled again in an evil knowing sort of way. "Yes. Fortunate for you, your escapade hasn't been publicized. Requests from parents have been pouring in. Your mother is eagerly deciding who your wife will be."

I tried not to look shocked, knowing this couldn't be true. More like coerced into deciding would be my guess. "And my sister?"

"Her upcoming promising has quickly become the talk of Natatoria. Azor has offered and she's accepted. She'll stay in the palace to help with preparations for the big day. Queen Desiree has become quite fond of Tatiana and can't wait to have her as a daughter. She's insisted we have a huge celebration and I've already had to dispatch mers all over the world to collect items she's specifically requested."

I fought my desire to rip his crown off his head and shove it down his throat, keeping a stoic expression. Mers typically didn't promise before their eighteenth birthday. No such luck for us. Maybe with all the extra preparations, we'd have extra time to plan our escape.

"After the ceremony, Azor will assist in assigning you a home and a job. I imagine we won't have any more incidents from you in the future."

Azor nodded his head.

Emotional blackmail. They intended to use the feelings a promising created to hold me captive in Natatoria. Good thing they didn't know they were already too late.

"Of course not," I lied and could hardly contain my smug smile.

Azor opened the lock on the cell door and swung the gate open, setting me free. I remained on the floor and felt strangely calm even after the King's dismal portrayal of my future. They might have thought they'd won, but I'd use their "promising" weapon against them; my feelings for Ash would fuel my escape. And I'd never let Azor look at, let alone kiss my sister. Ever.

King Phaleon turned toward Azor in satisfaction. "He's in your charge now."

"Yes, Dad." Azor bowed and the King exited with his body guards trailing behind him.

My weakened state prevented me from rising and strangling

Azor's neck once we were alone. He had a lot of nerve to force Tatch to promise him. I wondered if my sister had a matching bracelet as well.

"You're very lucky, Fin," he said, his voice laced with sarcasm. "I wouldn't have been so lenient."

"One day, Azor," I pledged, "you'll wish—"

"Fin!" Badger said, interrupting my threat. "I came as soon as I heard."

"Oh," Azor said in surprise. "Yes. I've had a little trouble with my star pupil."

Badger glanced at my wrist but kept a stony exterior. My guess was he knew exactly what the golden decoration meant.

"Aye," Badger shook his head. "Let me take him off yer hands. I'll straighten him out."

Azor laughed. "You can try—" he threw his arm out in an invitation. "He's all yours."

I exchanged hard looks with Azor for a minute before I tried to pick myself up off the ground. One day I'd get my revenge.

Badger reached out his hand and pulled me up. "Let's go, lad."

As soon as we were clear of the compound, I opened my mouth to explain what happened.

"It's okay, son," he said and held up his hands. "I already know."

"You do? How?"

Badger's frown pulled into a grin. "I keep thinkin' back to the day we met. I knew ye were gonna be a firecracker. But the promisin' is a right smart plan to get back on the King's good side. I'm honored at your choice."

I screwed up my face. "Choice?"

"Ah, don't pretend like ye don't know. My little Lily is a right fine gal and ye two will be so happy together."

My heart thudded a few haphazard beats. What did Lily have to do with any of this? "Oh, right," I said, playing like I knew what he meant.

But my breath came out heavily as my head swirled at the revelation. Did Mom decide Lily for me? If so, there definitely was no way I could tell Badge what happened with Ash now. He'd kick the crap out of me, especially if he thought I was two-timing his niece.

The logistics suddenly concerned me. Would our souls combine and free Ashlyn? Or would Lily bond with me too? I'd go mad being apart from Ash if it did. And I couldn't imagine being Lily's husband, the thought of kissing her was utterly disgusting. A life without Ashlyn wasn't a life at all and I planned to fight to be with her. If only it were some other girl, then Badger could help me escape.

Badger looked me in the eye as if he'd read my thoughts. "I'll be expecting ya to respect her or you'll be dealin' with me."

"Of course," I choked out as I cowered under his stare, worried he'd seen right through me. "You have my word. I'd never hurt Lily."

"I know that," he said playfully and jabbed me in the arm. "I'm just joshin' with ya."

I faked a chuckle and continued towards my underwater home-away-from-home. All I wanted was to close my eyes and wish myself out of Natatoria and into Ash's arms. I couldn't be forced to promise someone I didn't love.

Then I remembered I had to face my mother first.

40

ASH

The soft rapping on the door woke me up from my drowsy state. I'd been dreaming of my angel again and the blasted noise interrupted my utopia.

"Go away," I grumbled and pulled the covers over my head.

"Ashlyn, you've got company," Mom said through the door.

"I don't want to see anyone."

I heard the door creak open and cringed.

"Georgia came to see you," Mom said.

"Tell her I'll call her later," I said into the pillow.

"You can tell her yourself." Her soft footfalls stopped in the corner of the room just before the pulleys whined on the blinds, shooting light into the room. "It's time you joined the world again. Tomorrow, you're going back to school."

"What?" I sat up in bed, shielding my eyes from the sun. "I can barely walk."

"If you want, I've been able to get you a wheelchair and Georgia has offered to assist you to every class tomorrow."

"No, please—" I was about to object when Georgia peeked around the door frame.

"Plus we've got great news," she said with a huge smile.

"We've?" I stared at the door, expecting others to file in from behind her.

Brown hair and broad shoulders belonging to none other than Callahan came into view. I swallowed hard, tasting dragon breath that could kill small animals. Though today was the day I could finally take a shower, I hadn't yet and wore the same green pajamas complete with stains from dinner the night before.

I pulled the covers up to my neck. "Um, I need to go to the bathroom real quick. Can I meet you guys in the living room?"

"Good idea," Mom said as she plucked a few dead flowers from my collection of vases.

Once the door shut, I lumbered out of bed and limped to the bathroom. My toiletries sat untouched on the counter. After a good brushing, I finished up with a gurgle of mouthwash and pulled my greasy hair into a ponytail.

The warm washcloth felt refreshing over my face. But the swipe of deodorant and spritz of honeysuckle perfume did a poor job of covering up several days of stink.

I peeled off the jammies I'd worn for three days and dug through the clean clothes piled in a laundry basket. The sight of the swim team jacket stopped me. I ran my hand over the satin and my lips tingled remembering I'd worn it that day. I pulled my arms into the sleeves and felt comforted somehow.

"Hey," I said as I hobbled into the living room and took the couch opposite Callahan. He sat right where Fin had during his visit. My face tensed, remembering his plea for help—a plea that had to be deeper than just a request for clothing. I'd been so cruel.

"Glad to see you're getting around better," Callahan said with concerned eyes.

"Yeah, well—" I shrugged and tried not to care where he sat, forcing my feelings somewhere under the buffer of pain meds. The way Georgia and Callahan looked at me made me feel like an insect in a jar, every move watched. "What's the big surprise?"

Callahan turned to Georgia. She could barely contain her excitement, bouncing in her seat. "We found out why Brooke was suspended."

I got out of bed and cleaned up for gossip? Completely unamused, I raised my eyebrows and waited. "And?"

Georgia's lips curled up. "She and Kylie rigged the vote. A teacher found discarded votes for *you* in the trash. The office had a hidden camera. They were totally caught red-handed!"

"Oh, wow." I sat up, curious to what exactly would happen to the Senior Ball Queen now that she was dethroned. "So?"

"They're announcing the new winner tomorrow, so you have to be there."

I laughed. "I'm not going through this again. People will just vote for me 'cause they feel sorry for me, that's all."

"No," Georgia said and looked to Callahan for support. "They're taking the person with the second highest votes from the original count."

"She's right," he said.

I sat there and shook my head. What if other votes were tossed too? How unfair. Not only to put the other girls through the humiliation again, but to make me go back early to prove some point. All because of lies.

The irony suddenly seemed funny. My best friend, whom I trusted implicitly wasn't even human and neither was her brother—a foundation of lies. And Brooke needed the Senior Ball Queen title so bad, she was willing to do anything for it—more lies. And I almost died from my own actions, but allowed people I love to believe it was an accident—lies, lies, lies.

Where was my dishonor? My title stripping? I deserved to be exposed as well.

"I'm a liar, too," I said and began to laugh.

From inside, a week's worth of stress rumbled from my belly and strangely cleared my head. Georgia and Callahan both looked back in shock as I continued on. "I didn't get swept up by a wave off the beach. I took out our family's row boat on Sunday and fell out of it. The whole thing was my fault, and I lied about it."

"Ashlyn," my mother said behind me, her voice filled with disappointment.

I stopped laughing and stared at her. "Sorry, Mom."

She blinked back the tears in her eyes and remained quiet for a moment. Callahan and Georgia sat stiff like statues.

"I think it's time for your friends to go," she finally said.

In silence, they popped off the couch and filed out, looking shocked and disturbed, but I didn't care. I needed to come clean—to have them know what really happened. I wasn't worthy of the crown either.

But instead of relief, guilt swept over me and I burst into tears. The burden was so much deeper than just my mother's disappointment in me; grief for Fin and Tatchi's abduction and their faces right before they disappeared underwater haunted me. Not knowing their location or wellbeing wracked my nerves. My fragile psyche couldn't handle any more uncertainty.

I leaned onto the couch cushion and sobbed. A piece of my soul felt like it was dying and I didn't know how to fix it. The only time I'd felt whole since the accident was when Fin took my arm in the middle of my living room. And I'd forced him to leave, to go back to his evil cousin who wished nothing but ill will for both of them. I sent the one person who made me whole to his doom.

I begged God to protect them as I folded myself into a ball, rocking back and forth. Their fishy fins aside, I knew for certain I wouldn't last long if something happened to either of them, especially to Fin.

41

FIN

When I phased into legs and entered our house, Mom rushed me and hugged my neck so hard I thought it would break. Even though everything that had transpired only occurred over a few days, it felt like a lifetime since I'd last seen her.

"Finley," she said with a small sob, "I'm so glad you're safe."

"Mom." I let out a deep sigh and rested my chin on her shoulder, exhausted from the emotional journey. "I'm so sorry about everything."

She pulled back and studied my eyes. "What do you have to be sorry about? This is not your fault."

"But it is. I left Natatoria not once, but twice."

She laughed lightly, a gentle sound that cleansed my wounds. "Don't you think their reaction is a little extreme? What did they say your *supposed* crimes were?"

I looked back questioningly. "I—I left unchaperoned. That's against the law."

"Tahoe is your home and your uncle is there watching over things. You should be able to go there freely. Besides, you're practically eighteen. What are two months going to change? Nothing horrible happened."

But something did go wrong. "Mom, they aren't taking my crimes lightly. They put a bracelet on me so I can't leave Natatoria," I said with wide eyes. "Tatch has to stay in the freaking palace until it's time for her ceremony to Azor. We need to get word to Dad to stop it. Where is he?!"

Mom gently pushed aside a lock of damp hair off my forehead then took both my hands with a smile that didn't reach the uncertainty behind her eyes. "I don't know where he is."

"Can't we find out who does? Someone has to know."

Mom sighed, all the fight taken from her. "It won't be so bad. Once you partake of the bond, everything will change and you'll be happy with Lily. It's a beautiful thing."

"A beautiful thing?" I looked at her wrist to make sure she wasn't wearing some kind of mind altering bracelet herself. How could she be okay with this? "Mom, did you forget? Tatch hates Azor and I'm—" I looked away. The longing for Ashlyn burned an inferno I could no longer contain, threatening to consume all my logic. "Can someone be promised to more than one mer at a time?"

She dropped my hands and her eyes tightened. "Why are you asking this?"

I gulped as the fear of what I'd done gripped my stomach like a vice. "I've already kissed someone else."

Mom blanched. "Who? When did this happen?"

"It was an accident," I said and proceeded to fill her in on what happened with Ash.

She ran her hand through her hair when I finished and sighed. "Great Poseidon."

This time, I was the one consoling her. "It's not too late. If only we could get this bracelet off, then I could escape through another gate and find Dad. He'd stop Tatch's promising ceremony and we could all go back to Tahoe together."

She took my arm and traced her fingers over the Natatorian emblem. "How does it keep you here?"

"It'll inject me with poison if I leave a gate, or if I try to dismantle it."

She closed her eyes and held my wrist. "They're determined to break us."

"They don't have to win."

She turned around and kneaded her neck. "I've been trying to keep a good attitude and look at the bright side of things, but it's been one thing after another. First the mission, and now this—" she pointed to the bracelet. "I didn't want to believe Phaleon had it in for us, but we should have gotten word from your father by now and we haven't. Dad has no clue what's happening. This is Phaleon's revenge. His subtle plot to ruin our family."

"Mom?" I moved into her line of sight. "I don't understand."

"Did you ever wonder why we've never spent time in Natatoria and your father doesn't say why?"

"All the time."

She took a deep breath and sat down on the couch, already looking exhausted though she hadn't said a word. I took a seat next to her and waited while she collected her thoughts.

"You already know how your dad and I met, before I knew he was a merman. He told me he was visiting his aunt and uncle close to where I lived in Florida. He actually lived on land with his parents who were stationed to guard the Bermuda Triangle gate." She smiled at the memory. "We spent the entire summer together: laughing, swimming, and enjoying every sunlit moment together. We've told you kids he swept me off my feet and we couldn't live without each other, but what I didn't mention was Leon—which is what we used to call King Phaleon back then. He'd visit along with Jack."

Her smile faded. "It became increasingly evident they both liked me, but I only had feelings for your father. Leon became jealous. It was after I let him down easy that things took a strange turn. Unknown to me, your grandparents were accused shortly thereafter of becoming too familiar with humans. Overnight the family packed up and left without saying good-bye. This was right before my junior year of high school.

"Though utterly crushed, I never fully let go of your father's memory. A few years later, for my twenty-first birthday, I had a big party on a yacht out on the Keys. I had a little too much to drink and fell overboard. I'd hit my head and probably would have drowned if Jack hadn't been there to rescue me. He'd been underwater"—she winked—"spying on me the whole time. Once we were reunited, it was as if we'd never been apart. That was the day he kissed me. Our promising day.

"In the beginning, it was difficult, the distance—like now—was unbearable. But I had to finish college so I could get a job to support us. After a year, we couldn't handle the infrequent visits. Most of the time, Jack would have to sneak out of Natatoria, so he took the Tahoe Gate job, which was the least favorable place to guard at the time. The decision solved all our problems. I became a mermaid shortly after the move. Eventually, I had my aging parents move there too and retire so I could care for them until they passed.

"But we avoided Natatoria—one, because I was a new beta-mer and the other, to spare Leon's feelings. Once we heard of his promising to Desiree, we hoped he'd let go of the past. After he became King, though"—she shook her head and grimaced—"the laws changed. He stopped letting people live on land to guard gates. We are one of the last families to have that privilege. I believe it's because your father is on the Council. They see the value in him being in touch with human society, but by sending Dad on this dangerous mission and keeping me here, the King has put us both in a heart-wrenching place and he knows it.

"And if that wasn't enough, now he's sought to keep you and your sister here as well by using your emotions against you—and taking our daughter against our wishes and her will. The only problem is Ashlyn's soul won't ever allow her to move on. If the promising with Lily happens, they'll both be bonded to you, but only Ashlyn will own your heart. Naturally, you shouldn't want to be with Lily, which in normal circumstances would stop this from happening. The reality is Ashlyn's spirit will begin to consume you and there will be no rest until you're together. If you leave after you're promised to Lily, though, you won't feel it, but she'll suffer the same fate."

I closed my eyes and leaned my head back. My thoughts swam with the lies, betrayal, and deception while my soul ached, wanting nothing but to have Ash in my arms. Knowing she suffered just as bad, if not worse, sickened me. Though Blanchard attempted to mind-wipe her, unknown to him she'd been immune because of our promise, and now she was all alone and without any answers—her soul unbearably restless. What could she possibly be thinking? My decision was clear. No matter what, I couldn't condemn Lily to the same slow torture.

"Mom, we have to stop this."

"I know. But if they knew what happened, they'd find Ashlyn and kill her to free your soul and prove their power."

"NO!"

"So," Mom said with tears in her eyes, "maybe we can talk to Badger about it—"

"No," I interrupted. "How could I tell him? If he had any idea about this, he'd probably beat me up. He's excited about me becoming part of his family."

"Badger loves you. I doubt he'd do anything of the sort if he knew all the facts. He might be able to figure out how to help you and your sister escape beforehand. You have to go get Dad. We can't allow Tatiana to be with a man she utterly hates."

"I don't want Badger involved, but that doesn't solve this problem—" I held up my wrist.

"Right," she said with a pain-stricken face. She grabbed my hands forcefully. "Follow along like they want and I'll figure out a way to free your sister and stop this promising if it kills me. Maybe Tatiana and I could go together. Or—"

Mom's sudden determination horrified me. I suddenly feared

how far she would go to accomplish her goal—including leaving on her own.

"Please, Mom. I couldn't face Dad if something happened to you."

"Nothing's going to happen." A light of hope flickered from within the darkness that had consumed her eyes. "We're going to get out of here and find your father."

"Yeah, but—"

She smiled reassuringly. "Leon will not win, Finley. I promise you. But for now, we need to act like nothing has changed. Tomorrow morning at the festival, pretend you're happy about your engagement to Lily."

"The festival is tomorrow?"

"Yes, but it'll be okay. Being jilted at the altar is much better than being abandoned after being promised."

I rubbed my hand over my forehead, surprised Mom was being so optimistic when I had no idea how we'd get Tatch away from the guards in the palace, let alone get my bracelet off. "If you say so."

"I know so."

I couldn't help but shudder. Tatiana had spoken those same words just hours before and everything had gone horrifically wrong. I didn't want to jinx anything by agreeing.

42

ASH

Somehow, I managed to pick up the pieces of my sanity before Mom ordered the guys with the white coats to come and take me away. Of course, that wasn't before she arranged an appointment with a psychologist. I could only imagine the doctor's reaction if I explained the truth about what was really making me batty.

My little bout of hysteria kept me from school another day and Mom later apologized for pushing too soon for me to return. I'd retreated back to my room, away from the whispers of my family and decided to keep a watchful eye on the lake through the window. I had an eerie sense something bad was about to happen and that Fin and Tatchi needed my prayers.

Questions swirled in my head as I replayed the events of the abduction yet again. Little by little the pieces fell together. Unlike the old eighties movie *Splash*, water didn't necessarily make them merpeople. Then what did? Tatchi was never out past sunset, complaining her parents enforced a curfew. Did the sun have something to do with it? Was that why she couldn't spend the night at my house way back then? I gasped. That had to be it—the big secret her dad busted the cabinet over. Of course. They were merpeople only at night and they couldn't control it.

Criminy! How many had I come across and didn't even know it? Like their cousin Colin. Was the entire family merpeople? Were they born this way? Have they always lived in the lake? How have they kept it a secret for so long?

Then it hit me.

This whole time I believed an angel saved me from drowning when that wasn't what happened at all. I'd heard Fin's voice and saw his face right before I fell unconscious, but thought it was a dream. Had it really been him after all? My head ached in confusion.

As a merman he would obviously have been able to endure the frigid temperature of the water. But that was during the daytime. Could he will his tail in and out of existence? Then how did he get me to the Ranger station and why didn't the Ranger see him?

"Oh," I whispered as my lips suddenly tingled, a memory of Fin's lips touching mine.

He did. He carried me. It was his warm body next to mine, his voice that told me to fight, to live. My heart swelled. I no longer cared the facts didn't make sense. All that mattered was Fin. He was the one I'd been dreaming about this whole time. The one I wished for. The one I'd fallen in love with. The one taken from me.

Then I remembered all the horrible things I'd said, the way I'd overreacted when he came to my door. Was he about to tell me? Was my refusal to help why he was captured? My gut clenched. I'd turned him away and now he was gone, pulled under the waves by evil mermen to a place called Natatoria. Why didn't he make me listen? Was he afraid I wouldn't understand? Am I that stubborn he wouldn't even try?

Heartsick, I moved to the window and touched the glass, desperate to touch his beautiful face instead, wanting to beg for forgiveness. He had to come back. If he never returned, the longing would slowly chip away at my soul, robbing me of my sanity.

"Fin," I whispered as I brought my fists to my face, wiping my tears with my sleeves. "I'm so sorry. Please come home."

I couldn't stop the dread. I'd failed him.

43

FIN

Somewhere else in the palace, Tatch was getting ready, too. Mom had rushed off to find her, leaving me alone in a guest room. Of course, there was a guard outside the door preventing me from following or trying to duck out early. The King assigned my sister guards as well, along with a female chaperone instructed to stay with her at all times since she'd incapacitated all the men in my escape.

I clenched my hands to calm my nerves. Act happy. That was what my mother's orders were, but this whole charade made my stomach roll. I'd not seen Lily since we'd almost kissed at Badger's— a different time, a different me. The last thing I wanted to do was lead her on. Maybe I'd get a chance to let her off gently before the festival. Before we smiled and waved for all the mers to see.

In front of the mirror, I pulled at the silly sleeveless vest I wore and laughed. Who'd made this monstrosity? A beauty school beginners sewing class disaster, no doubt—mine being the first victim.

I turned to answer the knock at the door, expecting Mom, and tensed. Badger floated with Lily at his side instead. She'd never looked more beautiful in a long white gown.

"Oh good, it fits you." She smiled warmly, eyeing my attire. "You weren't around to measure. Everything happened so fast, I didn't think I'd have it ready in time."

I tugged on the bottom of my vest, glad I didn't comment first. "Like a glove."

Mom and Dad were right. Arranged promisings were awkward.

How was I supposed to act when I knew behind closed doors Lily's parents wrote up a proposal like we were cattle and sent it to my Mom via courier for approval? How was that romantic?

But to make things worse, Badger hovered behind Lily and beamed with pride, believing we'd be family soon. I took a deep breath and looked away. After the truth came out, he'd hate me for sure.

"I think we best be gettin' down to the festival," Badge said, breaking the uncomfortable silence.

"Good idea." I moved ahead of them, wondering if I should take Lily's hand or not, and decided the less attention I gave her the better.

I'd only been to a festival once as a kid so I had no idea what awaited us. Back then, the couples swam in a long line and waved to the crowd. It lasted way too long and was a complete and total bore. I imagined this would be the same.

The goon squad followed close behind and I caught Lily watching them and me with curious eyes. Part of me found her reaction comical. I guessed no one bothered to tell her she was engaged to a criminal.

As we exited through the palace doors, a line of buggies that looked like cars in amusement park rides spread as far as the eye could see on the shiny golden street. Dowels protruded from each corner of the car; shells and other shiny crap decorated the outsides. Most of the cars already held anxiously awaiting couples. We followed suit and waited alongside the other mer couples to speak with the coordinator, a woman dressed entirely in purple.

I craned my neck to find my sister, but neither Mom, Tatch, nor Azor were among the crowd.

"Tatch?" I asked mentally. *"Are you here somewhere?"*

No reply. Knowing her, she'd locked herself in a closet, refusing to come out.

"What a lovely couple you two make!" the woman in purple said to us as she held a thin slab of rock covered with writing. "Your names?"

"Finley and Lily."

"Elizabeth," Lily corrected.

I looked at her quizzically as the knot tightened in my stomach. We were complete strangers. How could she so easily want to form a lifelong bond together after only a few short visits?

"Here you are: Finley Samuel Helton and Elizabeth Katherine Oakley. Please report to carriage number twenty-five."

When I didn't move, too stunned by the craziness of the whole charade, Lily grabbed my hand and pulled me towards our carriage.

"Are you okay?" she murmured under her breath as we took our seats. Badger hovered off to the side, glancing from the car to the lady with the rock slab and back again.

"I guess so. You?"

She wrinkled up her brow, but continued to squeeze my hand. "I'm a little nervous."

Everything inside me wanted to take my hand back and refrain from skin contact, but I didn't want to hurt her feelings.

"I'll be back with ya in a moment, kids," Badger said and left to talk to the lady in purple again.

"This is coming about a little faster than I hoped," Lily said quickly. "I mean, don't get me wrong, I like you and everything, but—it's just—I don't know you all that well yet."

I exhaled, relief washing over me like a cool shower. This was my perfect escape. We could announce a long engagement that hopefully would never come to fruition. "You're right. We *should* get to know each other better first."

"What?" she asked and blinked back at me with a sudden frown. "*You* were the one who wanted to get promised right away."

"Me? No . . ." I backpedaled in my brain for a moment. The King said the families were coming to Mom asking me to become promised to their daughters, not the other way around. "How did you get *this* proposal?"

"By letter. How else?"

"What?" I jerked backward in my seat. "I'd never send a letter. I'd do it in person. I was told that you—"

I clammed up as soon as Badger appeared no longer feeling safe to talk casually anymore.

"Told what?" Lily demanded.

I looked up towards Badge and Lily let go of my hand.

"Aye. I'm supposed to be sittin' with ya accordin' to Purple Petunia over there. Sandy's goin' to have me hide fer not dressin' the part," he said as he settled into the seat behind us, tilting the carriage backward with his weight.

"Uncle Badge, you look fine," Lily said, flipping on the charm though I knew she was angry with me.

Four goons came over and took up our buggy—two at the back and two in the front. I glared at them, unappreciative they kept such tight tabs on me. What was the purpose of the bracelet if I had to have guards too?

"I don't want some bloke towin' me about," Badger grumbled under his breath behind us.

Lily turned and swatted his arm. "Shhh."

"Aye," he barked and got out. He shooed one of the goons away and took up the back right corner. "I'm more fit to be carryin' this jam jar than he is."

Lily threw her hands in the air and faced forward.

At the blow of a horn, the parade was officially underway. All the mermen lifted the cars in unison and everyone cheered except us.

"You could act a little happier about being promised to me," Lily said through her teeth while forcing a smile.

"I am." I grabbed her hand to prove it.

But she kept her hand limp when I tried to entwine my fingers with hers. Once the line proceeded away from the palace towards the town, Lily softened and waved to the cheering crowd. I tried to smile, but my lips pulled into a frown as I looked for Tatch again. They probably put her at the very end in some special float reserved for royalty.

"I need to talk to you later," I said as Lily blew kisses.

"It's a little late for talking, don't you think?"

True.

I sighed. So much for acting happy. All I could wish for was the dumb parade to end soon and a private moment so I could just break things off. Forget the long engagement idea.

Once we maneuvered around the last corner, the royal balcony finally came into view. My chest tightened when I spotted the royal couple—a sharp contrast. Queen Desiree appeared to be enjoying herself, while King Phaleon stayed stoic. But once he spotted our carriage, the corner of his lip lifted. I had news for him. His plan to grind my family into submission was about to come to a screeching halt. I'd never submit.

"Smile," Badger whispered behind us. "The King and Queen are watchin' ye."

Lily eagerly waved at the royal family, but when I didn't respond, she jabbed me in the side with her elbow. I finally raised my hand, but gave him an evil eye instead. Watching him birthed my deepest wish; that someone would overthrow him and set the people free of his overbearing command. Mers deserved to promise to the ones they loved without chaperones and parental interference, and they deserved to be given some credit and live where they wanted.

From the edge of the balcony, I spotted Chauncey floating over and he whispered something in the King's ear. Whatever he said wiped the smirk right off the King's face, his glare finding me. Normally I would have reveled in anything that annoyed King

Phaleon, but this time I had a feeling it had something to do with Tatch and why she wasn't at the parade.

a

When the parade ended, Badger didn't speak to me and immediately took Lily home. I was ushered back to the palace by the same annoying goon squad.

"Get comfortable," the scrawnier one said before he shut the door and bolted it on the other side.

Comfortable? All that was in the room was a mirror, a table and four ornate chairs carved from rock. Why were they still holding me hostage when I had the bracelet on? Dread choked me as I noticed bars covered the windows, making my guest room a renovated jail cell—a new addition while I was at the parade. *Nice.*

From outside I heard people chatter excitedly about their upcoming futures together. I wondered what Lily told her parents about how I behaved today. I could only hope the ceremonies wouldn't be for a while with all the Queen's lavish plans. Far enough away for us to escape.

I awaited news from someone about what happened with my mom and sister, continuing to telepathically call for Tatch without any return response. My plans when I got out weren't complicated: free Tatch, get the bracelet off, and escape Natatoria with my family. How, was a different question.

Could someone get word to Dad instead? Besides Badger, I didn't know who I could trust to help me. I was a pawn in a game the King controlled. He probably reveled in what was to come—Dad's not so joyous homecoming filled with news that not one, but both of his kids were promised in his absence. Nice reward for risking your life, leaving your family, and doing a secret job to help the King. Another insult to an injury Dad didn't inflict so long ago.

The bolt on the door unlatched. I stood upright.

"Son," Mom said and rushed to me, hugging my neck tightly.

"Mom?"

She wouldn't stop hugging me and then I realized she was crying.

"Mom!"

"I'm sorry, Fin," she said, her face pained. "I'm trying to be strong. Your sister—she fell apart today and refused to go to the parade. We did everything we could to convince her. I even secretly told her the plan to escape, but she'd wouldn't fake like she supported this. Once the King heard she wouldn't cooperate, he got very upset."

I stared into my mother's ashen face and my dorsal fin flexed. "What did he do?"

She looked up at me sadly—nothing but failure behind her eyes. "He's arranged a private ceremony for you and your sister. You'll be promised tomorrow."

"No," I said, backing up as if I was cornered. "I won't do it. Lily doesn't even want to. The King tricked her parents. She said I'd asked for her hand by a letter, but you said they asked you."

"It doesn't matter. There's nothing any of us can do. The King firmly believes if the two of you are promised, you won't cause him anymore grief."

"But I'm already promised!" I yelled.

"Shhh, I know." She pushed her hands downward. "This is such a mess. They sedated your sister, then she couldn't stay awake to attend."

"Really?" I scrubbed my hand through my hair. "I can't believe this is all happening."

She pressed her palms over her eyes. "This is all my fault."

I put my arm over her shoulder, suppressing the urge to tear apart the room instead. "It's not your fault. It's going to be okay, Mom. Like you said earlier, things could be worse. We still have time. I'll figure out something."

"Without your dad, I don't know how."

The fire in her eyes from the night before had extinguished, lighting anger inside me. I'd been looking at this whole situation like a child. What could Dad do that I couldn't? I was a man. It was time I started acting like one.

I swam to the door and pounded on it.

"I want to see the King," I demanded to the goon.

He looked at me with amusement. "Okay," he said before shutting the door.

I wedged my fin into the door jam and pushed it back open. "I'm serious. I want to see him tonight."

He gave me a wild smile; one tooth was missing. "Whatever ya say, Captain."

I drifted back, alarmed at the craziness in his eyes. Why did he call me Captain? Disturbed, I moved back to my seat and watched mom knead her hands. Once the King showed up, I'd let him know that Lily didn't want to be with me after all, that my father's word still stood. Dad said we'd get to choose and neither of us had.

Even if I had to tell him my sister and I wanted to be turned into a human, I would. We still had rights as citizens of Natatoria, and King Phaleon's rash decisions were breaking the law.

44

ASH

Though I was safely in my grandmother's room, subconsciously the water seemed to suck me under and hold me there. My family went about their business, coming and going, as they needed. I couldn't participate. Guilt made me watch the lake out the window and wait.

The appointment earlier with the psychologist didn't help either.

"How are you?" the older woman with glasses and white curly hair asked.

"Fine," I said and cracked a fake smile.

"Great. So what brings you here?"

"My mom," I said with a snicker. "You just talked to her. Remember?"

"That I did. So why did she bring you?"

"So you'll fix me—they all think I'm suffering from post traumatic stress."

"And are you?" She tilted her head and smiled.

I looked away from her probing eyes and stared at the sand garden on her coffee table. The sand reminded me of Fin and how he was trapped in Natatoria because of me. I bit my lip until it bled to keep from crying. "Heck if I know."

"Do you know what post traumatic stress is?"

"I Googled it."

"And what did Google say?"

"That you get all weird after a stressful or life threatening event. But really, it was no big deal."

She shifted in her chair but remained pleasant—shooting a

knowing smile. I wondered if the mention of "merpeople" would wipe it off.

"Why don't I tell you what I know about post traumatic stress and you tell me if that's what's going on?"

"Whatever," I said flippantly.

She ignored my rude reply and went on to tell me about how the traumatic events are like a strand of pearls. After the event, your brain doesn't know how to deal with the information so it's like someone has snipped the string, the thoughts bouncing in your mind. All your brain knows to do is replay the events over and over to try and put the strand back together again. Eventually, over time, you complete the necklace and put away the memories. Sometimes though, your brain gets stuck and the pearls keep bouncing.

"Nope. Not me. I guess I'm normal then."

She nodded and hummed. I wanted to rip the pencil from her hand and chuck it out the window.

"Have you been to the water since the accident?"

"Of course I have." The night Fin and Tatchi were abducted. I felt my lip quiver.

"And how'd that go?"

Pearls were an understatement. Super balls from the incident bounced around instead, smacking my temples as if it was a bull's eye. If I was having PTSD, it wasn't because I almost drowned in the lake, but rather that my friends were taken and I let it happen. "It was water. That wet cold stuff that will take your life if you try to swim in it right now."

"I see. Fear of the water seems to make you angry." She wrote something on a small white notepad.

She ripped off the paper and handed it to me. I assumed after seeing I wasn't going to cooperate, it was a prescription for some meds to dope me up, so I'd comply with my mother's wishes. An address and phone number was all she'd scrawled across the top.

"This is the number of a support group for teens going through stressful situations. I highly suggest you go and just listen to the stories."

I shoved the slip of paper into my pocket and creased my forehead. A hundred dollars an hour got me an address and phone number? Mom was going to love that one.

"Am I free to go?"

"Not quite I'm afraid. We still have forty-five more minutes."

I sighed and stared at the sand again.

She pried for the rest of the time, but I gave her nothing.

Earlier today, when spying on Fin and Tatchi's house, I noticed it appeared vacant. The traffic going in and out abruptly stopped after the abduction at the beach. Too late to demand answers. Though I doubted Fin's alluring cousin, who ended up being one of the bad guys, would have told me anything anyway.

My heart hammered knowing the enemy had been so close and I'd almost put myself at risk by going over and trying to talk to him again. Were all merpeople weird and hypnotic like that?

So I just watched the water and waited from a distance.

They had to return soon. They had to.

45

FIN

Somehow, I'd fallen asleep. This was the last thing I wanted to do as I waited for the King to show up. I'd only closed my eyes for what seemed like a half a second when someone grabbed me and sliced something sharp across my arm.

I looked up as a goon restrained me and another held a peculiar green plant against the cut. A tingling sensation began to trail through my limbs, taking with it all my fight.

"He won't be any trouble now," the third goon, who held the knife, said to some unseen person behind him.

I tried to stay upright, ready for my confrontation with the King, but slumped down, suddenly overcome with exhaustion. Through the doorway two tittering mermaids entered, carrying armloads of supplies and clothing. They came towards me, singing their sweet melodies. I forgot my anger and closed my eyes while they played with my hair and put different shirts on me. Off to the side I heard Mom interacting with someone as well.

I remained drowsy and eventually opened my eyes. The mermaids were gone. I brushed my hands over the shirt they put on me, which glistened with hundreds of tiny black, polished stones. The weight draped the garment snuggly across my chest and arms.

"I guess I'm all set to give up my life to Lily," I said sleepily as I grinned at Mom.

She looked like an angel with her hair pinned around her head, adorned with gems and shells. Only, she wasn't smiling back. "That's not funny. What about Ashlyn?"

Ash's beautiful face came to mind. "Oh, right," I snorted, "let's go find her."

She looked back horrified and shook her head. "Finley, you have to fight what they've drugged you with. Drink in some water."

I swallowed a few gulps, then burped. She sat down, resting her forehead on her hand. Even though my inebriated state made everything seem trivial, I couldn't deny her worry. Unfortunately for me, I didn't have the strength to care.

"Aw, Mom," I said and sat on the side of the chair, covering her shoulder with my arm. "It'll be okay, just like you said."

She shimmied away and continued to knead her hands together when someone unlocked the door. The same goons who'd poisoned me motioned for us to exit the room. My heart, which should have started to pound, remained at a steady pace.

They escorted us to a large ballroom in the center of the palace. I somewhat expected to see a mass of people, but found a small group of strangers in attendance—mostly females. The front of the room was typical of the décor of the rest of the palace: colorful sea anemones placed on marble columns were staggered between brilliant coral gardens. Vivid fish darted around the display. Definitely not lavishly decorated with items from all over the world, like the King said.

Mom leaned into me and whispered, "I'm hoping for a miracle."

I looked at her and snickered. "Miracle? I think it's a little too late."

"Just . . . just don't kiss Lily, whatever you do."

I shrugged and let her pull me inside.

"Welcome," a mermatron at the door said. "And congratulations. I'm the promising coordinator. Maggie, you'll wait here to be escorted once the ceremony starts and Finley, you'll stand on the dais to the right of the King's attendant. For now you can sit in a chair over there."

At the ends of her hot pink braids floating in the current, snake faces appeared and hissed at me.

"Eeew," I said and moved backwards.

My mother grabbed my arm. "Finley. Stop it."

I wrinkled my face and shook my head—the snakes disappeared. All I remembered her say was that the King would be standing up front with us. "The King is promising us?" I asked.

Her brow creased. "No, the King's attendant will be. The King is escorting Tatiana down the aisle."

"What?" I let out a gust that flapped my lips. None of this was right. Dad should be taking her down the aisle, not Leon. "And Tatch is going to let him?"

Mom nudged me in the side and gave me a hard look. "Fin—" She pointed to the front of the room. "Have a seat. I'll handle the details."

I rolled my eyes and followed her instruction, knocking over a sea star sculpture in the process.

Through the doors on the left of the room, a group of merboys filed in and hovered behind a huge harp. They were dressed in white long-sleeved shirts and stood stiff like statues. I tried to follow their example, but felt myself sliding off my chair. Instead, I leaned back and stared at the diamond chandelier that hung from the ceiling. Sunlight disbursed off the glistening stones and rippled in the water throughout the room. I wished the room was air-filled so I could exercise my legs.

The snake-haired lady nudged me. "Fin, it's time."

I opened my eyes with a start and maneuvered myself upright. Azor had taken his place on the stage already and to my surprise, our outfits matched. Still shrouded in a cloud of drug induced apathy, I swam up to him and gave him a big high five.

"Finley." He grinned smugly. "Ready for the big day?"

"Righty-O, dog." I formed my fingers into a gun and clicked my tongue.

He laughed half-heartily as snake-haired lady moved me over to the other side of the podium. Once she left the stage, the harpist, who had appeared from nowhere, began to play. The boys sang Natatoria's anthem as a school of seahorses pulled a small pram with my sister and Lily sitting inside. They both wore very ornate head pieces and white dresses, but my sister's head was tilted haphazardly back onto her chair and her mouth gaped open. The snake-haired lady swam over and jiggled her shoulder.

Tatch snapped her head up and shut her mouth. She canvassed the room and found me, then gave me a half-smile. But Lily's terror-stricken expression sobered me up. Lily's father swam to her side of the pram and escorted her to the entrance of the aisle. Behind them, the King entered and took up Tatch's arm.

At the sight of the King, my heart began to pound. He never came last night as I'd summoned. I'd have to confront him in front of everyone now. The music changed to a soft ballad and the four swam down the aisle behind two merlings who tossed starfish onto the white sandy runway.

Lily gulped hard as they came to the end and behind me, the attendant asked, "Who brings these mermaids to be promised to these mermen?"

"Her Godparents do," the King said and passed my tipsy sister to Azor.

I looked to my mom, who was horrified as Tatchi snuggled on Azor's shoulder. Where was my courage? Why couldn't I say anything?

Lily took my arm, her hand shaking as the attendant began the ceremony.

"We are gathered in front of friends and witnesses today to join Prince Azor and Tatiana, and Sir Finley and Elizabeth—"

46

ASH

In desperation, I decided I'd hallucinated the whole thing. Mermaids weren't real. It was time to put the "strand of pearls" away and think rationally. This wasn't me. I wasn't crazy. And no guy, no matter how handsome or wonderful, would drive me to act foolishly. I had a life to live and so did Fin. For whatever reason he wasn't with me, so I'd need to accept it and move on. Today would be day one of that journey.

I pulled out my homework and stared at the page filled with notes from my teacher. The words blurred and jumbled around, competing with the chaos in my head. Was a little peace too much to ask for? I flung my body back into the pillows and screamed at the sudden burst of pain from my leg.

I suddenly heard stomping and was startled when my door flew open. Dad stood in the doorway, terror splashed across his face. "What's wrong, Ash?"

"Dad," I said as the tears poured out. "I'm a mess. I can't stop all these feelings of dread all the time. But there's nothing I can do to fix the situation."

He came and sat next to me, fraught with worry. "Ash, you're not making any sense."

"I saw them, the other night. They were taken by their family to some strange place against their will. Something's wrong, I can feel it."

He closed his eyes and caressed my hair. "Ash. You imagined you saw them. Remember? We've been through this. They haven't been home. Mom would know. Jack hasn't been seen for almost a month."

"They weren't with Mr. Helton. They were alone. It was their weird cousin and some others. Can you please just go over and ask?"

Dad tightened his forehead. "If that would make you feel better."

I shook my head. "Yes, please."

As he stood, the bed squeaked, as if adding a small plea for my case. He grimaced and left me alone. I listened as he closed the front door, imagining him walking down the path and around the corner. Within minutes he returned.

"No one is home, Ash," he said quietly. "I'm sorry."

I rolled over and faced the wall, palming a hunk of hair and tugging. Something had to stop the madness and soon. The shell of my psyche was cracking and at any moment, I knew it would shatter to pieces.

"Why don't you come out and spend some time with me in the living room?" he asked.

I moaned but didn't move. He waited a minute and sighed, then shut the door.

47

FIN

"Phaleon, what is this all about?" A loud voice boomed from the doorway, interrupting the ceremony.

Everyone turned to stare at my father. I watched, my adrenaline trying to press past the drug barrier and kick in some liquid courage.

The King swiveled around, startled. "Jack, so nice of you to join us. Please—" he gestured, "take a seat."

"No. I will not," Dad said with hard eyes. "Why wasn't I told my children were being promised today?"

"I'd sent word. Obviously you got it."

"Word?" Dad laughed derisively. "Was this the same word that was supposed to be sent back to my family about my wellbeing?"

"Your messages weren't being delivered?" The King looked towards my mom with raised eyebrows. "I'm going to have to check into that. But still, let's not ruin this joyous affair—" He faced forward and motioned to the attendant. "Oberon, continue—"

"No, we will not." Dad moved into the aisle, taking a sympathetic look at each of us. "Fin, Tatiana. Do you wish to be here today?"

I gulped and shook my head. Tatiana remained stiff and bleary-eyed; she didn't respond.

Dad tightened his eyes and looked back at the King. "My children don't agree and I won't allow them to make a life decision under duress."

The King bristled. "It's not up to them anymore. They've broken the law."

"And what law is that?"

"Leaving Natatoria unchaperoned and without permission."

Dad's painful glance darted between Tatch and me, catching the glint of gold from the bracelet on my arm. My gut quivered. "Since when is the punishment an arranged promising?"

The King took a deep breath and flared his nostrils. "I know we are friends, Jack. But you've got a lot of nerve arguing with me. This is what I want to happen."

"With all due respect, I am still their father and get to decide who they are promised to. That is the law. Did you even ask why they'd left? Maybe they were concerned because they hadn't gotten word from me."

The King's face turned red with anger. "It matters not. They've accepted and will be promised today."

"And Maggie agreed to this as well?" Dad gestured to Mom who stayed frozen in her seat. "She probably wasn't aware that the parents' desires trump everything else in this situation and I'm stopping this ceremony right now. Don't press this, Phaleon."

"You are treading in dark water, Jack."

They stared at one another in silence, neither moving as the King's chest rose up and down. Dad stood firm, unwilling to cower in his presence.

When neither backed down, Dad lowered his head. "I have been a faithful servant to Natatoria and to you my entire existence, even when you were prince. You and I both know this goes further back than my children breaking the law. Even if you are King, you cannot break your own laws voted in by the people—your parents saw to that."

"Are you lecturing me?"

They drifted closer, now only a foot or two apart. The royal guard snapped up from their previous relaxed stance and poised themselves for an attack.

"So be it," Dad finally said with a shrug of his shoulders. "Maggie,

Finley, Tatiana, let's go. We're leaving."

"No!" the King shouted. "You will all stay where you—"

Dad moved to get into the King's face; his personal guard held him off. "You'll what? Have us banished? So be it. I resign from the Council. Me and my family will be leaving now."

Dad signaled us to leave the room, but the royal guard moved between us.

"Arrest them!" the King yelled.

The guards rushed in all directions. Dad let out a cat-call and mers dressed entirely in black charged into the room with spears drawn. The King's guards were outnumbered two to one, pinned against the wall.

The King bristled. "This is treason!"

"We have no wish to fight," Dad said while taking Mom's hand. "We only want to leave in peace."

A scuffle broke out at the door as more of the King's soldiers tried to enter the ballroom. The King's personal guard whisked him out the side door. In the hall, the King continued to bark orders to attack and rescue his wife and son.

"Come on, Fin," Dad called, holding open a door located on the opposite wall of were the King just left. "We haven't time."

Mom was at his side, motioning for us to come quickly. I turned to fetch Tatch, but Azor had his hand wrapped firmly around her waist.

My head whirred, still thick with drugs, unable to concentrate. More men tried to force their way past the stronghold and the guards along the walls fought back, pressing the rebels into the center. Someone grabbed Dad from behind and pulled him through the doorway. Mom screamed.

Lily dropped my hand and stared at me, as if I should do something. Should I rescue her too? Kiernan, the merman assigned to help me with community service, appeared from nowhere—his black hat askew and makeup smudged—and pulled her into the throng of bodies and, I hoped, towards safety. I stood, still half-dazed, trying to determine who these rebels were as mers from both sides clashed weapons together. Something seemed off with the fight, like they weren't really in combat but performing a practice exercise on Azor's field. Fighting was against the nature of our race, and with brother against brother the unspoken goal became "stun your opponent."

But with sharp weapons and the heat of battle, high pitched keening filled the room as blood clouded the water. Mermen of both sides began to drop one by one. Were they dead? A larger rebel dressed in black appeared at my side with an extra spear.

"Get yer sister outta here, lad," he said while placing the weapon in my hand and pushing me toward Tatch.

Badger.

Azor fought a rebel mer while Tatiana stood dazed and confused, leaning against the wall behind him. Fear pounded into my veins watching him. In Azor's eyes *was* the intent to kill. In the growing confusion, his attacker looked away for a moment and Azor plunged the spear into his chest. His high pitched wail changed the atmosphere of the room; one of ours had fallen at the hands of the King's son. He fell to the ground writhing in pain, blood gushing from the wound.

I locked eyes with the dying man momentarily and I felt fire race along my scales. This was the moment I'd been waiting for—an excuse to avenge the wrongs Azor had committed.

I let out a battle cry and charged Azor with my weapon. He whipped my sister around to face him, putting her between us. His mouth went to hers, kissing her outright. She struggled at first, but then went limp. I yelled for her to fight him, but it was too late. Tatiana wove her hands up into his hair, fully accepting the promise.

"No," I yelled, then cursed. "You're a dead man now, Azor."

He laughed victoriously as Tatch floated next to him, looking lovingly into his eyes. Then she spotted my weapon.

"Oh, no you don't!" she screamed and came at me, nails bared.

One swipe caught my cheek before I could catch her hand when she tried to do it again. The spear fell from my grasp. She thumped me in the gut with her tail, then picked up the weapon and floated in front of Azor, guarding him.

"I should have done that a long time ago," Azor said and placed his hands on her shoulders. She relaxed into his touch. Seeing them together washed dread over me.

"You're nothing but an animal," I said. "As long as I live, I'll hunt you down for taking my sister's choice away from her."

"Oh, will you?" He arched an eyebrow. "What are you waiting for? Let's do it right now."

"I'll never let you touch him," Tatch growled. *"Get out of here. I don't want to have to hurt you again."*

Her interference made fighting him difficult. I raised my tail anyway, my head still thick with whatever they'd used to sedate me.

"Fin! Tatiana!" Dad called from somewhere behind me over the horde of fighting men. "We haven't time."

"You heard him," I said and tried to snatch her hand.

"No!" She pulled her arm away from my reach. "I'm staying with Azor."

I turned my head quickly, catching my Dad's frantic eyes. Could he not see Tatch was guarding Azor? "She won't come with me," I called out.

"Leave her," he said. "Just come."

I tried to grab her again, but she hit my hand with the spear and moved closer to Azor's side. *"Please come with me, Tatch."*

She looked back at me, sorrow in her eyes. *"I'm sorry. You're right. The promise changes everything. Go while you can."*

I gulped down my emotion, unable to accept my defeat. *"I won't leave you here. I have to defend the honor Azor's stolen."*

"No, Fin. I'll be fine. I can't explain it, but I have to be with him."

"You won't get far." Azor's laughter burned in my ears as I turned to escape with my parents. "Maybe I'll ask the King to pardon you when they drag your sorry ass back, since you're my extended family now."

I clenched my fists as Dad yelled for me to hurry again. It took all my self-control to let Azor have the last word and to leave Tatch behind. Next time he wouldn't be so lucky.

I swam to the doorway through the bloodied water. Now I could see why Dad insisted we leave. The soldiers blocked the door and he had to fight to keep the royal guards at bay long enough for me to escape.

Mom squeezed my neck as the three of us swam from the palace with a group of rebel mers behind us. Dad headed directly towards the Tahoe gate. I remained quiet, stunned he'd leave my sister so easily until her piercing scream came from behind us. I turned. Two rebel mers had her within their grasp, writhing and thrashing her tail, as she demanded they let her go.

"Tatiana," Dad said as they approached. "This is ridiculous. You're coming with us, so settle down."

"No! I want to stay!"

One of her handlers attempted to pass her off when she sunk her teeth into his flesh, ripping out a huge hunk. The rebel mer yelped, releasing her. Free, she bolted away from us.

"Sorry, Dad. I can't go with you," she called out.

Dad's shoulders sunk as he watched her swim out of sight. He turned and pulled a grouping of kelp fronds out of the sand, yelling something inaudible.

"I'm sorry, Captain," the rebel mer said as he applied pressure to his wound with his other hand. "It's my fault. I shouldn't have let her escape."

"No, Jacob," Dad turned, his composure collected, "it's my fault. Please, go see Sandy. She'll tend to your wounds."

Jacob bowed before he swam away.

"The rest of you can go as well," Dad said to the rebel mers scattered among us.

One by one, they shed their black garb and wiped away their make-up, each giving Dad a quick bow, calling him Captain. I recognized them all—volunteers in Azor's army. They quickly swam away and blended back into society as if nothing happened.

I looked at Dad, stunned.

Mom put her hand on his arm. "Jack. We should go while there's still time. Once we've regrouped, we'll return for Tatiana. She'll be okay for the time being. Besides, you're injured too."

He looked down at the huge gash across his torso. "It's just a flesh wound. But we need the antidote first."

"No, Dad," I argued as rage flooded my body. "We can't leave her here. I know how to fight. Badger taught me. We need to get her back. Summon your men."

Dad's eyes met mine and glazed over. "I can't sacrifice any more lives. We have to put together a plan."

Mom kneaded her hands as she and Dad watched the palace off in the horizon, too far to see any activity. Dad put his arm over her shoulder. "He'll be here soon."

She sighed.

"Dad," I begged again. "We can't leave Tatch!"

Dad looked at me with pain in his eyes, but something over my shoulder made his face relax. "There he is."

I turned to see a rebel mer swimming in our direction.

"Aye, Captain," the rebel said and he embraced Dad. "There be no one followin' and I brought ya the 'lixer. Fin will be needin' it after ya cross the gate. Give it to him right away, or he'll have one nasty headache after he wakes up."

"Badger?" I asked.

He smiled at me under the black make-up. "You best be leavin'. I need to be gettin' back to the palace and figure who needs wounds attended. The girls have already doused the place with octopus ink, so they can pull out the victims. Don't want anyone dyin' on us or gettin' captured." He bowed his head.

"Please keep an eye on Tatiana." Dad put both hands on Badge's shoulders.

"Aye, Captain," Badge said somberly. "I'll guard her with me life."

Dad let out a huge exhale. "Thank you. Until we meet again old friend." They embraced.

"Stop it before I start blubberin'," Badge said with a chuckle and swam back toward the palace.

I looked to Mom who cried quietly as Dad rubbed her shoulder. He motioned for me to swim into the tunnel first. I wavered, still afraid the poison would kill me even with an antidote.

"It'll be okay, Fin. Once we get to the house I'll get the bracelet off you. Don't worry." He clapped my shoulder and I calmed under his loving grasp. "Let's go before the royal army gets here and tries to stop us."

Mom decided to swim through first, concern seeping through her demeanor of strength. Dad motioned for me to go next. I swam warily behind her and then felt the barbs under the gold sink into my skin. Within seconds, the world went dark.

48

ASH

I sat on the deck off the back of the house with an afghan pulled tight over my shoulders; a foreboding sensation seeped into my bones. No matter how hard I tried, I couldn't let go. The water whispered to me and I watched like I'd been compelled to do ever since the incident.

A loud boom rumbled the ground, forcing me to grip the arms of the chair. Then a large geyser of water shot into the air from the middle of the lake. I stood up in horror as the spray fell back downward. A wall of water began to build and came careening in slow motion towards the beach and the dock. And as if something jerked on *The Sea Star's* tether, the boat stood on end and submerged when the water rose up and covered the poor vessel. My hand muted my scream as the waves crashed up the hillside, almost hitting me where I stood.

"Fin?" I called out, my throat thick with uncertainty as my mother's potted plants rolled down the hill with the receding water.

Without thinking, I hobbled down the slick, muddied path to the dock and scanned the lake for any signs of life. The boat came back into view and righted itself as she knocked against the dock, drenched but whole. Fear gripped me. I wasn't sure what to do, but I couldn't just sit and do nothing. I got into the boat.

My muscles began to burn as I feverishly paddled the boat through the debris. I hoped to be the first to the spot and rescue survivors, for Fin and Tatchi. Helicopters appeared from nowhere and flew over the site I tried desperately to reach. I slowed as jet boats emerged on the water. *Too many people.* Would they find their bodies floating on the water? Would the world go crazy at the discovery of mermaids in Lake Tahoe?

Tears slid down my cheeks as I stopped and peered into the deep water, blue like Fin's eyes. Did they survive the blast? We'd learned in class the results of explosions underwater—effects far worse than above ground. I brought my hands to my mouth as more fish popped up on the surface, all dead.

"No," I cried as the possibility Fin and Tatchi could be dead as well haunted my thoughts.

I couldn't catch my breath, my heart racing too fast. I kept searching the water, hoping and praying they'd surface alive. If something did happen, how could I continue on? I grabbed the side of the boat, my body crawling for a way to help. There was nothing I could do but watch, wait. If Fin died, he'd never know how I truly felt about him; our last interaction was nothing but harsh words and rejection.

"No," I cried louder.

I reached my hand in the water, hoping they would see it and come to me. The bitter cold shocked my senses, awakening the painful memory of being fully immersed. I put my cold wet knuckles to my lips and rocked back and forth. The skin tingled like it had after I woke up in the hospital, after I remembered his lips on mine. How did this all happen? Why did I turn him away?

Shakily, I stood up in the boat, my eyes searching the water for the one I realized I loved. The one I had to spend forever with. The one who might not return.

My chest ached. I closed my eyes and turned my face towards the sun, praying for a miracle. My body swayed with the boat on the waves. Then insanity's black tentacles tangled its iciness in my thoughts. Fin had saved me before. Maybe if I fell in again, he'd come back to me. Then I could join them. I could go to the world that called to me in my dreams. With Fin. In the everblue.

I moved my foot and set it on the ledge, tempting fate.

49

FIN

"Fin? Fin?" my mother pleaded. Her voice echoed around in my head.

"I'm here," I tried to say, my tongue heavy in my mouth. The world, still black around me, was filled with oxygen. *Where was I? Heaven?*

I wriggled my toes; a warm blanket covered my human body. I pried open my eyes to see Mom and Dad hovering over me, staring. *I know this place. The living room in our house in Tahoe.* Mom had a mug in her hand and a tangy sweetness laced my throat.

I swallowed again. "I'm okay, I think."

Dad's shoulders relaxed as he squeezed my hand. "Welcome back, Son."

"The things the two of you put me through," Mom said with a sigh. "Are you feeling okay, Fin?"

I rubbed my temples, the pain zinging through my head like a fire poker. On the table next to me, the poisonous bracelet the King had slapped on my arm to keep me in Natatoria sat in two pieces next to a pair of bolt cutters.

"Here." Mom handed me two tablets of Ibuprofen and a glass of water. "Take these."

A circle of red dots surrounded my wrist. "What happened? What day is it?"

"It's only been an hour," Dad said. "I was hoping the bracelet was a decoy, but you fainted when we swam through the gate." Dad grimaced. "Once we got home, I couldn't find my tools. But after I threatened Alaster—"

Mom clenched her jaw. "Once Dad took off the bracelet, and I fed you the elixir Badger gave us, you came to."

"Where's Alaster now? Aren't they going to find us here?"

"Not for a while, I imagine. I escorted my good-for-nothing brother and nephew back to Natatoria and sealed the gate for good."

"You what?" I sat up, my body stiff.

"I activated the detonation device on the gate, just in case. Sealed her right up. No one's going to be coming or going from Natatoria through Lake Tahoe any longer."

Outside, helicopters hummed overhead. I swallowed hard again, my throat still dry. "And everyone saw the explosion?"

"Yeah," he said with a shrug. "Had to do it while I still had the chance."

My heart thumped hard. This would create a bigger hysteria than the waves I'd caused. Anyone within the vicinity would have seen or felt the explosion.

"I have to go find Ash." I threw off the blanket and stood up.

"No," Mom barked. "Sit down. You need to let the sedation wear off."

"I need to find her now!" I could only imagine what she'd think, especially if she saw the explosion firsthand. I took another deep breath to clear my swirling head, ignoring Mom's continued demands that I take it slow.

I cursed once I saw the mess on my bedroom floor—the board pried away from the hidey-hole, all my clothes and things scattered about. A lowly pair of folded jeans caught my eye. I slid them on with a black shirt that looked halfway decent, along with shoes and socks.

I was out the door and running towards Ashlyn's house within minutes.

What am I going to say? How is she going to react? Would she turn me away?

I didn't care. I had to talk to her, make her understand. We had to be together. I couldn't live another day without confessing my feelings to her.

I banged on her front door for several minutes without an answer. More helicopters flew overhead and the noise made me slightly fanatical. I held my ears and turned in a circle. Where was Ash? Footprints in the wet mud led to the dock. Off in the distance, a bevy of boats swarmed the water.

I spotted someone in a little boat a mile or so out. One I'd recognize anywhere. *The Sea Star.* The girl inside was standing, arms out.

"ASHLYN!" I screamed and ran for the dock, shedding clothing the entire way.

Unable to phase into a fin without ripping my jeans, I kicked with all my might. I had to stop her from doing something rash. Though I could save her again, I'd be naked once I got her on shore with nothing to put on—definitely a risk of exposure. Why didn't I put on my pack just in case?

I pointed my hands and butterfly kicked, speeding my progress slightly. She came clearer into view, still apparently deciding if she should jump or not. Her foot rested dangerously on the side, the boat close to tipping over.

"STOP!"

Ash startled and retracted her foot from the ledge, losing her balance and falling onto the seat with a thud. "Finley?"

I came to the side and treaded water next to the boat. "What are you doing?"

"You're alive?" She stared back as if she didn't actually believe she saw me for real.

"Of course I am. Why are you out here?"

She continued to stare in shock, her beautiful green eyes adding to my longing to kiss her.

"But the explosion?" She looked off into the horizon.

I grabbed the edge and tried to swim the vessel back towards her house. "Exactly why you need to be off the water. Everything is going to be okay now. I'm here."

"I'm confused. Shouldn't you be a—?" She pointed at my legs underwater and her cheeks flushed.

I hesitated telling her the truth, unsure how she'd react. I'd answer all her questions on shore. "It's a long story. Let's get you home."

Frustrated I couldn't swim as fast as I wanted, I climbed into the boat and took the oars.

50

ASH

I stared at Fin as he rowed the boat, the water dripping off his abs. All I wanted to do was touch him. Could he actually be here? Or was I having another splendid dream? I didn't trust my senses at this point after all that had happened. My heart pounded as my eyes caressed every inch of his body.

Tears spilt over my eyelids and down my cheeks. With each passing moment, I wavered between shock and disbelief. But there he was, in the flesh and blood. Fin. He was alive and here again—finally. And nothing coherent would come to mind to say. I hesitantly reached forward and touched his knee; the water on his jeans was hot under my fingertips. The sensation sent a chill down my spine.

He stopped. His blue eyes, burning with want, met mine.

"I can't wait anymore." He put the oars down and clasped my hands with his, taking away my breath. "Ash, I've done nothing but fight to get back to you since your accident" —I gulped— "and I can't live without you. We're bonded in a way I never knew existed. Something so wonderful yet so horrible when we're apart. You have to know I've been going crazy with worry for what you'd think after you saw what happened at the beach. I never wanted you to find out about us that way. Please know, I hated that I couldn't tell you the truth."

I wanted to say I understood, I didn't care. That I loved him. That I was relieved he was okay. Overjoyed he was finally here with me. But nothing would come out of my mouth.

"Ash—"

His eyes sparked as if he knew what I was thinking. Then he reached up, palmed my cheeks with his summery hands, and brought his mouth crashing into mine, soft and warm. Fireworks exploded between us as our lips hungrily devoured one another's. My hands wove into the back of his hair, my fingers wrapping into the soft, delicious strands. He crushed me into his body and I melted under his touch. All the grief vanished as his breath swirled into my being and healed my wounded soul. Though nothing made sense, everything finally felt right.

I couldn't be sure how long we stayed there, in the boat, bobbing on the water, our arms circling one another. I didn't care. We were together and nothing would break us apart now.

51

FIN

We finally disconnected ourselves enough to get the boat closer to shore. Though her face beamed now, I grieved at how much she'd hurt in my absence. Was she wearing the same swim team jacket from the time before?

"I wish I would have taken a shower today," she finally said, smoothing down her red fly-away curls.

"Ash, you've never looked more beautiful to me."

She blushed and pulled her jacket down over her hips. I docked the boat and reached for her hand, pulling her into my arms. She melted into me and I never wanted to let her go.

"I'm so glad you're safe," she whispered.

I planted feather-like kisses up her jaw line and she giggled. "Being apart killed me."

She moaned lightly in my ear and swayed. "Then don't ever leave me again," she said.

I inhaled deeply and hugged her tighter. "I promise."

She giggled again. "Can I please go shower? I look horrible and I'm pretty sure I reek."

"No," I said, wanting nothing more than to hold her all day.

She pulled back and gave me a crooked smile. "Please?"

"Fine, if you insist." I took her outstretched hand and kissed it.

She stood with a slight tilt, favoring her right foot. Then I remembered she was still injured.

"Wait." I had her sit on the bench on the dock. "This is going to be weird but I have something to help your leg. We need to take off your bandage."

"You do?" She pinched her eyebrows together, but folded up her pajama bottoms to reveal a large ace bandage that covered her thigh.

"Trust me."

Together, with our hands touching, we loosened the wrap. I winced once I saw the horrific bruise and jagged red line held closed with Steri-Strips.

She frowned. "Looks ugly, doesn't it."

"Not for long," I said with a wink and left her to return to the boat.

Earlier while rowing, I'd noticed the jagged metal piece she'd probably torn her leg upon when she fell into the water. With a quick flick of my arm, I made a matching gash.

"What are you doing?" she shrieked at the sight of my blood spilling onto the dock.

"Just trust me."

Horror crossed her face as I came back to her and held my arm over her cut. The blood seeped into her wound, absorbing like a sponge. I'd never witnessed a mer's blood heal human injuries before, so I wasn't sure if I was doing it right. Miraculously, the skin around the injury began to glow and change from a nasty red to a tender pink--the color of new skin. The trickle of blood slowly stopped as my own gash healed before our eyes, turning into a matching scar.

"Now I have a token to remember that day as well," I said and touched our scars together.

She looked up at me with innocence sparkling from her eyes. "What are you?"

I smiled and covered her lips with mine. "Yours."

She laughed and hugged my neck again.

I swooped her up into my arms and carried her to the house like I'd wanted to do the first time I'd seen her.

52

○

ASH

I showered quickly, afraid when I got out Fin would be gone, the whole thing a dream. The water trickled over the pink scar, tickling the new skin. I laughed, my insides filled with unexplainable richness. While hurrying to brush through my wet unruly hair, I heard a knock at the door.

"Ashlyn?" Mom asked, apprehension looming in her voice.

I opened the door, letting the steam escape. Her face brightened as she scanned my fresh appearance—my first shower in almost a week.

"Why didn't you call and tell me you had company for dinner?"

"I'm sorry," I shrugged. "He just got here. Would it be all right if he stayed?"

From down the hall I could hear Gran, Lucy, and Dad talking to Fin about the explosion on the lake. His presence made me giddy inside and I bit back my grin.

"Of course. I'm glad to see you're feeling better."

I smiled, probably for the first time since the accident and a tear glossed the corner of her eye. "Yeah, Mom. I'm feeling a hundred times better."

From nowhere, she wrapped her arms around me and sniffled in my ear. I rubbed her back, trying to soothe away all the grief I'd caused her the past few days.

She let go and composed herself. "Well, hurry up. I'm almost done reheating the lasagna."

I closed the door and counted my blessings for a moment.

Though it brought me Fin, what I did tortured my parents. I'd worried them needlessly and took everyone on such a crazy rollercoaster of emotions with me. I'd never do it again. I couldn't watch them suffer like that. Somehow, I needed to make it up to them.

A quick blow dry and a little makeup to cover the grey smudges under my eyes made a world of difference. When I walked around the corner without a limp, everyone gasped. The fact that Fin was here, hit me again, his gorgeous face melting my knees. His smile, a ray of sunshine after a storm.

"Man, I'm gone a few weeks and miss all the crazy stuff happening on the lake," he said with a wink.

"Totally," I said with nervous laughter.

Everyone's relief-filled giggles cleansed our living room now that I'd returned back to my old self. He patted the couch cushions and I joined him, feeling his warm thigh next to mine. As the conversation continued, I kept staring at him, marveling that he was here. All the questions I thought of in the shower tumbled in my brain: How did he escape the blast? Where did the bad mermen take him? How did he get away? Where was Tatchi? How did the whole mermaid thing work anyway?

But even if my family wasn't engaging him with their own theories of the explosion, including an attempt to bring Tessie to the surface, I knew once we were alone, I wouldn't be able to ask him mine. My lips would be busy kissing his instead.

And as if he knew I needed reassurance, his hand wove delicately with mine and my heart raced even more. How I could be so miserable one minute and elated the next, escaped me. But I didn't want him to ever leave. His presence blanketed all my fears I'd suffered from since the accident.

Dinner went smoothly and once the sun started to set, Fin grew nervous and asked if we could go outside. Mom shooed us out, insisting she'd do the dishes. We walked hand in hand into the dim twilight. I kept a watchful eye on him, concerned about the change in his behavior.

"I can't stay much longer," he said after we kissed again under the swaying pine trees down by the dock. "I *change* when the sun goes down."

I creased my brow.

"Into a m—" he looked off towards the beach where it all happened. "You saw what I am. Let's not pretend anything different and I'm sure you've got tons of questions."

My heart filled with compassion and I squeezed his hand. "And I'm okay with it." I looked at his luscious lips, finding it hard to concentrate.

He ran his finger along my jaw and tilted my chin up. "I promise to answer anything you want to know tomorrow. No school, right?"

I started to answer when he smothered me with another kiss. I pressed my body against his, feeling the strength of his chest and arms around me. He couldn't leave. Not yet.

Breathless, he pulled away. "Great. I'll see you then."

His lips pecked mine one last time as he attempted to leave, but came back for another. I giggled, watching him war with himself. Then the panic on his face took over as the sun made its final descent and dipped under the horizon.

"Good night, Ash. Sweet dreams," he called over his shoulder as he sprinted towards his house.

I swooned and waved back. "You too, Fin." *My love.*

53

FIN

I ran into the house and stumbled to the floor as scales burst down my legs. My fin pulled an *Incredible Hulk* routine and ripped my favorite jeans to shreds. "Crap."

"Finley, is that you?" I heard Mom call from the basement.

"Yeah," I said as I shuffled down the steps on my scaled butt like a seal, trying hard not to lose control and fall the rest of the way down.

In the pool, Mom and Dad swam together, dancing to an unheard melody, enjoying each other's company after being apart for so long. I understood, being promised myself and finally getting to be with Ash again.

"How was your visit?" Mom asked, looking at me briefly.

"Good. I almost didn't make it back in time."

She glanced over and handed me a coy smile. "I see."

I looked down and groaned. The waistband of my jeans still hugged my waist, making a frayed mess. I plopped into the water, ripped it off the rest of the way, and swam over to my floating raft, finding it broken.

Part of me wanted to swim out to the lake and stare up at Ash's window rather than stay here and watch my parents flirt. Another part of me wanted to call her, though I didn't know the number. Maybe she'd sneak out to the dock tonight instead. The thought of waiting all night to see her again killed me, especially since the pool suddenly felt too small with my parents in it.

"I'm going out," I finally said.

"I don't think that's a good idea," Dad said. "The lake is crawling with boats and divers looking for the source of the explosion."

I hit my fist against the water and groaned.

"Why don't you just call her on the phone?" Mom suggested.

I rolled my eyes. "How can I without the number?"

"Tatiana put it on speed dial," she said.

"She did?"

Mom smiled.

Without hesitation, I swam to the other end of the pool, and slithered to the stairs. I closed the basement door after catching Mom's giggle, happy to give them some privacy.

The upstairs bathroom, where I'd planned to hide-out with Tatch, had a super huge jaccuzi tub. The reasons Tatch escaped upstairs some nights suddenly made sense. Mom must have known she was making secret calls to Ash.

After the tub filled to the top, I stared at the phone, wondering when to call. Unable to wait, I pressed the speed dial button. If someone else answered besides Ash, the night would be mighty long. My pulse beat harder waiting for her to answer, my finger ready on the hang-up button.

"This is Ash. Leave a message."

"Ash—" I cleared my throat, wanting to hear her voice again even if recorded. "It's Fin. Call me when you get a chance."

I hung up and sunk under the water. Her face decorated the backs of my eyelids. Being apart, even for the smallest amount of time drove me crazy. Talking on the phone would hopefully help. We had to figure out how to manage this relationship the best way possible.

Relieved she hadn't rejected me, I marveled at our promising. If I knew how spectacular our love could be, I wouldn't have waited so long. Then I thought about Tatch and guilt gripped my gut. Did Tatch feel this way for Azor? I worried about her, wondering if the promise squelched all her dreams of college, of being human. I formed my fists into a ball as I remembered Azor laughing at me in the palace after he'd stolen a kiss. Revenge was going to be sweet.

So many decisions now. We couldn't stay in Tahoe forever. And if I became a man to join Ash's world, I wouldn't be able to avenge Tatch. Would Ash and I be able to survive until I could get Tatch away from his evil clutches? And once I became a man later, would our feelings for each other remain after the bond of the mer left our relationship?

I blew bubbles to reduce my nervousness, hoping the phone would ring soon.

54

ASH

I walked inside, sad and happy all at once. Fin was home. My heart was whole. Though we didn't have time to talk, I knew he'd answer my questions eventually.

"There's my girl," Dad called out once he saw me. "Come join us."

The family had retired to the living room to play cards.

"That was quick," Lucy said flippantly.

"Lucy," Mom said with a glare, "mind your own business."

"What I meant to say was, you went from Callahan to Fin so quickly. He's cute and all, but does he know you still have a boyfriend?"

If hissing wasn't socially unacceptable—especially since I'd gained my parents' favor, I would have. What happened to my nice sister? Though she was right, I wouldn't give her the satisfaction. We were practically broken-up anyway. Since his visit on Wednesday where I'd confessed my secrets and freaked them all out, I'd ignored his calls and texts. It would just be a matter of time before he stopped trying.

"I don't anymore," I muttered, shifting my weight in the entryway. "Callahan and I aren't really together anymore, so—"

She raised her eyebrows and blew out a quick gust of air right before she laid down her cards. "Whatever."

"Anyone who can pull my girl from her slump is all right in my book," Dad said, ignoring Lucy completely.

I wrapped my arms around Dad's neck and kissed him on the top of the head. His hair smelt of the firehouse: cigar smoke and old leather. "Thanks Dad. I really like him."

Gran's and Mom's eyes twinkled watching me. The general consensus (except for Lucy) was thankfulness. I could have brought home a tatted up guy with a lip piercing and they'd be happy at this point. Anything to get me out of Gran's room and back into the world of the living.

The faint ringing of my cell phone formed a knot in my stomach. Now was a good a time as any to tell Callahan. Better than at school.

"I think I'm going to move back into my room. My leg feels a lot better today."

"Good—oh. Gin!" Gran said and the rest of the group moaned.

I smiled. Things were back to normal, as if my accident had never happened. Well, as normal as they could be, considering I was in love with the merman who lived next door.

I shook my head and left to collect my things out of Gran's room. On top of the basket of clean clothes, I piled up my sympathy cards and toiletries. My cellphone on the nightstand beeped with a message.

The walk of shame up the stairs with the basket weighted my feet. The last thing I wanted to do was hurt Callahan. The phone started ringing again in my pocket and I sprinted the rest of the way.

To my shock, my room was cleaned: vacuumed and everything in its place. I plopped the basket on the floor and fumbled in my pocket to get the call. Caller ID said it was Tatchi.

Anxious to talk to her, my heart began to pound. "Hello?"

"What happened to my happy girl?"

"Fin?" My mind scrambled a second, not expecting to hear his voice. "How'd you get my number?"

He laughed, a fresh breezy sound that made me collapse on my bed in a wonderful heap. "You'll never guess."

"Did Tatchi give it to you? Is she there?"

"No." Fin said with sadness briefly in his voice. "But she did put it on speed dial."

"She's not there?"

"She decided to stay in Nat—our world."

"Oh." My chest constricted with disappointment. In our whirlwind of a day, I didn't even think to ask about her.

"It's a long story. I plan to go back and get her. Our family had to leave the colony."

"Fin, you're going to have to start from the beginning because none of this makes any sense to me."

That was when I learned all about the mers of Natatoria: where and how they lived, why human relationships where frowned upon, how sunlight allowed them to stay in human form, and how water was necessary for survival—his call placed while he lounged in the bathtub. I wanted to share my totally off base alcoholic theory, but didn't want to insult Fin's dad in the process. His warm voice, coupled with my snuggly blankets, kept me comfortable and entertained until morning. The "crazy" label I'd placed on myself peeled away like magic.

"So, you heard me scream?" I asked.

"That day, Ash—" he let out a huge sigh. "When you fell into the water, I nearly lost it. I didn't think you'd survive. And I didn't want to kiss you without your permission."

I snickered under my breath. "I highly doubt mouth-to-mouth can be considered kissing. But if it makes you feel any better, you have my permission."

"It's not funny." The seriousness in his voice was adorable, though, I had a feeling he was withholding something.

"Sorry. Thank you for being such a gentlemen," I said and tried not to giggle again.

"Kissing in my world is a very serious thing, Ash."

"And as a human, I'm very serious about my kissing, too."

"You're impossible."

I laughed. "Okay—I'll stop teasing. Next question. How did you manage to slip me past the Ranger?"

"Oh that." He paused again like he'd been doing after every question that required a lengthy answer. "Well—" he chuckled nervously. "I carry breakaway board shorts with Velcro seams, so when I phase into legs I have something to wear. So you could imagine what the Ranger thought when he saw me in nothing but your girl's swim team jacket—which was way too small—and board shorts, dripping wet."

"The Ranger never mentioned this?" I curled up my lip at the visual. "You put on my jacket? Why?"

"I was trying to dry it for you with my internal heater. Anyway, yeah, he freaked out. Especially after he saw the blood."

"Oh." My hand went to my mouth, the visual a little more grim. Why would the Ranger completely lie about this?

"And since mermen can erase minds, I told him, in my language, to forget what he saw."

I gasped. "Mermen can erase minds? Oh wow. That's . . . useful, I guess."

"Well . . ."

He got quiet and I heard the water swishing around in the tub. I assumed he wanted to confess something without me getting angry.

I bit my lip. "Did you erase my memories too?"

"After we were pr—touched lips, from mouth-to-mouth, I couldn't any longer, but since you were unconscious, it really didn't matter. And actually, Blanchard tried to mind-wipe you after you saw us in the water, remember?"

"Oh," I said in awe, remembering his musical words. "I thought he was going to punch my lights out or something."

"Mermen, typically aren't violent against humans. And mermaids—" he took a huge breath, "that's a story for another day."

I imagined him reclined backward with his fin hanging over the edge, like the mermaid did in the movie *Splash*. I yawned, noticing the clock read 4:00 AM.

"I should let you sleep for at least a few hours," he said in concern.

"I'm good."

"Good? You keep yawning," he said.

"Don't you need to sleep too?"

"I don't really sleep, more like rest. A few hours will work for me."

"That's nice." I would have liked to get away with less sleep too.

"I can come over in a few hours, if you like. How's nine sound?"

"Too long," I whined.

"You're adorable." I heard a smile in his voice.

I swooned. "Fine. I guess I can wait that long."

"Okay then. You hang up first."

"No, you," I laughed.

"You."

"You," I countered.

"How about we do it together. On the count of three. Ready? One. Two. Three."

I listened for the click that never came.

He laughed. "Hang up already."

"I said you first."

"Fine, since you won't do it and you need your sleep, I'll do it."

"Okay," I said with a lilting voice.

He paused for a moment, "Ash, you mean the world to me, I hope you know that."

Goosebumps covered my skin. "And you mean the same to me, Fin."

"If anything had happened to you today, I would have gone crazy. Please promise you won't pull any more stunts like that."

"I promise."

"Goodnight, my beautiful angel," he said.

I sighed after I heard him hang-up.

55

FIN

The sun rose and I caved at about 8:30, unable to wait any longer. Uncle Al and Colin had left a pile of dirty dishes in the sink and a rotting lemon, a loaf of stale bread, and a jug of expired milk in the fridge. My stomach clenched for some type of nourishment.

My parents weren't on the ground floor or in the pool, and I wasn't about to go looking for them upstairs. I understood the bond too well and being with Ash was all I could think about.

I was at her door in minutes, hoping she'd be just as anxious. Her figure, once she opened the door, took my breath away. I fought the urge to take her in my arms and kiss her right there.

"I'm early," I said and flashed the Jeep keys in front of her. "Wanna go get some breakfast?"

Her face lit up. "Yeah," she said and grabbed her coat off the wall. "Bye, Mom."

I took her hand in mine and squeezed as we walked back to my place for the Jeep. Her sweet honeysuckle perfume hit me in the enclosed cab. Desires to nuzzle my nose in her neck distracted me from driving and I missed the turn.

"Don't you mean to—?" She asked sweetly with a casual point of her finger.

"You make it impossible to concentrate," I confessed and enjoyed the color of her cheeks changing to a rosy red that matched her curls.

On a table inside the door of the diner, an abandoned *Tahoe Daily Tribune's* headlines said, "Explosion in Lake Tahoe Causes Tsunami." I swallowed hard. This was an unforgivable crime in the

King's eyes. Worse yet, we'd made a fool out of him during the attempted promising ceremony by challenging his word and escaping. Returning would be a death sentence. How could we ever rescue Tatch?

Ash and I snuggled in on the same side of the booth and pressed our bodies against one another. After ordering, Ash laid her head against my chest as I put my arm over her shoulder. I still wanted to get closer.

"So, if you've managed to upset the—" She looked up with thoughtful eyes and paused for a moment. "—the King, won't he come back and arrest you or something?"

"It's a little difficult to come back with the gate destroyed," I whispered. "He'd have to get across the state somehow from the Pacific Ocean to Tahoe during sunlit hours and he just ruined his only West Coast connection—my dad. And his insistence that mers avoid human contact is now going to work against him."

"So I've made you a wanted man?" she asked with a coy smile.

I kissed the top of her head. "Ever since you stole my heart, yes."

She giggled before becoming serious again. "Do you think you're safe here?"

"Dad seems to think it's okay for now and that's a good thing. I can't imagine leaving you."

She hummed and drew her finger over my knuckles, tickling my skin and driving me crazy. In her presence, I'd lost my appetite and wondered why we even ordered food. A secluded place to curl under a blanket sounded so much more appealing than a restaurant. Our bond made my desire to let my hands wander increase a hundred-fold.

In the early morning, I'd decided to do the right thing and make an honest woman of her first. Her parents seemed to like me and I wanted to keep it that way. Would they approve of her marrying at such a young age? I'm sure they wouldn't if they knew my secret.

"What are you thinking?" she asked, breaking my moment of life planning with her sweet voice.

"What to do next," I said and hugged her tighter.

"As long as I'm with you, I'm up for anything," she purred in my ear, nibbling my earlobe gently.

I curled my toes to restrain my hands. Luckily the waitress showed up with our food before I could return the favor.

We hurried up and ate, then headed for the park. The ground was still wet from the melted snow, which meant we'd have to sit on a bench. We found a spot with the lake in view and snuggled under a blanket.

"So," she said hesitantly and I knew the question before she asked it. "How'd you become a merman actually?"

"I was born this way."

"Born? Hmmm. I bet you were the cutest little merboy in Natatoria."

"We call our babies merlings. But I don't know. You'll have to ask my mom."

"Aw, that's cute," she giggled but tensed next to me.

I wasn't sure what I'd said that made her uncomfortable. Was she afraid if we had kids, we'd end up with merlings? I actually didn't know what kind of kids we'd have, her being human. But that was definitely something we could discuss in the future. I didn't plan to force her into a lifestyle she'd rather not be a part of, or even tell her it was an option.

To be safe, I changed the subject. "I didn't spend tons of time in Natatoria growing up. My parents liked living on land more than under the sea."

"Do you like it there?"

"It's a very beautiful city. The mers before us created a pipeline of mirrors that reflect sunlight in from all over the world. The entire place is covered in gems, gold, silver, and platinum. With the sunlight bouncing all over, it's like being inside a huge crystal ball. The only frustrating thing is you have to remain a mer the entire time. Only in a retrofitted oxygenated room can you change to legs."

"There are rooms underwater?"

"That's why I carry around my board shorts. Nakedness isn't accepted in our colony, unlike the pictures you see." I maneuvered two strands of her hair to create makeshift legs walking on her arm.

She giggled again, her voice high and cheery. "I'd love to see it."

I frowned, completely confused. She wanted to see Natatoria, but didn't want merlings? Then I cringed. Could she have guessed there was a way to be changed into a mermaid? She had no idea the sacrifice, the uncertainty now that we were fugitives, separated from our kind. I wasn't going to let her know there was an option, at least not yet.

"We won't be going back for a long while, that's for sure."

"But you said Tatchi is there."

My gut tightened. "Yes, she is. It's complicated."

"Is that why she didn't want to go to college with me? I guess being a mermaid and all would make that pretty difficult."

"No," I said quickly. "She did want to go. Originally, she kept trying to get me to leave our way of life, too, but I wanted to be loyal to our people which ended up being a major mistake. It's different for the men than the women in Natatoria. She tried to tell me, but I wouldn't listen."

"Oh." She crinkled up her nose.

My heart thumped harder, knowing where this conversation was headed. Was it time to tell her about the promising? Why a kiss with a mer is so powerful and revered?

"I'm sure you've heard the fables about mermaids luring men into the sea to their deaths." She watched me with wide-eyes. "It's true. Whoever a mermaid kisses, their soul will bond with hers and her absence will drive them mad."

"Honestly?"

I raised my right eyebrow. "You tell me."

She watched me with curiosity and touched her lips. Recognition sparked behind her eyes. "Is that the same for mermen too?"

I nodded my head. "Our weddings are called promisings. All it takes is one kiss to bond with someone for life. Then you'll need them almost more than—"

"—life itself." She reached up and trailed her fingers down my stubbly cheek. "That's what you meant when you said a kiss is very serious. It all makes sense now. I thought I was going insane this past week. I kept dreaming and thinking about you all the time, hoping you'd come back. But it was only mouth-to-mouth resuscitation. That's hardly a kiss."

I looked down. "It still counts."

"Oh," she said and her face brightened. "Is that why my lips tingle all the time?"

I marveled at her innocence and then frowned. "I wouldn't have done it without giving you full disclosure on me, on us. But, under the circumstances—"

"Are you trying to apologize again for saving me?"

"Well . . . it was way more than saving. I've high-jacked your life."

"Hardly," she laughed and squeezed my hand. "I've actually got a confession of my own. Of all the guys I know, you'd be the only one I'd pick to be promised to. I've had a crush on you ever since the sixth grade."

Her confession gave me the chills. "Really?"

"Totally. I don't know how you couldn't tell. I'm always a complete bumbling mess around you. I mean, you've always been flirtatious, but I didn't think it meant anything. And once we got older, you stopped hanging out with us."

"Oh," I said, thinking back to my actions on the beach. "I wanted to take things further, but tried not to give it a second thought because you were off limits. Our way of life is—well, you know. Complicated."

"But you couldn't resist me," she said, her lip curling up.

"You were sort of dying." I'm sure my smile gave away the truth, that she was right.

"I think it would have been super awesome if you'd just shown me. Like when we swam to Fannette Island."

"You would have freaked out." *Which you did once.*

"Never." She cocked her head.

I chuckled, biting my tongue.

Her eyes sparkled. "I've always known you were special."

"Or genetically mutated."

"In the most adorable way." She mussed up my hair and planted a kiss on my nose.

"But what about *that* guy?"

She pursed her lips. "What guy?"

"I saw you k—" It hurt to form the word let alone say it. Everything inside me wanted to punch his lights out. "—with him on your porch. You were all dressed up."

She sat back, her eyes darting back and forth as if trying to remember. "Was that you?" She gasped. "It was you!" She busted into peals of laughter. "Oh, my gosh. You were spying on me!"

"Was not."

"Then what were you doing in the water?"

I shifted in my seat. "I was just visiting. I couldn't stand being trapped underwater for so long. And then I saw you with *him* and he had his hands all over you."

"You're jealous." She crawled into my lap with a huge smile and I melted. "There's no *him*, so don't worry. I'm all yours now, apparently until death. So don't get all green merman on me."

"Good. One less guy I have to—" I caught myself before saying *kill* "—take out."

"So dramatic. Are you purposely trying to avoid telling me about what happened to Tatchi?"

"No," I said and hugged her tight. "After they took us back, she ended up getting forced into a promising and—" I cringed "—that really left her no choice. She had to stay. We don't know what we're going to do now. We can't force her to come home. She'll suffer without him."

"Who's she promised to?" she asked.

"The King's son. He's the reason she didn't want to go to Natatoria in the first place. He's had a crush on her forever. The day I came to the beach to get Tatchi, it was for a family meeting with him. She knew we wouldn't return. I didn't listen."

"I don't think it's your fault, Fin. From what you said, the King manipulated the situation."

"Yes, but—I don't know anymore—it's become so confusing. Before the promising, Tatch wanted nothing to do with the King's son, and after, we couldn't pry her away from him. Without knowing what she really wants now, I don't know what to do. Should I try to bring her home? Only death will set her free."

She gasped. "Her death?"

"No! His. Only after *his* death does her soul become free again."

She grabbed her chest at heart level and sucked in air. "Don't do that to me."

"Sorry," I said, admiring her theatrics. "You're stuck with me."

"I guess I am." She wrapped her arms around my neck. "And you with me."

"I'm glad no one is at this park."

"Me, too."

We finished the rest of the conversation wordlessly with only our lips doing the communicating.

56

ASH

After more people showed up at the park and we caught a few glares from moms at our display of affection, we high-tailed it back home.

"I think you should meet my parents officially," Fin said out of nowhere as he turned the corner, our houses in view.

I swallowed hard. "Meet your parents? Now?"

Somehow I'd assumed they'd be reopening their shop for business today.

"Heck, yeah. We're practically married now in mer standards. They know everything."

I tried to speak but stuttered something incoherent and couldn't finish. *Did he say we were practically married?*

"Look," he said, taking my frozen nervous hand into his burning hot one. "This is cause for a party. You're family now. They're your in-laws."

"Not in my world they aren't. If my parents even knew what happened—my dad would flip and he's the most understanding of the two. I can't even imagine my mom's reaction. She might just keel over with a coronary."

He tilted his head and looked at me over the top of his sunglasses. "Am I scaring you?"

"No," I said. "This is all a little fast. You just came home. We just got together."

"It's eternal. You can't fight it. We can't be apart. We're a match made in water."

The lump in my throat made talking difficult. "Hardly. I can swim like a fish, but my talents are limited. I doubt I could keep up, let alone survive." *Besides, we aren't even a matching race.*

He chuckled. "Please. Come meet them. They'll be cool. I promise."

"They don't really know me," I said, still in a panic.

"Well then let's remedy that."

We parked out front and my legs turned to mush. My last memory of his dad, though unrelated to drinking, still scared me. Though Fin said he'd already told them about me, I couldn't imagine them liking me. First off, I wasn't a mermaid. How could I give them merlings in the future?

Fin popped out of the Jeep and went around to open my door. I sat quaking in my seat, gripping the leather with white knuckles. This wasn't how I wanted my date to end—fighting with his parents and them forbidding us from seeing one another again. It had to be a set-up.

"It'll be okay. I promise," he said and kissed my hand before he led me out.

Memories of coming here and looking through the window as a child hit me hard. I tried to dig my heels in, but Fin looped his muscular arm around my waist and ushered me inside.

"Mom? Dad?" he called out. His voice echoed through the vaulted ceilings of his lavishly decorated home.

A scuttle from upstairs preceded a "Be right down," from a female voice.

"Fin, let's go. Come on," I whispered and pulled his arm with all my might. "They're busy."

He shook his head.

"Fin," a woman said with a smile as she flowed gracefully down the stairway in a white cotton dress. Long, flowing blonde hair covered her shoulders, and eyes bluer than Fin's sparkled at me behind bronzed skin. She was 100% mermaid material if I'd ever imagined one. "Who's this beauty beside you?"

Beauty? Has she looked in the mirror today?

"This is her, Mom. My Ashlyn," he said, pride bursting forth like he'd just won the lottery.

Fin's mom took my hands before she enveloped me in the warmest hug. "Welcome to the family, dear." She pulled back and studied my fingers. "Oh, I see it. It's coming in lovely."

She traced over the spot on my ring finger where a wedding band would go. I studied the spot and noticed raised discolored marks on my skin.

She took off her own wedding ring to uncover a gorgeous colorful tattoo underneath. "Yours will look like this soon."

My mouth fell open. Now my parents were definitely going to kill me. A tattoo? "How—?"

Fin showed me his hand. He also had faint markings like mine. "They'll match once they completely fill in, after a month."

I blinked. "Holy crawfish."

Both Fin and his mom laughed as she hugged me again. "You are too adorable."

"What's all this laughter happening in my kitchen?" A gruff voice spoke from the stairwell.

I nearly peed my pants when I turned and shook in Jack's presence. Standing six foot three with a gnarly beard and broad, naked shoulders, he towered over us. Off-white drawstring pants were all that he wore.

"I told you to put on a shirt," Fin's mom said and disappeared for a moment. She reappeared and threw one at him.

I didn't move, blink or speak as he pulled on this shirt, and inspected me.

"Come on, Dad," Fin finally said.

"Aw, love. You're as pretty as a picture. Come here!" He grabbed me and squeezed the life out of me. I coughed as he pounded me on the back. "Well, this is such a wonderful day. Have you two made official plans yet? What did her parents say?"

Fin opened his mouth and nothing came out.

"Jack, give the boy a chance to see his girl and get reacquainted. There's a lot to discuss. She is *still* human after all."

The word "still" rang through my head a few different times. I turned to Fin and studied his stoic expression. He'd only told me we bonded, not that I was going to sprout scales in the near future.

"We haven't talked about the details yet," he said quickly.

"You need to start because we can't stay here forever."

My heart thumped wildly. "You can't stay?" My frantic glance ping-ponged between the three of them.

"No," Fin said, looking hard at his father and then softer towards me. "We've got time to work everything out. We aren't going anywhere. Don't worry."

I couldn't stop from breathing faster. He was my world. He couldn't leave without me.

"I'm famished," Jack said, unfazed by the invisible grenade he'd launched in the room. He moved towards the fridge. "You kids hungry?"

I felt unstable, my reality toppling over.

He opened the fridge and cursed. "Great Poseidon. I swear my idiotic brother would die if he ever lost his scales."

Fin leaned over and whispered. "There's nothing in the fridge."

I gaped. Who could care about food at a time like this? Mermaids? Merlings? Tattoos? Leaving? I couldn't focus as the blood pounded louder in my ears. I needed fresh air—now. "I need to go outside," I choked out, grasping onto Fin's hand.

"Oh." Fin looked at me and furrowed his brow. "Hey, Dad. We just ate and besides, I need to get Ash home."

"Lookie here, some pancake mix." Fin's dad removed himself from the pantry for a second and took a quick look over his shoulder.

"Oh, sure. Good to meet you, Ashlyn."

"Yes. Come back soon," Fin's mom said, enfolding me in another warm hug. "Don't worry. Everything will work out."

I gave a feeble smile as Fin led me out the door by the hand.

57

FIN

Ash stumbled outside. Her glassy eyes indicated she'd reached information overload—something I'd hoped my parents would avoid.

"That went over well," I said with a fake grin. "I told you they'd like you."

She nodded but the uncertainty creased her forehead like a paper fan. She stopped and stared at the lake once we got to the Jeep. I turned her to face me. "We'll get through this. I promise."

"Please drive me somewhere," she mumbled as she opened the door and robotically climbed in.

I took a deep breath before climbing into the driver's side and starting the Jeep. "Where do you want to go?"

"I don't care."

She remained quiet for several minutes as I drove down the secluded lakeside road with no destination in mind. Would this be the time she told me she couldn't handle this? That she wanted out of the promise? Her silence gnawed at my gut.

"Please talk to me," I finally said. "What are you thinking?"

"Everything . . ." she stopped.

"What do you mean?"

"Everything has to change." She started to sniffle.

Seeing her tears, I pulled to the side of the road and got out. She remained inside with her door opened a crack, only her foot propped on the running board.

"Look at me," I said and put her cheeks between my hands. "I love you and I'm not going to let anything keep us apart, or make things difficult with your parents, or ask you to move away, or assume you'll want to become a mer, like me. This will all work out."

"You love me?"

"Of course I do." My shoulders dropped. "I knew it the day I wanted to punch that idiot's face when he had his hands all over you."

She sniffled, but smiled—the first time since we'd left the house.

"I love you, too," she said softly.

My heart expanded, filling with indescribable bliss hearing the words. I pulled her off the seat and into my arms. She whimpered sweetly as I covered her lips with mine, tasting the salt on her skin, kissing away the tears. I never wanted to see her cry again. If the mer life scared her, I'd become a man in a heartbeat. Her happiness was my everything.

I looked into her green eyes and pushed back the red, loose curls falling around her cheeks, worried how to help. She had no idea she'd fit in perfectly and put all the mermaids to shame with her beauty. She smiled at me, as if she read my adoration of her on my face.

I pulled her back into my arms, and cradled her body against mine. She finally relaxed.

"I was thinking," she said in my ear. "Why don't I go to college here in Tahoe next year instead."

"What? Why?"

"'Cause—" she nuzzled deeper into my chest "—it would be less complicated."

I pushed back, wanting to study her eyes. "Complicated? You didn't think I'd let you go alone, did you? I'd like to see you stop me."

Her lips curled into that adorable grin as her face lit up with new hope. "Tatchi and I specifically picked Florida Atlantic University because it was close to the ocean. And I can get a job and we can live by the sea. Or . . ." Uncertainty clouded her eyes.

"What's wrong?" I asked, brushing a curl off her forehead.

"Am I going to . . . " Her cheeks flushed as she bit her lip.

"Are you going to what?"

She dropped her eyes and rubbed her finger over the promising mark. "This is so embarrassing."

"Tell me," I demanded.

"Fine." She let out a quick gust and straightened up. "When am I going to turn into a mermaid?"

I blinked for a second, confused why she thought she'd spontaneously change. Then smiled, filled with relief. "You mean because we're promised?" I chuckled.

"I knew it was silly." She grimaced.

"No, don't feel like that." I folded her back into my arms and squeezed. "A promise doesn't make you turn into a mermaid, though I'd really like that—" she giggled. "Our *essence* does. There's a spring in Natatoria under the palace that bubbles up a blue liquid from within the earth. If you drank it, you'd transform into a mer. I'm sure you've seen it. Tatch has a vial on her bracelet."

She thought for a moment. "Oh, right. So, if I drank that, I'd poof into a mermaid?"

"Something like that. I've never actually seen it happen. It's a fashion statement for mermaids to carry it around. They continue to drink it—like it's a fountain of youth."

I laughed, but suddenly realized we might not have brought back any *essence* with us.

"That's kind of cool," she hummed as she leaned against my shoulder.

I kissed her temple and inhaled the honeysuckle scent in her hair. "Just know I don't want you to feel any pressure. I can become human, if it comes down to that."

"There's a way to do that?"

"Yes," I said and took her hand. "The bond of our souls might go away, but we'll be together on land without any mer restrictions."

"But you'll have to leave your family and you won't be able to go get Tatchi."

"Then I'll go get Tatch first. My family will still be around. Maybe they'll take up residence in Florida, too."

"That's huge," she said with a sigh. "I don't want you to have to choose between me and them."

My chest tightened. "It won't be like that. It'll all work out."

She looked down and traced the raised emblem on my ring finger that signified our eternal connection. "Will this go away, too?"

I grimaced. "I don't know. Possibly."

She sighed again and laced her fingers with mine. "I don't want it to go away."

I moved our hands up and brushed her tattooed finger against my lips, kissing it. "Maybe I'll put something else in its place."

She smiled, her expression warm. "Are you proposing to me?"

My heart thumped wildly in my throat. This wasn't how I wanted to ask her. Not without a ring. "What?" I said and looked away with a sheepish grin.

"Brat." She hit my arm and I grabbed it to pull her toward me again, brushing my lips against her neck.

"I like being your brat."

"This is all so crazy," she whispered in my ear. "But as long as we are together, I'll do and go where you want me to."

"Music to my ears," I whispered back and swayed with her body as we heard music. "It would be nice to be able to be free from always worrying about the sun setting."

"Tell me about it," she said as she moved in for a kiss.

a

The afternoon flew by faster than I wanted and after another wonderful dinner with her family, the eventual decision of who would leave whom became heartbreaking to think about. Ash fidgeted and hid her left hand under the table during dinner. Once the sky turned rosy and cast long shadows across the kitchen floor, we both looked at each other in sadness. Another early good-bye.

"I'm sorry," I whispered as I moved a stray lock of red hair from her face and peered into her green eyes. "I hate leaving so soon."

"Can I meet you later at the dock? I'd love to see your—what do you call it?"

"It's just a fin. I'm appropriately named for my appendage," I said with a wink. "How about later this summer, when it's warmer? I'd hate for you to freeze outside."

She curled her lips downward and pouted. "Please?"

I laughed. "We'll see. I'll call in an hour, how's that?"

"Fine. I guess."

I kissed her irresistible lips again before dashing to get home. I didn't want to ruin another pair of jeans.

"Finley," Mom said as I walked through the door, "she's adorable. What did you two decide?"

"Nothing yet, Mom," I said and went towards the basement stairs, "but I want to talk to Dad."

"He's downstairs fixing one of the soda taps on the bar."

"They broke that too?"

"Among other things. They have no clue how to use or work anything around here."

Dread hit me. I hadn't thoroughly checked my room yet. Did Colin break anything of mine? I went to my room, but knew I wouldn't have time to look. Scales had already begun to appear on my legs. I slid out of my jeans and sat on my bed. My tail burst from my skin like magic and I wondered what Ash would really think of my fishy side. The time spent living as separate species would make for an interesting relationship.

I slid across the floor and maneuvered down the stairs. Mom was testing out the new tap, while Dad moved to fix the filter.

"Son," Dad called out, waving a wrench in his hand, "I like her."

"She is something special."

Mom dangled a vial filled with *essence* on a chain for me to see. "I can't wait for the day she officially becomes one of us."

I exhaled, relieved she grabbed some before we left, but felt a pang of dread after spending such a great time with Ash's family.

"One thing at a time, Mom," I said quickly. "I'm not in a rush to take her away from everyone who loves her. Don't you remember what it felt like to leave your humanity? What would you think if I chose the opposite? To become a man instead?"

Her smile pulled into a frown; a tear glinted in her eye. "I'm sorry, Son. You're right."

"It's not an easy decision," I dropped my eyes, "for now she's going to finish high school and go to college. It's near the Atlantic in Florida. And once she graduates, things will change. You guys managed it."

Mom looked to Dad with a faint smile on her lips. "Yes, we did."

He swam over to her and hugged her shoulder. "You endure much to be with the one you love."

Mom sniffled and I swam away from them, over to my floating lounge chair, needing to escape the tension. Dad had reattached the arm to the seat.

"Thanks," I said and tested it out by relaxing back and closing my eyes. All I wanted was the hour to pass quickly, so I could call Ash and not feel pressure to make these tough decisions.

"How Colin managed to break so much stuff in such a short time, I'll never know. Why I'm even bothering . . ."

I sat up at the sudden silence. "What do you mean?"

Dad sighed. He crawled into the closest floating lounge and paddled over to me. "Since we're going to be leaving, I don't see the point. Mom and I are planning to get out of here once I wrap up the business and our finances. Florida is actually where we'd planned to go. It's close to home base."

Home base. I'd forgotten about the mer safe house for runaways Dad had set up a while back, unbeknownst to the King.

I ran my hand through my wet hair. "Badger gave me an earful while you were gone—"

Dad laughed lazily. "I'm sure he did."

"You didn't tell Tatch and me anything about anything . . ." My cheeks burned. "It was quite embarrassing at times."

"Well," he scratched his belly before Mom swam over and handed him a beer from the tap, "ever since you were little merlings, I've been contemplating leaving the colony. I didn't want you too attached and interwoven into a life that I'd have to uproot you from. And with Phaleon in control, it's become too unstable. The so-called secret mission I was on was actually to find his runaway daughter and he didn't want anyone to know."

"What?" I laughed under my breath. "Wow. Now that says a lot."

"Yeah." Dad chuckled, too, while Mom handed me a Coke. "And I wanted to bring you along, but I needed you there for your mom and your sister. I had a feeling Phaleon would twist things around to his advantage in my absence somehow, but—" he groaned and slapped the water "—Azor stealing Tatiana's promise should have gotten him stripped of his fin. If it were anyone else—"

"We'll get her back," I interrupted.

"I know. But I can't help but think this is all my fault. I should have talked with her earlier, let her go to home base when we had the chance. She, of all people, shouldn't have to endure Natatoria. All she craved was human life. She constantly got in trouble for gallivanting all over with Ashlyn and staying out 'til the last minute. Have you seen her room? It's covered in posters of human boys and her bookshelves are filled with those gossip magazines. I just thought we'd have more time."

Mom swam up and touched Dad's arm. "Don't be too hard on yourself. Fin's right. We'll go back and get her. I'm sure Azor is treating her fine."

I gritted my teeth to keep from responding. Mom didn't know what Azor was really like—what an animal he was. I could just imagine his treatment of her—more like a possession than a person. Even with the promise binding her to him, I had a feeling once the lovey-dovey feelings dwindled and real life set in, he'd have her locked up in his compound to do chores for him all day—and night.

Dad and I exchanged hard looks. He clenched his jaw and nodded. We knew the truth and we had to get her out.

"Once I find out what happened after we left and get my men together, we're going in," Dad said, softening his expression and placing his hand on top of Mom's. "I'm not leaving her there any longer than I have to. And Fin, you'll get to escort Azor out of Natatoria. How's that?"

A malevolent grin spread across my face. "With pleasure."

Mom tensed. She knew this meant a war—the first of its kind for our people.

"And we promise to be careful, Mama," Dad said quickly and gave her a kiss. "So don'tcha worry."

They looked at one another; pain of longing in her eyes. "Just bring her back," she said quietly.

"I promise."

"So," I said slowly, breaking the tension again. "Did you find Phaleon's daughter?"

"Aye," Dad said. His response made me think of Badger and miss him. "What a mess. We found her, barely alive and in the middle of a botched attempt to become human. There were people and authorities all over her apartment complex. I've never had a bigger mess to clean up.

"Apparently her roommate found her finned up and bleeding to death in the tub. Of course she freaked and called nine-one-one. Poor girl was working completely alone and off rumor. With all the people involved—it got ugly fast.

"But we managed to mind-wipe the witnesses and erase most of the evidence. But with smart phones nowadays, pictures get on the internet so quickly, it becomes impossible to retract. But luckily, only a few really bad pictures leaked out and they don't look any different than the mermaid lore online now anyway. We got lucky this time.

"But I blame Phaleon. His insistence of forbidding the teaching of how to become human and keeping mers trapped in Natatoria just fuels the desire to explore."

Mom agreed.

I shivered at the image. Dad had told us how to switch when we were younger. The visual scared me from ever wanting to do it. The graphic description of allowing yourself to bleed to death, but capturing your blood (like in a bathtub) and lying in it so it can heal you from the outside during the transformation was a horror show in the making. But you weren't supposed to do it alone, in case of trouble or a complication. And then afterward, a male mer needed to erase your memories so you wouldn't tell the secret. I wouldn't have though, let alone imagined doing that, until now. Until Ash became my everything and I'd go through anything to be together, forever.

I looked towards Mom who watched Dad with empathetic eyes. "Did she live?"

"Yes, but she's not going home. We've got her in the safe house with friends for now. But if it wasn't for my connections and computer skills, this could have been our undoing. Phaleon's fear of humankind has become his downfall and the mer are no longer satisfied with just having merlings and tending to the colony. One day people are going to revolt."

"So then who were those warriors?" I asked.

"Friends of mine and Badger's. We've been grooming men for such a situation as this for several years under the guise of Azor's army training. Due to Phaleon and Azor's poor treatment of their people, the mermen have been eager to join our cause and keep it secret. Even when it came to this mission, I was the only person who was willing or even able to lead it. But what he doesn't know is that my connections with people on land is what made me successful. He's got a thing or two coming, especially now that his son has stolen my daughter from me against her will."

I looked him straight in the eye. "Mom told me about what happened when you were younger, with Leon wanting Mom but she chose you and then your parents getting banished."

"Yes, it was time you knew the truth. I've never trusted him fully after that. He's always wanted to keep me under his thumb, but he's too much of a coward to do anything directly. That's why this mission became something to his advantage. It's too bad his parents aren't still on the throne. They were true leaders."

My chest tightened. "Do you think he'll seek revenge? How long do you think we've really got here?"

Dad looked to Mom and shrugged. "I'd say a month or two."

"Really?" The hope calmed my nerves. Ash could finish school and then we could leave for Florida in June—to get her all set up for college, of course. "This is good news. Ash has been so nervous about when we'd leave and how things would work out."

"But I'm going back to get Tatiana sooner than that."

"Oh, right," I said, worried what Ash would think of me leaving so soon.

Mom touched my arm. "Ash will come around. Just let things marinate. With the promise, she'll follow you to the ends of the earth."

"And I her," I said quickly. "I'm going to tell her now."

Mom smiled. "Enjoy your talk."

I shimmied up the stairs and checked the time. Exactly an hour had passed. The phone barely rang before she answered.

"Hey, baby," I said, intending to be cheesy. "Where have you been all my life?"

"Right here. Waiting for you."

58

ASH

Just hearing his voice made me whole again. In the time waiting, I'd chewed my nails to the nub, worn a new groove in my carpet, eaten half a box of chocolate chip cookies, and yelled at my sister for messing up the bathroom.

"I've got good news," he said.

"Tatchi's home?"

"Well, no. Not that good. I've talked to my parents and the Florida thing works in perfectly with their plans. There's a safe house for runaway mers, so we'll be together while you go to college."

"Great," I said and pulled in a deep breath.

A safe house sounded more reassuring than him living alone in the Atlantic. But I still didn't know how to tell my parents we were getting serious, so serious I'd want to marry him if he asked. Being only seventeen and jobless without a place to live wouldn't stack in our favor. And Fin seemed apprehensive about me becoming a mermaid. Would I have to wait long? The thought of swimming around with a real live tail exhilarated me. Would college end up being the cover-up? Would my family notice I'd changed? Heck, if we lived in the Atlantic together, why would we need jobs anyway?

"Ashlynnnn," he cooed, "what are you thinking about?"

"Life."

"Sounds serious," he said with a little laugh.

"Since our first kiss, I can't think of anything else."

"That wasn't entirely my fault. You were the one taking a pleasure cruise in freezing waters."

"I'd heard that there was a hot merman stalking the waters around Fannette Island. I had to look for myself," I giggled.

"Hot, huh?" he asked with a smile in his voice.

"And sexy."

"I've been told that."

"By whom?" I asked with pretend outrage.

"By all the mermaids."

"Oooh, if you were here I'd—"

"What?"

"I'd pin you down and kiss you so you'd never think of anyone else but me."

"Can I come over now?"

We both laughed.

"I wish," I said

He continued to flirt with me and plan our future. In the back of my mind, I started to envision the wedding as well. I couldn't imagine anyone except Tatchi being my maid of honor, but worried if I waited any longer, and let him go to Natatoria without me, they wouldn't come back and I wouldn't have the power to find him. My dreams and worst nightmares swirled together in a multicolored cloud of uncertainty.

"Geez," Fin said in exasperation. "Who keeps trying to break in on our call?"

"What?"

"Call waiting. Hold on. I need to tell this fool where to stick it."

"Okay."

I heard the click and waited, imagining him chewing out the poor telemarketer who was trying to make their sales for the night. Out of my window I saw the bathroom light in his house filter through the trees and smiled. We were so close, yet so far away. After two minutes passed, I wondered if my phone still worked properly. I clicked a button so the screen would light up and the seconds counted away. After three, my heart began to speed up. What was taking so long? After ten minutes, I was about to put on my clothes and walk to his house myself.

"Sorry, Ash," Fin said, finally clicking over. "It was an important call for my dad. Something's come up."

"Is everything okay?"

"Yeah," he said, but I didn't believe him. His edgy voice told me something very bad happened.

"Is it—?"

"I'm really sorry. I can't talk anymore tonight. I'll come over first thing in the morning. I love you."

I slid off my bed onto the floor, gripping the phone. He couldn't hang up without telling me who called. "I love you, too."

"Don't worry. It'll be okay. Goodnight."

He hung up before I could tell him goodnight back.

Okay? How could it be okay if he's worried?

My chest ached as I put down my cell phone and turned to watch his house. The bathroom light wasn't on anymore—the entire house dark. Who called? What news did they bring? The fear I'd felt the entire time Fin was missing came back and scratched its nails down the chalkboard of my soul. I wanted to run over and bang on the door. Why didn't he tell me? Why did he make me wait?

I began to pace again and ate the rest of the cookies. In times of stress, a swim always did the trick to calm my nerves. I just wanted the phone to ring. I willed him to call me back.

An hour passed, then two. The rest of my family had gone to sleep and only the wind whistling through the pine trees kept me company. I couldn't stop my mind from racing. I had to know what was going on.

Against my better judgment, I picked up the phone and called. Once the answering machine picked up, I hung up. He must have been in the pool in the basement with his parents.

I tried to sleep, but only tossed and turned. Nothing would ease my mind. In desperation, I grabbed my pillow, a sleeping bag, and four blankets from the hall closet and snuck outside to the dock.

I curled up in a ball on the cold wooden slats and draped my arm over the edge, just barely touching the water. I hoped to send Fin a little SOS with my finger tips. The brittle cold distracted me from the whirlwind of chaos haunting my mind. I hoped in some crazy way he'd know I needed him and swim to find me.

"Fin," I called out over the water. "Please . . ."

59

FIN

"What does Badge mean 'they're coming'?" I yelled in the basement.

"Badger called from Scotland and apparently Alaster helped Azor and his buddy's get vehicles in Sacramento. They're hiding in the river tonight and going to drive here at dawn. We've only got about two hours to get away from the lake before they arrive."

"No," I roared. "I'm not leaving without Ash. It's not fair to her or me. I'll hide and stay in Fallen Leaf Lake instead. Leave the Jeep and I'll catch up with you in Florida in a few months."

"Impossible, Fin," Dad countered. "I know how much you love Ash, but they aren't leaving Tahoe once they get here. They're going to try to reopen the gate."

"What?" I plunged myself backwards into the water and let the air escape from my lips as I sunk to the bottom. Then I yelled and pounded my fists on the pool bottom, wishing it was Azor's face.

"Fin," Dad said underwater. "It's only for a few months. Maybe Ash can come to Florida early for the summer. For a trip?"

"But how are we going to travel across the country? We're fish."

"I got an RV today. We'll use the GPS and find rivers and lakes along the way. We'll make due until we reach Florida."

I closed my eyes and didn't move off the pool floor. "I can't, Dad. I can't leave her."

"This time we don't have a choice. There's too much of a risk of them spotting you if you stick around."

My heart felt like it was going through a meat grinder. Ash would never understand. This was going to break her. "Then make me human. Anything to stay."

"Fin," Mom said, sitting on the pool floor next to me. She took my hand. "Have you considered where you'll live? Once you become human, you'll be subjected to the elements, to the cold. You need to stay a mer, at least for now—Tatiana still needs your help to free her. And the promise will be broken. Ash's feelings could change."

I rolled over and hid my face. As selfish as it was, I didn't want my promising feelings for Ash to go away, for either of us.

"You have to be strong, for her," Mom said.

I didn't want to be strong. I wanted to break things. "I have to tell her good-bye in the morning?"

"We'll be leaving as soon as we can." Mom's shoulders slunk down. "I'm so sorry."

I darted over to a corner in the pool and sulked the rest of the night. I wanted to call Ash and listen to her sweet voice. If only Ash could tell me this was a joke, but I wouldn't be able to withhold my disappointment. This was something I had to tell her in person.

I tried to visualize a ray of sunlight so I'd phase into legs. I'd do anything to have one last night together, to curl up in each other's arms and hope the morning never came. How could we survive this? Being apart for a few hours was hard enough, but months?

I groaned and put my face in my hands, the impending doom rocketing through my body. The night ticked by slowly but eventually the sun rose and rays peeked through the basement windows.

Without a word, I left the pool and ran to my girl.

60

ASH

"What are you doing out here?"

My eyes opened to the morning sunlight dancing around Fin's silhouette.

"Waiting for you?" I choked out, my throat sore from the chilly evening.

"What am I going to do with you? You can't be doing insane things like this. You're going to drive me mad."

I rubbed my eyes and sat upright, anger suddenly burning in my veins. "Drive you mad? If my being outside, hoping you'd come here last night to calm my frazzled mind is going to drive you mad, then maybe you shouldn't leave me hanging like you did."

Fin exhaled sharply, his nostrils flaring. "Please, promise me you won't do anything like this again."

My tense shoulders dropped as I curled my lips down into a frown. "Promise me you won't let urgent calls interrupt us and then hang up abruptly. You have to be honest with me. That's what relationships are all about."

He squatted down, piercing his baby blues into my balloon of frustration, deflating it instantly. "I'm sorry. We got some bad news."

"I figured." He opened his arms and I collapsed into his chest. "What happened?"

He waited forever, rocking me gently, sniffing my hair and kissing the top of my head. I hummed and relaxed, but didn't like the way he ignored my question. Fear prickled down my spine.

"We—we aren't safe any longer," he barely said, almost as if our reality would break if he talked louder.

"Who isn't safe?"

I felt him tremor as his eyes grew glassy, grief swirling within the dark pools of blue. Why did I ask the question when I knew the answer? The mermen from his world were coming for them, pure and simple. The denial this day wouldn't happen blew up in our faces. But why now? Why so soon? His dad was so confident everything would be fine. I willed him to tell me something else. Anything else.

"My family isn't safe. Mermen from Natatoria are coming today to reclaim the house and reopen the gate. We have to leave."

The air whooshed from my mouth and I grabbed his arm. "NO!"

He pulled me into a tight embrace and hugged me hard, like I was going to vanish before his eyes. I felt him convulse—just once—as my own tears fell down my cheeks. I couldn't handle this. I had to go with him.

He took my hands into his and pulled me to my feet, taking one moment to wipe his cheek with the back of his hand. "Listen to me. We're going to Florida and I'm going to contact you every day. I'm not going to let distance drive us crazy. We'll be together, just get to Florida as soon as you possibly can."

I started breathing faster and faster, my head dizzy, my body shaking. My voice pitched, hoping he'd listen to reason. "But I don't want to be alone. I can't be alone. I—I'll never survive. I'll go mad without you. Please... can't you stay?"

He paused with a pained expression. Then he shook his head. "We have to survive. We can do it. It's only for a few short months," he said somberly.

I pressed my eyes closed and felt myself sinking down. He had no idea the pain I felt without him, the torture. I practically went mad.

He took my shoulders, stopping my descent. "Ash, open your eyes."

I sucked in a quick gust and felt myself unravel inside. "No. If I do, you'll leave."

"Ash, open your eyes. Please."

His voice stirred something deep within my soul. Desperation? Hope? I couldn't be sure. Unable to fight him, I opened them slowly.

He removed something small from his pocket. At first I couldn't tell what it was until the stone reflected shards of crimson light as he held a ring towards me.

I stared at the ring, then into his inquiring eyes. My pulse hammered as he lowered himself to one knee.

"Ashlyn, will you marry me?" Excitement and fear danced across his glorious face.

My mouth went dry. Was this really happening? The worst and best moment of my life?

I peered down at him, then at the ring again. Married? Goosebumps covered my skin. I'd be Mrs. Helton. Visions of a minister asking us to repeat vows and our family and friends in the audience filtered in my mind. I couldn't imagine being with anyone else—ever.

"Yes," I choked out. "Of course. Yes!"

He slid the ring onto my finger and it fit perfectly. I studied my shaking hand through blurred vision.

"A red stone for my ginger girl."

I glanced back up. Tears trailed down his cheek. He scooped me into another tight embrace and I squeezed back with all my might. If I held on, he couldn't leave, he wouldn't go.

"We'll be together soon," he whispered in my ear. "Please be strong for me."

I fought back the sob stuck in my throat. "It's going to kill me."

He took my cheeks within his hands. "Me, too, but it'll be worth it. I promise. I'll call you every day."

"You'd better," I said and his lips came crashing into mine.

We devoured each other, our gasps for air few and far between. Our hands hungrily explored each other, tugging and pulling to fill the ache of the inevitable. If we stopped, then our bliss would be over and the longest wait of our lives would start. His hands grasped at my cheeks, at my neck, sliding across the tears staining my skin. Though I didn't want to stop, our kiss wasn't going to prevent the mermen from coming. I had to make a decision. Either I'd let this consume me and cause madness, or I'd decide to endure. I already knew what the madness felt like. This time, I needed to be stronger. And he was worth every second I had to wait.

We pulled back, both of us holding each other's cheeks. We studied each other's eyes, both red, swirling with anxiety.

"I love you," he said again.

"I love you, too," I said.

And inside, I let go.

Evergreen, book #2 of Mer Tales is coming Summer 2012.

Acknowledgements

I thank God for turning around a dark time in my life to show me a new passion and for his mighty blessings in healing my son. Second, I thank my ever-patient husband, Mike. If it weren't for his care of our home while I entertained my imaginary friends, we all would have starved, been buried in dust bunnies, and worn smelly clothes. Your encouragement helps me continue to see the big picture when I want to fall apart over the small stuff.

To my mom and dad for loving me and cheering me onward towards my dreams.

For my siblings, for enduring yet another book.

To Savannah, my über babysitter, for your help day after day. I'm so glad my kids love you as much as I do.

To the fab duo of Lisa Langdale and author Lisa Sanchez, for being the best bomb beta's ever and encouraging me to continue on when I felt like quitting.

To author Kristie Cook, I give you a million bazillion hugs for being honest and patiently helping me make my manuscript something others will love too and for being a sounding board in this crazy experiment—may the KM dream press on.

For my friends and girls in MOPS, for your support and friendship while I balance life, motherhood, and writing.

To Donna Wright, for finding most (smile) of my mistakes.

To Rhonda Helton (my #1 fan) and Tracy Lanski, letting me use your last names.

To Eleni from LaFemmeReaders, for hosting my book tour and being such an encouragement.

To Yara from Once Upon a Twilight, Jen from Extreme Readers, Jessica from Bookaholics, Jaime from Two Chicks, and all the other book bloggers: my work wouldn't see the light of day without your endless enthusiasm and promotion as fabulous wordsmithers, booklovers, and networkers.

And to you, my dear readers, for your emails and letters of praise that always seem to come at the right time. Really, I write for you! I hope you enjoy Everblue as much as I've enjoyed writing it.

Follow me at:

http://brendapandos.blogspot.com

Follow the Author

Sign up for the author's newsletter to enter contests and find out about future installments at: www.brendapandos.com

Twitter: @brendapandos

Facebook.com/brendapandos

Email: brendapandos@gmail.com

Connect on Goodreads

Also by Brenda

The Emerald Talisman

The Sapphire Talisman

The Onyx Talisman

Coming 2012: *Evergreen, Book #2, Mer Tales*

About the Author

Brenda Pandos lives in California with her husband and two boys. She attempts to balance her busy life filled with writing, being a mother and wife, volunteering at her church, and spending time with friends and family,

Working formerly as an I.T. Administrator, she never believed her imagination would be put to good use. After her son was diagnosed with an autism spectrum disorder, her life completely changed. Writing fantasy became something she could do at home while tending to the new needs of her children, household, and herself.

You can find out more about her daily challenges and discoveries on her blog at:

http://brendapandos.blogspot.com

4/16   ll   12/15

CPSIA information can be obtained at www.ICGtesting.com
Printed in the USA
LVOW081654031012

301362LV00012B/61/P